MAIL ORDER BRIDE

Montana Rescue

Echo Canyon Brides
Book 1

LINDA BRIDEY

Dedication

This book is dedicated to all of my faithful readers, without whom I would be nothing. I thank you for the support, reviews, love, and friendship you have shown me as we have gone through this journey together. I am truly blessed to have such a wonderful readership.

Contents

Chapter One

Smoke and noise filled the air in the saloon simply known as Spike's. Spike himself, a man in his mid-sixties, tended the bar in the small place, enjoying the comradery of the usual crowd. He was a modest man who owned a modest bar and made a modest living. Spike didn't ask for much and he didn't like to draw a lot of attention to himself; he was happy just to work and be around his friends.

Spike looked around, spotting most of them in the place. They were either drinking, gambling, or playing darts. Doing pretty much what they always did. This included Evan Taft, sheriff of Echo Canyon, the man could do the job he'd been hired to do just fine and then some, but his methods were sometimes questionable.

So was his personal behavior. He did things that most men would never admit to doing even if they actually did them, such as crocheting—and in public at that. Spike looked down the bar to where Evan now sat on the cold March night, working on what looked like a baby blanket.

He smiled as he heard Evan humming some tune. He had no idea what the song was because Evan couldn't sing worth a damn. Spike had to admit that Evan could crochet up a storm, though.

"Who's that for?" he asked as he delivered a fresh beer to the sheriff.

"Meagan Humphries. She told me this morning that her and Fritz are having another kid," Evan said in his calm, smooth tone of voice. "She's due in July sometime, poor thing. Right during the worst of the heat."

Spike said, "Well, that's almost five months away, Evan. Why make the blanket now?"

Looking up from his work, Evan's green eyes met Spike's blue-eyed gaze. "This isn't for the new baby, this is for the ones they have now. It's still cold out and you know they don't have much money. I figure they can always use another one for the twins."

"Oh," the older man said. "I wish you would just say what you mean and not talk in riddles."

"I did. I told you who it was for, Spike. That's what you asked."

Spike rinsed out a glass and dried it. "Yeah, but then you told me that she was pregnant again."

"That was just new information. Try to keep up, ok?" the sheriff said with a smile.

"You're a jerk," Spike said.

Evan said, "Yep." He held up the blanket done in a soft yellow and green granny-square pattern. "What do you think?"

"It's comin' along real good, I'd say," Spike said.

There was no denying that Evan was talented at the craft. As Spike admired the blanket, Jerry Belker came in the door. The tall, colored man smiled when he saw the blanket.

"You at it again, Taft?" he asked, sitting down at the bar.

"Yep. It's for the Humphries' twins. She's pregnant again, by the way. Fritz needs to control himself a little more. They can't afford the kids they already have, let alone another one," Evan said.

"Ain't that the truth?" Jerry agreed. "There's things you can do about keepin' from makin' babies nowadays, you know. Maybe someone needs to tell Fritz that."

Evan grunted. "Don't look at me. I'm not bringing up that subject with him."

Jerry looked at the blanket and said, "That's pretty. I'm sure Meagan will appreciate it."

"Well, I wish I could do more, but you know that Fritz won't take money from anyone," Evan said. "I even tried to give them food one time, but that didn't go over good, either."

Spike said, "I sure pity her all right. It's too bad she don't divorce him."

"She's got no grounds," Jerry replied. "Fritz doesn't sleep around or beat her, so by Montana standards, she's not gonna be granted a divorce."

Evan said, "She could get a separation, but who's going to support her? That's where he's got her. He won't let her get a job, either."

Jerry said, "There ain't many jobs to be had right now. This town is gonna die out if something ain't done pretty soon. Then none of us'll have a job and we'll have to move on."

Evan nodded and sighed.

It was true. Echo Canyon was dying a slow death, being choked out by the success of miners in other towns as they found big veins of gold. Echo, as it was affectionately called by the townspeople, had had no such luck. All of the gold had essentially been gone as of five years ago in 1885 and with it, many of the families around the area.

The men needed work and there just wasn't enough of it to go around in Echo. There were also a lot of single men who'd come to work the gold mines and now they had no gold to show for all their work. However, they liked where they lived and so they stayed, working various jobs at some of the ranches and the businesses that were able to keep their doors open. So that was the situation in Echo in 1890.

Spike said, "There's gotta be something we can do to get some more businesses here."

"And women," Jerry said. "Don't forget about women."

"What do you care about women for? You got one," Spike said.

Jerry grinned. "That's right and I aim to hang onto her. My Sonya's the light of my life and we're hopin' to have a little Belker soon. To answer your question, Spike, I'm sure the other fellas around here would like to have a family, and in order to do that, we need women because us men just don't have the right parts to make babies on our own."

Spike said, "I get that, but what I don't get is how you think we're supposed to make that happen? It's not like there's a lot around here to attract women. Plus, once they're here, they've got to be supported, don't they?"

Jerry said, "Let's get the women here first and then figure out the rest later."

"What's this 'we' stuff?" Spike asked. "What do you want *me* to do?"

"Yeah, you're too old," Jerry said.

Spike bristled. "Too old for what?"

"To advertise for a bride, that's what. A lot of other men around Montana and other places out West here did it to get women. I heard of a place up in the northern part of the state where it worked out real well for them and their town has gotten bigger," Jerry said. "It seems like the more women came to their town, the more it's grown."

Spike said, "Well, that's great for them, but it don't help us none. You're right about me bein' too old. Besides, there'll never be another woman like my Irene, so I don't even want to look for a wife."

Jerry nodded his understanding. "I know."

"So even if this plan would work, who we gonna get to go first?" Spike asked.

Jerry flicked a glance in Evan's direction, but the sheriff had his head bent over his work again.

"Well," Jerry said, "it's gotta be someone good-lookin'. Someone strong and decent. He'd better be smart, too." He smiled at Spike and then looked pointedly at Evan. "Someone who's good with his hands. Ladies like it when a man's good with his hands."

Although he kept on working on the blanket, Evan had been actively listening, just like he always did, and he smiled a little at that remark.

"Yep. I think I know just the man, too," Jerry said, staring at Evan.

It got quiet and Evan waited for Jerry to continue. When he looked up, both Spike and Jerry were looking at him. Gazing from one to the other, Evan understood that they were talking about him.

"Oh, no. You're not roping me into this crazy idea of yours. I'm just fine on my own," Evan said. "I'm not looking for a wife."

Jerry said, "But as an elected official, isn't it your sworn duty to help Echo?"

"I wasn't elected. They advertised and I answered," Evan corrected him.

"Point taken, but you do get paid, correct?" Jerry said.

Evan said, "Yeah, but that has nothing to do with looking for a wife."

Spike said, "But it would help the town stay alive. Think about all of those kids who would have to leave their home and think about all of the history here. It'd be a real shame to let it, and Echo, die."

"That it would, but you'll have to find someone else who's looking for a wife to do it," Evan said as he began gathering up his yarn and blanket.

Jerry said, "But you're the sheriff and if other men see you getting a bride that way, they'll follow your lead. You'd be setting an example for them."

Evan finished shoving everything into a saddlebag and said, "Find another example. I'm not doing it."

With a warning glare at his friends, Evan left the bar and found his horse, Smitty, a buckskin gelding. He mounted and turned Smitty for home, a small house on the outskirts of Echo. It didn't take him long to get there and put Smitty away for the night.

Entering the small parlor, he saw his Aunt Edna sleeping in one of the two wingback chairs, her feet propped up on an ottoman. He smiled at the sweet sight the older woman made. Sitting his saddle bag on the floor, Evan took off his coat and hung it by the door.

Going over to his aunt, Evan crouched down and gently shook her. "Aunt Edna."

She roused and opened her eyes. "Evan. Goodness. What time is it?"

"Late. Time for you to go to bed," he said.

She chuckled and ran a hand over his jet black hair. "You need a haircut young man. I thought you were gonna get that done last week?"

He smiled at her. "I was, but then we had all that stuff happen with the Trasker's. I never got around to it. Remember?"

"Yes, I remember, Evan. I'm old, but I haven't gone senile yet. Get it done by Friday or else I'm not making you those cookies you wanted," she said, sitting forward.

"Yes, ma'am."

"That's more like it." She grimaced as she stood up. "Damn arthritis. I'd be just fine if it wasn't for my knees being riddled with the dreaded stuff."

"I know," Evan said sympathetically as he helped her over to the stairs. "I don't know why you won't let me switch our rooms so that you don't have to go upstairs at night. It would be a lot easier for you, Aunt Edna."

"Maybe, but I like my room. Besides, I'm not ready to give in yet," she said. "If you're hungry, there's some leftover steak in the kitchen."

"Ok."

As she started climbing the stairs, she asked, "How were the boys tonight?"

"Same as always."

"Did you know that Meagan Humphries is expecting again?" she asked.

With each step she took, one or the other of her knees creaked, making Evan wince each time. This was their normal routine. He'd come home, she'd be asleep, and he'd make sure she got up the stairs safely. They didn't sit and visit like normal people; they talked about their day as they went up the steps.

"Yeah. I know."

Edna said, "That damn husband of hers needs to learn how to keep the barn door closed a little more or else go to Billings to see a girl or two."

"Aunt Edna!" Evan objected.

She snickered and he knew that she'd intended to shock him. "Well, it would be better than pestering her all the time, and that's what those women are for."

Evan broke out laughing at her attitude. It was funny to hear a supposedly Christian woman extoling the virtues of prostitution, but then again, that was Aunt Edna. A contradiction to everything in her own way.

"Here I am, a sheriff, and you're condoning illegal behavior," Evan said.

"Why do you think I said he should go to Billings? That's not your jurisdiction, so you wouldn't have to worry about it," she said as she reached the top of the stairs.

He chuckled. "Thanks, I think. What if Uncle Reb had gone to see one of those women?"

"Well, that's different. If he would have, he'd have sat down to pee the rest of his days," she said with a dismissive wave of her hand.

This was Evan's favorite time of day, talking with his aunt like this. He never knew what was going to come out of her mouth and the later it got, the more outrageous her statements became.

Done laughing over her last remark, he said, "I think it's time you went to sleep."

"And I think it's time for you to shut your mouth and do the same," she retorted.

"I aim to."

Turning to him, she embraced him and said, "Goodnight, Evan. What do you want for breakfast?"

"Whatever I make," he answered, looking down into her blue eyes.

"Good boy. I'm a lousy cook," she said. "It's a good thing Reb cooked or we would have starved or had to live on cookies since it's all I can make. Thank God you take after him and not me."

"Don't I know it," he agreed, hugging her back.

Releasing him, she moved away slowly. "Now stop bothering me and go to bed."

Smiling, he said, "You're the one bothering me, remember?"

"I'm allowed since I finished raising you," she shot back.

"Sure, hold that over my head again."

All this was said as he was going back down the stairs.

"I will until they plant me in the cemetery, sonny boy," she said.

"Don't call me that."

"Sonny boy, sonny boy," she sang out.

"Go to bed, old woman, or I won't cook for you!" he shouted from his room.

This was another part of their nightly routine. Evan knew that their banter would continue for probably another ten minutes as each of them changed for bed.

"Guess what cockamamie plan Jerry and Spike have cooked up for me now?" he shouted.

"God only knows with those two. Are they coming for dinner on Sunday?"

"I don't know. I didn't ask them because they were spoutin' a bunch of crap about mail-order-brides. Can you believe that?"

"About what?"

"Mail-order-brides."

"Jerry has a wife. Spike wants one?" she asked.

"No. They want *me* to get one!" he said.

Silence.

"Hey! Did you hear me?" he asked as he pulled off his pants and slung them over a chair.

"Yes, I heard you. Why do they want you to get one?"

"Some nonsense about helping the town by increasing the population and business. I'm not sure how they expect us to support a whole lot more people when we can't support what we got now," he shouted.

"That still doesn't tell me why they want *you* to do it," she said.

He could tell she was at the top of the stairs again, so he went to the bottom and looked up at her. Neither of them cared that he was in his underwear and she was in her nightgown.

"Jerry said that since I'm the sheriff, I should lead by example. If I do it and it works out, other fellas will do it, too. Like I said; nonsense."

She put a hand up to her chin and rubbed it a little. "I don't know about nonsense. It's unusual, but it might work."

"I hope you're kidding," he said. "I'm not going to order a woman by mail. I'll meet the right woman on my own."

"Yes, because you've done so well by yourself, Evan. Why, I just adore your wife and all of the children you have running around here," she said.

Evan narrowed his eyes at her heavy sarcasm. "Very funny. It's not like I can afford a wife and kids anyway."

"Evan, where there's a will there's a way. It's always been my wish for you to have a family. Once I go, you won't have anyone," she said.

"Aunt Edna, there's no way I'm doing this and that's it. I don't even know how to go about it anyhow. I'm done talking about it," he said.

Hearing the genuine irritation in his voice, Edna decided to drop it for now. "Oh, all right. It wouldn't hurt to think about it. That's the last I'll say about it."

"Thanks. Now go to bed," Evan said. "Goodnight."

"Goodnight, Evan," she said and shuffled into her room, closing the door.

Hearing the latch click, Evan sighed and put on his robe. He wasn't ready to go to sleep yet, so he found the plate of steak and potatoes she had left in the kitchen for him. Sarah Powell, a neighbor, had come over and cooked the dinner with the ingredients he'd left for her. Not bothering to warm the plate, he went out onto their small back porch and sat on a wooden chair. The moon was hidden, so it was a darker night. He gazed out over the small valley their house overlooked. At the bottom of it lie a small streamed that ambled along a relatively flat terrain.

Lush vegetation grew up around it as a result. One of the reasons

Evan had bought the house was because of the easy access to water; the well never went dry and it was certainly easy growing a garden. Looking over to the right, he saw the one steer they owned and their milk cow standing in the small pasture.

At twenty-six Evan was young for a sheriff, but he'd learned at the elbow of his Uncle Rebel Taft, one of the toughest sheriffs ever known to Gallatin County. From the time he'd been old enough to carry a gun, Evan had been taught by his uncle all about being a lawman. When Evan had been eighteen, he'd started working alongside his uncle and both men were feared and respected. However, after his uncle had passed, no town or city in the county except Echo would take a gamble on hiring a twenty-two-year-old deputy to fill the role of sheriff.

He heard a screen door swing shut over to his right and smiled to himself as he took a bite of steak. There was no sound until Billy Two Moons jumped up onto the porch. At eighteen, Billy was tall, lean, and very handsome. He called himself a mutt because he was a mix of this and that. According to his foster parents, his heritage included Lakota, Cheyenne, and Nez Perce Indians with a dash of white thrown in for good measure.

While his eyes were as dark as obsidian, his hair color was medium brown with red highlights that were more prominent in the summer. His skin tone fell in between the shades of the two races.

"So, Billy, you wanna share this with me?" Evan asked.

"Nah. I'm fine. How's the blanket coming along?" Billy asked.

Around a bite of steak, Evan said, "Good. I should be done with it tomorrow night, I think."

Billy nodded and sat down on another chair. "How's Edna tonight?"

"Fine. Asleep when I got home like normal," Evan replied. "What were you up to?"

"Drawing."

"You gonna be able to get that painting done I want to give Spike for his birthday next week?"

A talented artist, Billy sold his paintings and drawings, which was his main source of income. Once every couple of months, he took whatever he had finished into Dickensville, a town closer than Billings, and sold it there.

"That's why I came over," he said. "Come look at it."

Evan raised an eyebrow and looked pointedly down at his state of undress.

"Come around the back way. Besides, the folks are in bed," Billy said.

"Only if you finish this steak. I can't," Evan said. "These were cut too big. I tried to tell Ross to cut them smaller, but he never listens to me about it."

"That's because Ross thinks that everyone eats like he does." Billy swept his long hair away from his face.

Evan eyed him and said, "You oughta get your hair cut. Then it wouldn't always be in your eyes."

Billy gave him a level stare. "Can you really see me with short hair?"

"Probably not. You could try it once. It'll grow back."

"Nah. Why bother? Besides, the girls like it," he said, grinning.

With a chuckle, Evan said, "You're gonna get shot one of these days."

Billy lifted his shoulders in a shrug. "Look, I make no bones about not being serious, so none of them can say I haven't been honest with them."

"Tell that to their fathers. How many do you have on the go right now?" Evan asked. Billy's exploits with the opposite sex ranged from amusing to shocking and were always entertaining.

"Just three," the boy said.

"Only three, huh? What happened to the five you were seeing last week?"

"Two families moved away, or didn't you hear?" Billy said.

Evan shook his head. "You're kidding. Which ones?"

"The Hinkleys and the Smethers."

Evan stopped chewing. "Smethers? You mean the barber left?"

Jerry and Spike's remarks about Echo dying out came to him, and he began thinking that they were right.

"Yep. Closed up shop over the weekend and they left yesterday," Billy said, stretching his legs out in front of him.

"Damn. Now I'm gonna have to go to Dickensville to get my hair cut. I didn't get it done, what with that whole Trasker affair last week. Wait until I tell Aunt Edna. I'll bet she hasn't heard. She'd have told me if she did. Here." He handed Billy his plate.

The youth took it and stood up. "Come on. I'll show you that painting."

"Ok. Aren't you cold?" he asked.

Billy smiled. "Nope. I'm never cold."

He ran around without a shirt whenever he could get away with it no matter what time of year it was.

"Must be that mutt blood of yours," Evan said.

Far from offended, Billy laughed. "Yep. Us mongrels are more hardy than you purebloods."

Evan shoved him off the porch in response for his jibe. "Move it, kid."

Billy hung onto the plate and kept his footing, despite Evan's rough treatment. As they walked across the large yard that separated their houses, Billy tore off a piece of steak and chewed. "Mmm. Sarah makes good steak."

"Yep," Evan said.

Billy led Evan around the back of the white clapboard house in which he and his foster parents lived. His father, Remus Decker, had built on an art studio for Billy. It ended up that Billy had also decided that he was going to sleep out there, too. So, Remus, being the doting father he was, had installed a small woodstove and insulated the place better so that it was airtight and would hold the heat well.

Before leading the way inside the studio, Billy threw the bone from the steak to his dog, Homer. Even though the red coonhound had some quirks, Evan borrowed him once in a while to help track down the occasional criminal or missing person.

As soon as he stepped inside the door, Evan was enveloped in the scents of paint and turpentine. Several canvases sat on easels at various places around the large room. A full-sized bed was situated along one wall with a dresser next to it. Billy didn't care much about neatness and a few of the drawers were partway open.

This habit drove Evan crazy and he went over and closed them.

Billy laughed. "I can't believe how fussy you are about a house for a man. And you crochet. Oh, and you cook. Are you sure you weren't a woman in another life?"

"Shut up. Show me the painting so I can go to bed," Evan said.

"I don't know why you're in such a hurry to go to bed," Billy said. "There won't be anyone in it but you."

Evan said, "If you don't shut that smart mouth, I'm going to help you do it. The painting, please?"

"Right here, Sheriff."

Walking over to an easel, Billy removed the protective cloth draped over it and stood back. Once again, Billy stunned Evan with his talent. The painting of Spike's late wife, Gwen, was exquisite. Using a photograph that Evan had snuck out of Spike's house the week before, Billy had recreated it, adding color and breathing life into the woman on the canvas.

If Evan didn't know better, he would have sworn the woman was alive. He also could see why Spike had no interest in marrying again. Gwen had been a gorgeous woman with deep brown hair and dark eyes. No wonder Spike always sang her praises and was still in love with his late wife.

"Dang, Billy. That's amazing. Spike's gonna love it. I can't wait to give it to him," Evan said.

"Give me two days and it's all yours," Billy said. "She was a beautiful lady. Oh, you can have the picture back. I don't need it now—I got all I need up here." He tapped his temple.

"You ask me, you need to have a lot more up there than you do," Evan said.

Flashing Evan a devilish smile, Billy said, "I make up for it by having more in other places."

Evan groaned. "Is that all you think about?"

"I'm eighteen. What did you think about at my age?"

"Being a sheriff."

"Well, being a sheriff isn't keeping you company at night, is it?"

Evan took the photograph of Gwen from Billy. "What is it with everyone tonight? Suddenly you're all concerned with my marital status."

"Who is?" Billy asked.

"Spike, Jerry, Aunt Edna, and now you."

"I don't care if you get married, I'm just saying it wouldn't hurt for you to—"

Two shotgun blasts rang out in rapid succession, cutting into their conversation. Evan and Billy ran outside just as someone ran past their houses.

"Let Homer loose! He came from the direction of the Pattersons' house. Go check it out. I'm going after him," Evan directed.

"You don't have a gun and you're in your robe!" Billy hollered after him.

"Won't be the first time I've ran after someone half-naked. Do as I say," Evan shouted back.

The sheriff gave chase to the unknown runner. Homer caught up to him in no time.

"Homer! Sic 'em!" Evan commanded.

The dog ran happily beside him, tongue lolling.

Rolling his eyes, Evan said, "Sic 'em, *please*?"

That was the magic word. Homer shot forward, disappearing into the dark. Evan kept going until he heard Homer sound off somewhere to his left. Evan changed direction. Ignoring the cold and the fact that he was running barefoot over rough ground, he followed the sound of Homer's baying.

He entered a densely wooded area and had to slow down a little. Even so, his powerful legs kept him speeding along at a good clip. Homer bayed again and Evan reduced his speed as he closed in on him. The dog jumped up and down at the base of a large oak tree.

Evan looked up into the branches, but it was too dark for him to see much. "Hey! This is Sheriff Taft. Come on down from there!"

A shot rang out and Evan hit the ground.

Chapter Two

Slinking around the side of the Pattersons' house, Billy peeked in one of the parlor windows and was shocked at what he saw. Ellie Patterson lay sprawled out on the floor, blood oozing out from underneath her body. He ran to the door, flinging it wide open, and hurrying to Ellie's side.

"Mrs. Patterson!" Billy cried, beginning to look her over. He had to fight to keep the steak and potatoes he'd just eaten down as he saw the small river of blood running across the wooden floor.

Two gaping wounds were torn into her chest. Billy looked around and grabbed an afghan from the sofa and pressed it over the wounds, but he knew it was a losing battle. Even as he did so, Ellie's eyes glazed over and her last breath left her in a sound that resembled a sigh. Billy struggled against tears as he covered her body with the afghan.

Then he remembered her kids and knew they had to be scared out of their minds. Jimmy and Amy were eight and four, respectively, and they were very sweet children. Billy ran to the stairs and called out to them.

"Jimmy! Amy! It's Billy! It's ok to come out," he said, running up the stairs. "Where are you guys? Come on out."

Going into the kids' room, he saw the door of a large armoire crack open a little.

"It's ok. It's me. Billy," he said.

Little Jimmy crept out of the armoire, followed closely by Amy. Both of them were in their night clothes.

"Come here," Billy said, kneeling and opening his arms to them.

The two toe-headed little ones ran to Billy, clinging to their friend.

Jimmy said, "He shot Ma."

Billy closed his eyes as he hugged them tightly. "You saw it?"

"Yeah, but not Amy. I came up and got her in the closet with me," Jimmy said, sniffling.

"Good job, buddy. You did the right thing. You're a brave guy," Billy told him. "Do you know who it was?"

"No. I never seen him before. He was skinny and he had a big nose. That's all I saw of him. He shot Ma and I ran upstairs," Jimmy told him.

"Ok," Billy said. "I'm gonna take you over to our house, ok? Where's your pa?"

"I don't know. Maybe Spike's," Jimmy said as Billy rose.

Amy had yet to speak. She shivered in Billy's arms as he lifted her up.

"Jimmy, when we go downstairs, you go straight out the front door, ok? Don't you look anywhere but straight ahead. Do you promise to do that?"

Jimmy nodded solemnly. "I promise."

"Good boy. Let's go," Billy said.

Remus stood in the kitchen of their house, listening to his son's story. His wife, Arlene, sat on the sofa with Jimmy and Amy, trying to comfort them.

"Jimmy's description doesn't ring a bell with me," Remus said.

"It could fit a lot of guys," Billy said.

Remus nodded. "Has anyone gone looking for Shane?"

"No. Evan's after the guy who went running by here." Billy's mouth curved up in a smile. "He's in his robe and barefoot, but he's chasing him. He took Homer."

The older man rubbed his forehead and laughed. "That sure sounds like Evan. I've never seen anyone like him. He coulda stopped for a gun at least. Well, I'll check at Spike's and see if Shane's there. I hate like hell to give him this kind of news. You stay here with your ma and help with the kids, ok?"

"Sure, Pa."

Remus nodded, shrugged his big shoulders into his coat, and told Arlene where he was going. Before leaving, he kissed each of the kids.

Two more shots rang out as Evan lay on the ground. Evan could tell that they came from a revolver. He didn't know what the culprit had done with the shotgun, but they had apparently changed weapons. Intent on catching his prey despite the fact that he was almost naked and weaponless, Evan put his keen mind to use and assessed the situation.

He was going to have to get the person, whom he assumed was a man, to use all the ammunition in their gun and then hope that they didn't have more on them. There was no way for him to crawl silently up the tree, so sneaking up on them was out of the question. He looked over at Homer, who had backed off a ways.

The dog sat on his haunches, looking up into the tree. Every so often, he licked his chops. Evan smiled. Homer liked to get his teeth into bad guys if possible. The sheriff knew that if the guy hit the ground right now, Homer would help take care of apprehending him.

That's it! I have to get him down somehow. Then Homer and I can nab him.

"Now look, jackass. Make it easy on yourself and come down. I'm going to find you no matter what, so you might as well just come down here."

"Is that really you, Sheriff?"

"Yes. It's Evan. Who's that?"

"Calvin Parker, sir," the voice said.

"Calvin?" Evan asked, as he began rising from the ground. "Why the heck are you shooting at me?"

"Because I thought you were him," Calvin said.

Evan could hear him begin to climb down the tree. "Stand down, Homer. Please?"

The sheriff had never before seen a dog who understood asking politely for things, but that was Homer for you.

Homer laid down, but still watched Calvin as he progressed downwards. Once the man had dropped to the ground, Evan snatched the revolver from him.

"Where's the shotgun, Cal?"

Calvin shook his head. "I wasn't the one with the shotgun."

"Get walking, Cal. We're going to the office," Evan said. "What do you mean you didn't have a shotgun? Who did?"

"Shane."

They had come out of the trees and as the moonlight hit them, Evan looked into Calvin's blue eyes. "Shane? Was he shooting at you?"

Calvin's face crumpled and the man dissolved into tears.

Evan sighed and waited a few moments before asking, "What happened? Start at the beginning."

Wiping away tears with his coat sleeve, Calvin said, "Shane was trying to shoot me, but he got Ellie instead. She's dead. I'm sure of it."

Evan's eyebrows shot up and his heart began hammering in his chest. "Ellie's dead? Where are the kids? Are they safe?"

"I th-think so. I didn't see them," Calvin said.

"Let's go. I don't understand what's going on here, but I'm gonna get to the bottom of it," Evan said.

Calvin looked Evan over as they walked. "Do you know you're in your underwear?"

"Yeah, I know. We better stop by my place so I can get dressed. If you try to run, Calvin, I'll track you down no matter what I have to do.

I'll find you. Do you hear me?" Evan said.

"Yeah, Sheriff. I won't run off. I swear," Calvin said.

Evan rubbed his tired eyes and said, "So let me see if I have this straight, Cal. You and Ellie have been having an affair. Shane caught you tonight and tried to shoot you, but he got Ellie instead. Is that right?"

"Yeah. That's why I ran," Cal said. "I didn't want to be shot."

Evan regarded Calvin in silence for a few beats and then smacked him hard alongside his head. "What the hell is the matter with you? Why would you do that?"

Calvin rubbed his head and said, "What? Run so I didn't get shot?"

Evan smacked him again. "No! Have an affair with a married woman! Because of you two kids are motherless now."

"She started it!" Calvin objected.

Evan glared at him. "You didn't have to take her up on her offer, you idiot!"

"Well, if it wasn't me, it would have been someone else," Calvin said. "I wasn't the only one she was after."

Leaning back in his chair, Evan sighed and looked at the ceiling of the simple brick building. He'd heard rumors about Ellie's carrying on, but he hadn't paid much attention to it. Although he listened to gossip, he didn't usually give much credence to it. He could understand why Shane would be enraged, but murder wasn't the answer. Not only were Jimmy and Amy now without a mother, but a father as well because he was going to go to prison.

"Well, I'm putting you in lockup until I can find Shane to verify all this," Evan said. "C'mon."

Calvin stood, but balked a little about going back to a holding cell. "You mean *if* you find him."

Shoving Calvin along, Evan said, "Oh, no. I'll find him. You know me better than that, Cal. I'm like a Mountie. I always get my man. One way or another, I'll find Shane."

Calvin felt chills break out along his spine as he heard the somewhat malicious note in Evan's voice. He did indeed know Evan well enough to know that the sheriff never quit when it came to catching criminals, no matter how dangerous. As Calvin went into the cell, he thought about how glad he was that he wasn't the one Evan was after.

By ten o'clock the next morning, all of Echo had heard about the murder of Ellie Patterson. Evan avoided town as much as possible because he didn't want to have to answer questions about it all. He had yet to locate Shane, but he would. If he didn't personally, one of his law enforcement buddies would. Not only that, but he had one of the best bounty hunters in all of Montana working for him.

Thaddeus McIntyre was one of the toughest and craziest men Evan knew and he backed down from nothing or no one. The grizzled, middle-aged man knew the state like the back of his hand and if anyone could find Shane, it would be him. He'd been a friend of Evan's Uncle Reb since the two had been kids and he'd transferred that friendship over onto Evan when he'd been just a boy.

Evan had come by his uncle's sense of duty and decency by inheritance and Thad's recklessness and determination by association. The mix was very effective, and Evan's success rate and experience was what had landed him the job in Echo despite his young age. He'd proven himself time and again and other towns now regretted not hiring him. A few had tried to woo Evan away from Echo, but he'd told them to kiss his behind and leave him alone.

Strolling into the sheriff's office, Thad walked up to Evan and thumped him on the shoulder. "So, we got us a murder, huh?"

"Yeah. Thanks for coming," Evan said.

"Well, I'm a little bored at the moment and a manhunt sounds like a good way for me to occupy my time. So, Shane, huh? Ellie wasn't very good at hiding her, um, indiscretions. She even propositioned me a couple of times. I think she did it just to get Shane's goat."

Evan shook his head in disgust. "I don't understand that at all. Shane's a good man. Why did she want to do that kind of thing?"

Thad sat in a chair and said, "Because she could. You gotta admit she was a fine lookin' woman with that red hair and big brown eyes. Nice figure, too. She liked the way men looked at her. There's more men around here than women and I know you know that. So, if a woman's offering, chances are that at least a few men are gonna take her up on it."

"Yeah, I know that. Well, that's not important right now. We gotta get Shane and bring him in. He'll have to stand trial, no matter what the circumstances."

"Yep. How're those poor kids?" Thad asked as he took out a cigarette and lit it.

"Shaken up. Jimmy saw it. He said the guy was skinny with a big nose. When I asked him about it, though, he told me that he'd just made that up because he didn't want Shane to get in trouble. It's a damn shame. He'll never get that out of his head."

Thad nodded and cocked his head. "You know what that's like."

Evan nodded. "Yeah. It's hard to forget seeing your family killed." Not wanting to get into that, he asked, "So, when are you leaving?"

"Straight away. I just wanted to stop in first to let you know I got your message. You need a deputy. Then you could go with me and leave him in charge," Thad said.

"That would be nice—I might actually get a day off now and again. But Echo can't afford a deputy. They can hardly afford me."

"Is that the reason you don't want to look for a wife?"

Jerking a little, Evan said, "Jerry opened his big mouth, didn't he?"

"Yep. Last night. You musta just left right before I got to Spike's. He said that you didn't cotton to the idea of ordering a bride. You should do it," Thad said, his dark eyes zeroing in on Evan. "You're a young man. It's only right that you'd want to have a family."

"You don't," Evan retorted.

"Nope, but that's because I'm not built that way. You are. You're just like your pa and Rebel. Family men. It's in your blood. Don't bother fighting it, son. Just because something terrible happened to your family, doesn't mean that it would to your own." Thad rose and came over to Evan. "Did you really chase after Cal in only your underwear?"

Evan grinned. "Yeah."

Thad laughed and clapped his shoulder again. "That's my boy. Well, I gotta go catch a bad guy. I'll be back with his sorry hide. Think about that bride business."

Evan's amused smile turned into a hard scowl. "I'll find one sooner or later."

"Well, you're not doing too good at it on your own, but that's only because there just ain't enough women around. If you find a wife, other fellas will follow your example. Jerry's right about that."

Evan said, "Yeah, but if it doesn't work out, then what?"

Thad said, "Long as I've know you, you've been a risk taker. Take a risk and see what happens. You're also determined. A determined risk taker is sure to succeed. Well, see ya."

After Thad left, Evan leaned forward, putting his head in his hands. Thad made it five people in the space of twenty-four hours who had hounded him about marriage. He would like to have a family, but finding a wife by mail? He just didn't know about that. He also didn't know anyone who'd ever done it.

"Where would I start? I guess put an advertisement in the paper. We don't have one. The closest one is in Dickensville." Evan often talked to himself when he was working through a problem. This annoyed others because sometimes they never knew if he was talking to them or not. "What do you say in one of those ads? I can't believe I'm even considering this. I must be insane."

Thad's remark about him being a risk taker was right on the mark—when it involved anything but his heart. Maybe it was time to change that, though. His mind made up, he rose from his chair.

"Cal, I'll be back after a bit," he called out.

"Ok!" Cal hollered back.

After locking up, Evan mounted Smitty and headed out to Jerry's wagon shop located on the west end of town. As he trotted along, Evan nodded to folks as he went. He soon encountered little Pauline Desmond. Seven years old and full of herself, she'd attached herself to Evan for some reason.

"Sheriff!" she shouted from across the street.

Evan recognized her sweet little voice and grinned. He turned Smitty in her direction and crossed over to her. "You again?" he teased her. "What do you want?"

She laughed, her brown eyes shining. "A ride."

"Well, I can't right now. I'm on my way somewhere and then I gotta get back to the office. Tell you what. When I get back in town, I'll come get you and we'll go for a quick ride then, ok?" he said.

"Do you promise you'll come get me?" she asked as her mother, Jenny, came out of the general store.

"I promise, if it's all right with your ma," Evan said. "Hi, Jenny."

"Hello, Sheriff. Is she pestering you again?" Jenny asked with a chuckle.

"Nope. Is it ok if I take her for a little ride when I get back?" he asked.

"Sure, as long as you don't mind," Jenny said.

"Nope. I sure don't," Evan assured her.

"All right, then. Oh, Travis said to tell you thanks again for helping with the roof the other day," Jenny said, speaking about her husband.

Evan said, "Glad I could help. I'll see you after a bit."

"'Bye, Sheriff," Pauline said with a little wave.

Tipping his hat to them, Evan rode off again.

Jerry was surprised to see Evan walk into his workshop that morning.

"Don't you have a murderer to catch?" he asked.

Evan said, "Hello, Jerry. It's nice to see you, too. How are you?" in response to Jerry's abrupt greeting.

Jerry carried some lumber over to where he was working on

repairing the sideboards of wagon and dropped it onto the floor. "Hello, Evan. Good to see you. I'm fine, and you?"

"That's better." Evan grinned. "Thad's going after him since I can't leave town."

"Yeah, I know. I just had to harass you. Now that we've exchanged pleasantries, what do you want?" Jerry put a board up on two sawhorses and started measuring them.

Evan grew a little nervous as he said, "Well, since everyone isn't gonna leave me alone about this, I guess I'll put an ad in for a wife. I can't believe I'm saying that, but what the hell? I might as well give it try."

Shock made Jerry drop the pencil he'd been marking boards with and he gave Evan his full attention. "You're serious?"

Evan's determination rose as he said, "Yeah. I mean, look what happened because there aren't enough women around here? I hate to say it, but you were right about that. If the men around here had their own women, maybe we could prevent this kind of thing from happening again. Where do I start? I don't know how to write an ad like that. Do you? You said there was some town up north who did it. How did you hear about it?"

"You know that fella I bought Alonso from last month?" Jerry asked.

Alonso was Jerry's new Clydesdale he'd bought to haul lumber. He was a beautiful, intelligent animal and Jerry's pride and joy.

"Yeah. What kind of name for a horse is that, anyway?" Evan said.

"This from the sheriff who crochets and chases bad guys in his underwear," Jerry said with an ironic look at Evan.

Evan just stared at Jerry and said, "Just answer the question."

"Well, this Dwyer fella said that he got his wife that way. She's a good-lookin' woman, too. He said it was easy. You just write down what you're lookin' for and tell the lady what you're like and then put in the ad. He said he was almost buried with letters. Of course, he's a rich, handsome man, so I'm sure that had something to do with it. You're handsome, just not rich. So I'm sure you'll get a lot of letters yourself."

"So that's all there is to it?" Evan asked.

"Yup. Piece of cake. When you gonna do it?" Jerry asked.

"Might as while do it before I change my mind. I'll write it up tonight and get Billy to take it to Dickensville for me. They can put it out on the wire to other papers. Oh, Aunt Edna wants to know if you and Sonya are coming for dinner on Sunday."

Jerry smiled. "You bet we are. She owes me a poker game."

"Good. I gotta get back. I promised Pauline a ride before I have to go babysit Calvin again. I've half a mind to release him. If Thad isn't back by Monday, maybe I will. He confessed to the affair and all," Evan said. "I don't think he's lying to me."

"I don't think so, either. You're a great judge of character, so go with your gut. That'll come in handy once you start gettin' all those letters, too."

Evan laughed. "I hope so."

Chapter Three

"Aunt Edna, will you look at this for me?" Evan asked that evening.

He'd written up an advertisement, but he was no writer, and he was worried that it sounded stupid.

"What is it?" she asked, looking up from the doily she was working on.

"An ad for a bride," he said.

She broke into laughter, but when Evan just smiled, she said, "Oh, you're serious. You're actually doing it?"

Evan pulled over another ottoman and sat on it close to her chair. "I got to thinking about it today. If we had more women, maybe we can avoid things like what happened between Ellie and Shane. Thad also said some things to me that got me thinking. Maybe it *is* time to look for a wife."

Beaming, Edna took the tablet from Evan and said, "I think you're making a good decision. Now hurry up and choose a wife and make some babies."

He laughed. "I have to get the ad in the paper first."

"Ok. Let's look at what you have here," she said. After reading the first sentence, she tsked and reached for his pencil.

Evan gave it to her and then watched with dismay as she crossed things out and mumbled over what he'd written. "What's wrong with it?"

"Well, it's just that a man wrote it and most men just aren't skilled in writing romantic things. You've given bare facts, like what you write in your reports, but that's not gonna get you a woman, sonny boy. Give me a couple minutes and I'll fix it for you," she said.

Evan said, "Ok. I'll go get some more wood while you do that. It's gonna be cold again tonight."

She didn't answer because she was already busy with the task at hand.

Going out back to the wood pile, Evan began gathering a good armload. Taking it in, he put some in the wood box in the kitchen and then loaded more on the fire in the parlor.

"There. That's much better," Edna said. "Take a look."

Evan took the tablet and began reading.

Handsome small town sheriff desires to marry a lovely woman between 21 and 28 years old with good domestic skills, and she must be willing to start a family right away. He is 6' 2" tall and weighs around 185 lbs. Trust me when I tell you that he is quite a fine male specimen. I should know since I'm his aunt. With his ebony hair and jade green eyes, he's very pleasing to the eye. He's polite, hard-working, and has a good sense of humor. Please send letters to Sheriff Evan Taft, General Delivery, Echo Canyon, Montana.

He smiled and said, "You actually want me to leave this in here about you being my aunt?"

"Of course," Edna said. "It shows that you're a family man. Women like to know these things. Mark my words, sonny boy, you put that ad in and you'll be knee-deep in letters in no time."

Evan said, "Ok. You've never steered me wrong yet. I'll go give it to Billy."

"You tell him to come to Sunday dinner, but not to wear a shirt," Edna said.

"Aunt Edna, you're terrible," Evan said as he put on his coat.

"He is a very scrumptious boy, Evan. Even us old ladies like to look," she said with a naughty laugh.

Groaning, Evan left the house.

Twisting wheat-blonde hair around her forefinger, Josephine Bainbridge drank her morning coffee and looked through the window of the small kitchen. Birds flitted here and there, but she wasn't really paying attention to them. She was waiting for her friend Opal to arrive with the newspaper.

Josie, as she was known, scrimped and scraped just to survive so she couldn't afford a paper of her own, but Opal always gave hers to Josie. She tapped her foot agitatedly on the floor and then got up. She wasn't one to stay still or waste time, so she began looking over her finances again and trying to figure out how to make some more money.

This was something she did every day even though there really wasn't a solution. She didn't have many unique skills. Cooking, cleaning, and sewing were things that most woman were skilled at, so it didn't make her stand out that she could do those things.

The only thing that set her apart from other women was that she sang and played guitar. However, there wasn't any call for such a thing where she lived in Pullman, Washington. The only other skill she had was creating beautiful quilts, but again, many women could do that.

At twenty-two, she felt as though her life would never start. Other women were getting married and having families and she was being left behind. Opal was getting married in two weeks and she was the last of Josie's single friends. The problem was that, unlike some other places in the country, Pullman had an abundance of women, but not enough men. Finding a man in her age group was hard because the men had their pick.

Since she was slimmer in the hips and lacking somewhat in the bosom department, Josie didn't have the hourglass figure that was in fashion at the moment. She'd had some suitors over the years, but no one that she'd want to marry. Josie was looking for love and she wasn't going to settle for just anyone.

As soon as she heard the knock on her door, Josie ran to it and opened it. Opal smiled at her and came inside Josie's little bungalow.

"Hello, Josie. Here you are," she said, handing her friend the paper.

Josie took it and promptly sat down on her threadbare sofa to read it. Opal sat down, spreading her skirt neatly about her. The pretty brown-eyed brunette looked around Josie's place and frowned. In some disrepair and a little dismal in nature, the bungalow was not an ideal residence, but it was all Josie could afford on her own, Opal knew.

Her best friend had done her best to brighten the place up, but there was only so much to be done with it without it being completely remodeled. William Stanton wasn't about to do such a thing since he was such a miserly man.

Once she'd read all of the articles that interested her, Josie turned to the classifieds and began looking through the personals. She was hoping to find a husband in Pullman, but so far none of the ads had struck her fancy. Josie had begun to accept the fact that she was going to have to go farther afield to find a man to marry.

Carefully, she read each ad, not missing a thing. She slid a small notepad off the coffee table and wrote down the ads that she liked. After writing down two, she came across one from a sheriff in Montana. She chewed on her pencil as she read it. The man certainly sounded like good husband material and his job was probably exciting. Could she handle being a sheriff's wife?

Also, there was the traveling to consider. She had been hoping for someone close by since she wasn't sure she could scrape up the money to get somewhere farther away. She really liked the sound of him, though, and thought it was cute that his aunt was vouching for him. It sounded like he was good to his family and that was an important thing to Josie.

She wrote down the ad, deciding to see what came of sending him a letter along with the other men. Laying the paper aside, she looked at Opal and said, "Well, there are three that seem promising."

"Let me see," Opal said.

Josie handed her the notepad and waited while Opal read what she'd written. As Josie watched Opal, she felt a moment's jealousy of her friend's good fortune in finding a great catch like Sean Everett. He was a good-looking, successful doctor and kind besides. It was no wonder the blond, blue-eyed man had fallen for Opal. She was a beautiful, intelligent woman and she would make a good doctor's wife.

"Well, I think you have some good candidates here. I like this one from Montana, but I don't want you to move so far away," Opal said.

With a sigh, Josie said, "I may not have a choice. We'll see what happens."

"Right. Are you ready to go to the dress shop with me? I have my final fitting today," Opal said.

Josie nodded as she felt that stirring of envy again. "Yes. I'm ready. I'll just get my coat."

Opal felt sympathy for Josie. She'd heard the sad note in Josie's voice and knew that she tried hard to hide it. Opal hoped that one of the men to whom Josie had been writing would be the right one for her. She knew that Josie was lonely and that with her getting married, she wouldn't have as much time for Josie as usual. Even though she didn't want Josie to move away, she wanted her to be happy. So if that meant that she had to move, then Opal would support her.

"Ok. I'm ready," Josie said as she put on her black kersey cape. She'd made it herself out of heavy wool with a silk lining. She'd splurged and bought some pretty black pearl buttons to adorn the front of it.

They left the house, walking the few blocks to Madam Bernadine's Women's Boutique, where they were greeted by Bernadine herself.

"Oh, Opal, Josie. How good to see you both. You're here for your fitting," the fifty-ish blonde said.

Opal smiled. "That's right."

Bernadine smiled. "You must be so excited. Not long now."

"I can't wait," Opal said, her eyes shining with happy anticipation. "Our house is ready and we've already bought our furniture and arranged it." Opal clapped her hands a little and Bernadine laughed.

"Well, it certainly sounds like it's all coming along nicely," Bernadine said.

Opal nodded.

Sean had built a very roomy, two-story house with three bedrooms, a large parlor, dining room, kitchen, and an office for him. It was white with green shutters and they had a nice lawn all the way around it that would be perfect for playing with their future children. Sean had let Opal decide on much of the home's décor, saying that she knew much more about it than he did. The young woman had been happy to do the job and Josie had helped her.

Bernadine turned to Josie. "Do you need to be fitted a last time, too?"

"No. I'm the same as I was," Josie said with a little laugh.

"All right, then. Let's get you taken care of, Opal," Bernadine said, leading the women to the dressing area.

As Josie watched Opal being fussed over, she prayed that one of these men she was writing to would be the right one for her.

Chapter Four

D^{ear Sheriff Taft,}

My name is Josie Bainbridge and I'm writing in response to your advertisement. My given name is Josephine, but I prefer Josie. I'll cover the formalities first. My hair is blonde and I have blue eyes. I'm twenty-two and I'm 5' 7" tall, with a slender build. I've been described as "willowy."

I'm very good at keeping house and I help some people around Pullman with childcare, so I'm also what you're looking for in that department. I've always wanted my own family and I'm very ready to start one. While I would worry about you, your profession doesn't bother me. What you do is very important to the community and I would never try to get in the way of that.

Based on the way your aunt wrote your ad, I can tell that she loves you and that you have a good relationship with her. It's important to have that kind of connection with family and it seems like the two of you have that. I lost my parents when I was nineteen within six months of each other. My mother passed first, and I think my father was so brokenhearted that he couldn't bear to live without her and went to be with her.

I work part-time at a restaurant here and also babysitting. I don't make very much money, but I have shelter, food, and clothing, so I can't complain. There are many people less fortunate than me, so I'm thankful for what I have.

My Uncle Gilbert taught me to play guitar and I sing. I've written a few songs of my own, but I don't think they're very good. It's something I do that's relaxing and it helps keep my uncle alive for me. Do you do anything creative? I also like to quilt. What's Echo Canyon like? It sounds like an interesting place. Have you always lived there?

I was born and raised in Pullman. It's a nice place to live, but we have a shortage of men here, the same as some of the Midwest has a shortage of women. That's why I'm not married by now. Well, I'll close for now, but I look forward to hearing from you.

Sincerely,

Josie

The day Josie's first letter arrived was a busy one for Evan. He'd barely gotten to the office when Thad arrived, hauling Shane Patterson inside.

"Here you are, Sheriff. One murderer, just like you ordered," Thad said, grinning.

Shane's brown eyes looked haunted and he looked thinner to Evan.

Wherever he'd been hiding, food must have been in short supply. He didn't smell very good, either.

Taking Shane from Thad, Evan said, "Shane Patterson, you're under arrest for the murder of your wife, Ellie Patterson."

Roughly, he shoved Shane along to the left-hand side of the room and through a doorway. A row of three cells lined the wall in the second room. To lessen the chances of escape by prisoners, there were no windows in the cells, but there were windows on either end of the cell area. They could be opened to allow ventilation, which helped prevent heat exhaustion and keep the stench down in the summer.

Evan's predilection for cleanliness carried over to the sheriff's office, and he performed regular housekeeping duties. This even included keeping fresh linens on the cots in the cells. A small cook stove in the main room not only provided heat in the winter, but also gave Evan the ability to feed prisoners and himself.

Pushing Shane into the first cell, Evan said, "You make me sick, Shane. How could you do it?"

Shane said, "I was tryin' to get Calvin, not Ellie."

Evan shut the cell door and then banged on it. "It doesn't matter! Either way, you'd have been leaving your kids without a father and now they have no parents at all! Jimmy saw the whole thing! Did you know that?"

Tears flooded Shane's eyes. "No. I didn't know. I didn't mean to do it. I was just so damn mad when I came home and found the two of them kissin' like that."

Evan slammed his hand repeatedly against the door, venting the rage that suddenly consumed him. "Jimmy will never get the image of his father murdering his mother out of his head! Never! I oughta know because I watched my whole family get murdered! He lied for you, Shane! An eight-year-old little boy lied to protect his cowardly, murdering father! I can't look at you anymore."

Before he opened the cell door and gave Shane a beating, Evan walked out into the main room, past Thad, and out of the office into the bright sunshine. Pacing back and forth a few moments, he got a handle on his emotions, putting the past back in the iron box in his head and locking it up again for a while.

He didn't take those memories out much, but sometimes, when something like this happened, the box just wouldn't stay shut.

He heard Thad come outside, but his friend didn't say anything. Thad knew there was nothing to say about the subject that could help Evan.

Instead, Thad asked, "So how's the whole bride thing going?"

Thankful for Thad's sensitivity, Evan laughed a little. "Pretty good. I've gotten some letters, but I haven't had time to read the one I got today. A couple seem promising, I guess. Thanks for hauling Shane in. I'll get your money."

Thad followed Evan back into the sheriff's office. "So do you want me to help you take Shane over to Dickensville so they can get him up to the state prison?"

Evan nodded. "Yeah. Let's do it tomorrow morning, ok?" Evan said and handed Thad his money.

"Thanks," Thad said. "Ok. Leave at seven?"

"Make it eight. Aunt Edna moves a little slow in the mornings," Evan said.

"Sure. No problem," Thad said. "I feel so bad about her knees. Other than that, she's fine."

Evan looked into Thad's eyes and said, "Actually, I think she's started with it in her ankles, too, but doesn't want to tell me. I've noticed a difference in her walk the past few months."

"Aw, hell," Thad said. "It's a damn shame. She's not all that much older than me. There's nothing they can do for it?"

Evan shook his head. "Nope. I've had her to several doctors, but they all say the same thing. It's just gonna get worse."

Thad said some other choice words and sighed. "Well, at least she has you and you know you got a lot of friends to help you out."

"I know," Evan said. "Thanks."

With a nod, Thad said, "Well, I'll leave you to your letter. I hope one of those gals works out for you."

"Me, too," Evan said as he sat down at his desk.

<hr>

Evan had read Josie's letter three different times, along with the other six he'd received. But hers stuck in his head and he found himself thinking about it over the last two days. For some reason it resonated with him, but he didn't know why. It wasn't a funny letter or very exciting, but there was something about it that spoke to him. It was strange.

Two of the other letters had interested him, but not like Josie's letter. After mulling it over for a third day, he sat down to write her back that night.

Dear Josie,

Since I'll call you by your first name, feel free to do the same for me. I've never heard a woman play guitar before, but I'd like to hear your songs. I'll bet they're better than you think they are. I might as well tell you now. You asked if I do anything creative and I do. I crochet. I'm completely serious about that. My Aunt Edna taught me when I was about eleven and I've been doing it ever since.

Like your guitar playing is a way for you to relax, crocheting relaxes me, too. Some of my buddies harass me about it, but everyone knows not to really make fun of me for it. Being a sheriff can be exciting. My Uncle Reb taught me everything I know. He was a sheriff for a long time and I was his deputy. He died about four years ago and I miss him a lot.

I bounced around for a while after he died because nowhere wanted a twenty-two-year-old for a sheriff.

They all thought I was too young. When Echo put out an ad for one, I answered it and they hired me. My uncle was known around a lot of the state and they were only too happy to have me. So I moved my aunt here with me since we're all the family each other has. My parents and two sisters passed away when I was eleven and my aunt and uncle finished raising me. I'm sorry to hear that you lost your parents young, too.

We definitely have a shortage of women here, which is why I advertised for a bride, of course. Echo is a small town with two restaurants, a post office, a wagon shop, two saloons, one church, a general store, a small school, and a couple of other businesses. It's normally a fairly quiet place, with your occasional fight or some drunk getting rowdy, but for the most part it's peaceful.

My next door neighbor, Billy, is a good artist. He's eighteen and full of himself, but he's a good kid. I sometimes use his dog to help me at my job. Homer is a coonhound and he's a great tracker. I'm glad to hear that me being a sheriff doesn't put you off. Any woman I marry has to be able to help me a little with my aunt. She's a terrible cook, so I have a couple of neighbor ladies cook for her when I can't be home. I like cooking and I'm good at it, so I don't mind sharing that duty.

I like a clean house, so I keep up with ours since Aunt Edna has trouble getting around on account of her bad knees. She has arthritis really bad and it makes it hard for her to be on her feet real long. She's stubborn, though. She won't switch rooms with me so she doesn't have to go upstairs to bed at night. I usually follow her up the stairs to make sure she's ok.

I guess it's my good fortune that there aren't a lot of men to be had where you are. Write me back.

Sincerely,

Evan

Josie was excited about Evan's letter. He certainly sounded like her kind of man. She smiled as he talked about his aunt. She sounded like a sweet lady. It didn't bother her that Echo wasn't a big town; Josie wasn't looking for excitement. She was after a good man with whom she could have a family and a nice life together. Those were the most important things to her.

After reading the letter again, she realized what time it was and hurried off to her job. Halfway to Bart's she stopped walking as it hit her that she'd need a job once she got to Echo, if things went well with her and Evan during their correspondence. She would have to ask Evan if there were any positions available anywhere.

Arriving at Bart's, she sighed and put on an apron. She was grateful for employment, but being a waitress certainly wasn't her dream job. All throughout her shift, she thought about Evan's letter and it made her smile. Once work was done, she hurried home to write back to him.

When the end of May came, she'd made up her mind to go to Echo Canyon, depending on Evan's response to her telling him she'd like to meet him. Josie checked the post office every day to see if a letter had come. Opal was nicely settled into her and Sean's new home and she was a happy woman.

Josie enjoyed going over to their house for dinner, but she always felt like a third wheel, which was why she preferred going to Opal's family dinners. She was still the only single person there, but it made her feel better when there were more people around.

Finally, a letter from Evan came and Josie took it over to Opal's to open it with her friend there for moral support.

"Josie, calm down for heaven's sake," Opal said as she watched Josie pace back and forth across their parlor.

"I can't. What if he doesn't want me to come? I've wasted all this time and I'll be back to square one," Josie said. "What if I've bored him and he hates me and has just been writing to me out of pity?"

"I doubt that's the case. Now, c'mon and sit down so you can read that letter."

Josie blew out a breath and flopped down on the sofa next to Opal. "Ok. Here I go."

She opened the envelope and unfolded the letter, cringing as she began reading.

Dear Josie,

I'm really glad you want to come to Echo. I know you said that you could be ready sort of quick so I took the liberty of checking the train schedule. It looks like if you left on June 10th you could be here by the 20th. You'd come into Corbin, which is only a county over from Gallatin. I'd pick you up and bring you back to Echo. There's a couple here who run a small boarding house and they'd have a room for you. I wish we had a nice hotel here, but we don't.

As for your question about a job, I've been thinking about that. You said you can sew real well, so you might be able to pick up some work doing that kind of thing. There are men here who don't have anyone to do that since some families have left Echo, taking the women who used to do it with them. It might not be exciting, but it's honest work.

Well, let me know if all that sounds all right to you. Keeping my fingers crossed.

Evan

Josie jumped up from the sofa, letting out an excited cry. She jumped up and down a little and handed the letter to Opal, who read it.

A smile spread across Opal's face. "I told you! I'm so excited for you, even if it means you'll be leaving me."

Josie sat down and hugged Opal. "Don't worry. It's not all that far so I'll come see you. You and Sean could come there, too."

Opal's eyes lit up at that idea. "That would be fun! Maybe we'll plan it for next year so Sean can have time to make sure things would be covered at his practice."

"See? It'll be fine. I'll miss you, too," Josie said. She sobered and bit her bottom lip. "It's a little scary; I won't know anyone there. I know it'll take a little getting used to, but I have a good feeling about it."

Opal nodded, "I do, too. I want you to be happy. I know how much you've wanted to find a good man and start a family. This Evan seems like a sure bet. He'd better be good to you, or I'll go there and give him a piece of my mind."

Josie said, "Don't give him too big a piece. You need to hang on to what little you have."

Opal gasped and pinched her arm. "Just for that, I'm not helping you pack."

Rubbing her arm, Josie laughed and said, "Yes, you will. Not that I have all that much. I need to get a few suitcases. I only have one. They should have some cheap ones at the thrift store. I'm going to go on June 10th because then I won't have to pay rent for July. I can put that money towards my train ride. It's so much easier traveling now that the railroad goes that far."

Opal nodded. "I know. It'll make it easier to visit that way, too."

"Come with me to the store and help me pick out suitcases," Josie said. "Please?"

"Of course I will. We might even be able to get Mr. Phillips to come down on his prices," Opal said. "We'll bat our eyelashes at him a few times."

Josie laughed. "You do the batting. He'll be much more interested in you than me, even though you're married."

Rising, Opal said, "Stop that. You're a beautiful woman and Evan is going to see that."

Sighing, Josie said, "I certainly hope so."

"Trust me. He will. Now, let's go shopping."

"Are you sure you don't want me to go with you?" Billy asked the night before Evan was leaving to go pick up Josie in Corbin.

He'd planned to go a day ahead of time and stay overnight so he was right there to get her the next day. That way he'd make sure to be on time. He didn't want her to think he wasn't coming.

"No, Billy. I don't need you to go with me. Thanks for the offer, though," Evan said.

Billy nodded. "Sure. I just thought you might need some moral support since it's been so long since you were out with a woman or anything," he said with a grin.

Evan raised an eyebrow at him. "What makes you think it's been all that long?"

Billy's eyes widened. "Who is she? I've never seen you with a woman."

"None of your business," Evan said. It was his turn to laugh when Billy made an annoyed face. "Unlike you, my young friend, I don't kiss and tell."

Billy grinned. "You're the only one I tell. It's not my fault that the girls like to brag. Half the time it's not true, but they like to make more of it than it is."

"Are you going to stand there and tell me that you don't ever have girls over?" Evan asked as they sat out on the back porch.

"I've had a couple over, but nothing ever really happened," Billy said.

Evan looked at him in surprise. "Nothing?"

"Nope. Kissing and stuff, but nothing else. I'm not stupid, Evan.

Yeah, I like to play around, but I'm not looking to be a father or a husband right now. And there aren't many young guys around here. If one of those girls get pregnant, I'm either gonna wind up dead or married," Billy said. "Most likely dead, though."

Evan grunted. He was surprised at Billy's admission. "So ... never mind. It's none of my business. I'm glad you're being sensible about it. I don't want to have another murder on my hands, especially yours."

Billy smiled at him. "The answer to your question is, yes, I've been with a woman. A *woman*, not a girl."

"A woman? What woman? Where? Please tell me she's not married," Evan said, closing his eyes and leaning his head back against the house.

"She doesn't live around here. She lives in Dickensville," Billy said.

Evan gave Billy a sharp look. "That's why you want to go with me. You want to see her."

Billy's bashful grin told Evan he was right. "Is she a prostitute?"

"Nope. She's a lonely single woman with a couple of kids. Every so often I go see her."

Evan passed a hand over his face. "Has it ever occurred to you that she could get pregnant?"

"I told you I wasn't stupid. We take precautions. I can't do that around here or the girls will talk about that. So I only go so far with them. I guess you'd call it keeping up appearances," Billy said.

"Well, that's smart about taking precautions, but have you ever thought about the fact that you're giving these girls false hope? That one of them or more thinks that maybe you'll fall in love with her?"

Billy became quiet a moment and then said, "No. I've talked to them about it and told them that I'm not going to fall in love with them."

"Why not? As I recall, the girls I think you're talking about are pretty. What's the matter with them?"

"If I tell you this, do you promise not to tell my parents?" Billy asked.

Evan found Billy's eyes in the dark and said, "I promise."

"You're like an older brother to me, Evan. Please don't tell anyone," Billy said.

"I promise not to say anything."

"I won't fall in love with them because I'm already in love with someone," he said.

"You are?" Evan asked. "With who?"

Billy pursed his lips and almost didn't tell Evan. Then he blurted, "The lady I go see."

Evan scratched his chin a little in confusion. "So let me get this straight. You're in love with the woman you see in Dickensville who has how many kids?"

"Two."

"And you're in love with her?"

"Yeah."

"Does she know it?"

Billy nodded.

"Does she love you?"

"I think so, but I think she's scared to admit it," Billy said.

"How old is she?"

"Twenty-three."

Evan could understand why it would be difficult for a woman five years Billy's senior to admit she might have feelings for him. "Are you confusing sex with love?"

Billy shook his head. "No. I'm not. I really like her kids, too. Bruce and Renee. Bruce is five and Renee is three."

"How long have you been seeing her?" Evan asked, not sure what to think about the situation.

"Since last year around Thanksgiving, I guess. Her husband was killed in a mining accident a couple years ago, so it's just her and the kids. I mean, her parents help. That's another reason I think she's scared to admit she might have feelings for me. There's a lot of prejudice against Indians in Dickensville and you know it," Billy said.

"I know," Evan said softly. "I'm sorry, Billy. You're in kind of a tight spot, but you have to know that it wouldn't work out. Even if she did want to marry you, you can't support her and two kids. I mean, would you even want to? You just said you weren't looking to be a father."

Billy nodded. "Yeah, I would. I know that sounds crazy, but it's the truth. I meant that I didn't want to have kids with any of the girls here. You're right, though. It'll never go anywhere. So I just go see her when I can."

Sympathy for Billy's plight filled Evan and he knew it was hopeless for the boy. Billy was well-liked in Echo, but it wasn't that way in other places. Most of the Indians were now on reservations, and even those that weren't were often still treated little better than animals.

That Billy had been raised completely without contact with others who shared his heritage didn't matter to a lot of people. An Indian was an Indian in their eyes. It was another reason why Billy hadn't sought to court a girl in Echo. Such a union wouldn't have been accepted, no matter how much he was liked. The prejudice still existed and it angered Evan no end.

So who was the boy supposed to marry if no one was going to let him marry their daughter? Was it so wrong for him to go see this woman? Evan didn't usually condone premarital sex, but he couldn't be a hypocrite since he'd been with a couple of women outside the bonds of marriage. His moral principles felt a little mixed up at the moment as he looked at Billy's dejected body posture.

It was a shame, because he really was a good-looking, kind, funny, and smart young man. Evan felt that any girl would be lucky to land him. Sympathy won out over morals.

"I'll tell you what; you can come with me. No one but me has to know that we spent some time in Dickensville before going on to Corbin. I can only give you a few hours there, but it's better than nothing."

Billy looked at Evan in wonder. "Do you really mean that? Don't tease me about this."

Evan smiled. "I'm not teasing you, Billy. Not about something like this."

In an instant Billy was off his chair, hugging Evan tightly. "Thank you! God bless you! What time do we leave?"

Laughing as Billy released him, Evan said, "Six. Be ready and on time."

"I will. I'll go pack right now! Thanks again. I owe you," Billy said with a big grin.

"You bet your behind you do," Evan said.

Billy was so elated that he could barely keep from shouting. "Whatever you want. Ok. Goodnight. See you at six."

Evan chuckled as he watched Billy run over home.

Chapter Five

The train on which Josie was traveling moved along at a good pace and she smiled as she thought about the fact that the day after next she would be meeting her future husband. At least she hoped he would be her future husband. She hated to think that things might not work between them and that the trip would have been a waste of time.

Pushing away negative thoughts, Josie reread Evan's letters, memorizing the things he'd said in them. He sounded like such a nice man and she was both impatient and nervous to meet him. She thought that the name Echo Canyon had a romantic sound to it and hoped that romance would blossom between her and the sheriff.

Because she didn't have much money, her seating wasn't the best. She was crowded in with a rather large woman who had insisted on taking the window seat. This gave Josie the advantage of being able to get in and out of her seat quickly since she was on the aisle, but it also made it uncomfortable since she was slightly in the way of passengers who were trying to get by her.

There was a man across the aisle who had offered to let her sit by him since the seat next to him was empty, but Josie didn't like the looks of him. She had politely declined his offer, but he kept looking at her in a way that made her nervous. Josie was hoping that he would be getting off at the next town.

In the meantime, she ignored him, keeping to herself so she didn't draw his attention any more than necessary. The lady next to her shifted a little and Josie found that she'd been bumped out more into the aisle.

Josie said to her, "I don't mean to trouble you, but could you slide over a little? I'm sticking out into the aisle."

The woman gave her an irritated look, but scooted over enough that Josie could sit more fully on the seat.

"Here now, lass," a voice from behind Josie said.

She turned around to look into bright gray eyes set in a handsome, slightly angular male face. "Pardon?" she said.

"Why don't ya come sit with me?" he said in a song-like Irish brogue. "That way ya don't have to be bounced out of your seat by her Sowship there and ya don't have to worry about the likes of him up there."

Josie blushed as she realized that he meant the woman next to her and the man across from her. She chanced a glance at each of them and saw that both of their expressions were angry.

"Come, lass. My mother raised a right respectful man and no harm will come to ya while you're with Lucky Quinn," he said, patting the seat next to him.

There was something about Lucky that made Josie trust him. Quickly, she gathered up her satchel and newspaper and scooted back to sit with him.

He grinned at her and she thought he was a very nice-looking man with those gray eyes of his and light blond hair. Holding out a hand to her, he said, "Ya know my name, but I don't know yours."

Josie smiled and shook his hand. "Josie Bainbridge. It's nice to meet you."

"The pleasure's all mine. What's a fine lady like yerself doin' travelin' all alone?" he asked as his strong hand released hers.

"I'm on my way to meet a man. I'm a mail-order-bride," Josie said with a bashful smile.

Lucky said, "Ah, just my luck to meet you only to find you're already taken. Well, he's a lucky man. It always sounds funny to me to say lucky since it's my name."

"It's not a nickname?"

"It's not. My mother was blessed with nine children, of which I'm the youngest, and by the time I came along, she just couldn't think of any more names, so she picked somethin' very obvious because it was so easy. Da didn't much care at that point, either. So, Lucky I was and Lucky I am," he said.

She laughed at his explanation. "Well, Lucky, I'm very grateful to you for taking pity on me."

"Like I said, I was raised to respect a lady and if I didn't help ya, well, Ma would give me a tongue lashin' for sure," he said. "So where ya headin'?"

"A place named Echo Canyon," she said.

Lucky's eyes grew wider. "Ya don't say. Now, I'm tellin' ya the truth when I say that 'tis the same place I'm goin'."

She smiled. "Are you teasing me?"

"I'm not." Lucky lowered his voice and leaned towards her a little. "I heard there was a small vein of silver around there that I might be able to mine. Since I ain't got nothin' to lose, I figured I might as well take a looksee."

Josie couldn't resist saying, "With a name like yours, you're sure to strike it rich."

He let out a robust laugh and she again thought what a good-looking man he was. She judged him to be in his late twenties or so and somewhere a little over six feet. With broad shoulders and strong-looking arms encased in a fairly nice suit, he was very easy on the eyes.

"Well, I hope so. I'll let ya know," he said.

"I'll hold you to that," Josie said, happy to have made a friend.

Without warning, the train lurched a little and both she and Lucky grabbed the seat ahead of them for support. It happened again, only harder, and then they were being hurtled sideways as the train went completely off the tracks. Their car went flying, flipping over on its side and plowing across the arid ground and vegetation along the side of the tracks.

With his quick reflexes, Lucky had grabbed Josie on the second hard jolt and wrapped his large body around her to protect her as much as he could. They and the other passengers were thrown about the car. Lucky's back collided with the roof of the car, knocking his breath from him. Somehow he managed to hold onto Josie, still shielding her from the worst of it.

Their car eventually came to a halt and Lucky and Josie came to rest on the windows on the opposite side of their car. They lay there for several minutes, trying to get their bearings as people around them cried out in fear and pain.

"Are ya all right?" Lucky asked Josie in a raspy voice.

Josie assessed herself and found that other than some scrapes, the only other injury she seemed to have was a sprained wrist. "Yes. I-I'm all right. Are you ok?" she asked, twisting around to look at him.

Lucky began releasing her. "My back hurts from being slammed against the ceilin' and my knee's a little banged up, but I think I'm fine."

Slowly they sat up and started looking around at the others. Not everyone was as fortunate as they had been. Several of the windows had broken and some people had cuts from the shards of glass. Other people were shouting that various body parts were broken and there were a couple of wails that told Lucky and Josie that deaths had occurred.

Tears stung Josie's eyes as their cries reached her ears. "Oh, Lucky! How horrible. How did this happen?"

"I don't know, but we need to get out of this car and go for help. It looks like we're in a lot better shape than most. I don't know if it's just our car or not," Lucky said, looking around. "We should be able to get out the back door there."

Josie nodded. Lucky stood up, groaning from the pain in his back. Even so, he helped Josie get up. After getting their bearings, they began walking out around other passengers, assuring them that they were going to send help to them as soon as they reached the next town.

Upon reaching the back door, Lucky had to shove against it hard several times before it opened. He gingerly dropped from it, favoring his knee. He reached up for Josie, grabbing her around the waist and lifting her down.

He grunted in pain and she said, "I'm so sorry. You should have just let me climb down."

Lucky smiled and said, "Nonsense, lass. I'm fine." Looking around them, Lucky saw two other cars that were in the same shape as theirs.

Going over to them, Lucky and Josie called out to their passengers. They received a response from a man who opened one of the car doors and introduced himself as Larry.

"Larry, are ya able to handle things here? We're gonna go get help since we're not hurt so bad, but there's no sense in a whole bunch of us walkin' around. We'll send help, of course. When the rest of the train gets to the next stop, they'll tell 'em what happened, but maybe we can find help closer, Lucky said.

Josie smiled a little. "I didn't think about the rest of the train."

Larry said, "Well, I did and unfortunately, it didn't make it, either. Here."

Lucky caught the small binoculars that Larry tossed him. Looking through them up ahead of the wreckage, Lucky could make out more train cars off the track and what looked like the engine sitting across them.

"Bloody hell," Lucky said. "I guess we better get a move on, Josie." He threw the binoculars back to Larry. "Like I said, we'll send help."

Larry nodded and said, "Much obliged. I'm a doctor so I'll start doing what I can here. Be safe, you two."

Josie nodded. "We will."

Looking down, Lucky said, "I'm glad you're wearin' boots, otherwise walkin' with me would be out of the question."

"Why do you want me to go with you?" Josie asked. "Won't I slow you down?"

Lucky shook his head. "No. I don't want you stayin' behind with that eejit back there. I don't trust him and he ain't the only one's looked at ya. You're safer with me."

"Me? Men were looking at me?" Josie said, looking back at the train cars they were leaving behind.

"Aye. At you, fair Josie. You're a bonnie lass and those chancers wouldn't hesitate to take advantage if they had the chance," Lucky said.

"How do I know you weren't one of those men?" she said, suddenly a little fearful. "And what is a 'chancer'?"

The hurt look in Lucky's eyes made her instantly regret her words.

"Josie, I told ya already. My ma raised me to do right by a lady and I'll not harm ya," he said. "A 'chancer' is what you Americans would call a suspicious character."

"Oh, I see. I'm sorry, Lucky. It just scared me a little to know that men were ogling me that way. Thank you for your help," she said.

He nodded. "Don't worry yourself about it. We also need to get ya to your man. He'll be worried, I'm sure."

"Oh my gosh! Yes! Oh no! He'll think I'm not coming, Lucky!"

"I'm sure they'll send a wire up ahead to let the next place know what happened. We'll send him a wire, too, so he knows you're all right," Lucky said.

"Money! All my money is in my satchel." Josie began to feel panicky.

Lucky stopped. "All right. Wait right here. I'll get your bag. At least you'll have your money. I remember what it looks like."

"Ok. I'll stay right here," she said.

With a nod, Lucky ran back to their car, his gait a little uneven as he favored his right knee slightly.

When Shelby pulled open her back door, Billy was the last person she'd expected to see.

"Billy," she said, masking the initial joy the sight of him brought her. "What are you doing here?"

His bright smiled dimmed a little when he heard the displeased note in her voice. "I came to see you since I had a chance. I missed you," he said, looking into her pretty brown eyes. "I know you're happy to see me," he said with a beguiling grin as his eyes swept over her curvy, petite figure.

Shelby tried not to smile back at him, but it was a losing battle. "Get in here," she said with a laugh.

He came in and shut the door. "How have you been?"

She said, "Fine. I got a raise at work, so that was a good thing." Turning away from him, Shelby attempted to ignore how good he looked with his toned, muscular body and handsome features.

"That's great. I'm glad they appreciate what a hard worker you are," he said, putting his hands on her shoulders from behind. He frowned when she pulled away from his touch. "What's wrong?"

Steeling herself, she turned to face him and said, "Billy, I can't see you anymore. It's not right. You're just a kid."

"That's not what you said last time I was here," Billy said, closing the distance between them.

Shelby smiled at his cocky attitude. "That was then and this is now."

"Let me remind you why you didn't mind my age before," Billy said. He cupped her face and proceeded to capture her lips in a toe-curling kiss.

Her body reacted him and she let the kiss go on for a little. Somehow she found the strength to tear herself away from him. "No! I can't do this anymore! It's not right and it's not what I need."

"What do you mean?" Billy felt a growing sense of alarm.

"Billy, I need to find someone who can take care of me and help raise my children," Shelby said. "It's been fun and you're so sweet, but it's over. You need to find someone your own age."

"I love you, Shelby. I've told you that I would take care of you and the kids—that I'd do anything to make you happy," Billy said.

Shelby forced a hard note into her voice as she looked into Billy's black eyes. "Billy, the fact is that you're just too young and immature.

You're also an Indian. I can't marry you. I'd be an outcast and so would my kids."

Billy's nostrils flared and Shelby could see the hurt in his eyes. It almost made her relent, but she was doing what she knew was in his best interests. Even as she thought this, she also thought he was so beautiful and, right or wrong, she wanted him.

"My being an Indian has never bothered you before. Besides, I don't think of myself as an Indian."

"Don't you see? It doesn't matter. Everyone else sees you as an Indian."

Staring at her, hardly believing what she was saying to him, Billy asked, "What do you see when you look at me? Your opinion is the only one that matters to me."

Putting a hand to her forehead, Shelby said, "I see a very handsome, sweet, funny, kind boy who I should have never started anything with. I'm sorry if I led you on. We're through, Billy. Leave and don't come back. It's over."

Billy stepped closer again, but Shelby backed off. "Get out!" she yelled. "Go and don't come back! I can't be with an Indian boy. Go!"

Her cutting words had their intended effect. Billy's head came up and his expression registered a combination of hurt, confusion, and anger. "Fine, but I know you love me. I won't bother you again, but one day you're going to be sorry about ending things. Goodbye, Shelby."

Proudly, Billy turned and walked out, slamming the door behind him. Shelby hurried to the door, parting the curtains on the window and watching him mount his horse and ride away.

"I already am," she said as tears began rolling down her face.

Evan and Billy had agreed to meet at one o'clock at the Golden Lion Hotel since they'd made it to Dickensville by nine. There were usually some people there that Evan knew and he also liked to visit Sheriff Lyle Stratton, a friend of his.

He had stopped at the hotel, but not many people were in the dining room at the moment. He ate breakfast and chitchatted with those he knew to kill some time. Just as he finished and was paying the bill, Billy came walking into the hotel restaurant.

"That was quick," Evan said by way of greeting. "Wasn't she home?"

Billy's jaw clenched. "Can we just go?"

Evan's dark brows drew down. "Do you want something to eat? We won't be stopping for a while."

The boy leveled a stare at Evan. "I don't want anything to eat. I just want to go."

Uh oh. I don't things went very well with his lady friend. "Sure. That's fine," Evan said.

Billy nodded and turned away, but not before Evan saw the glimmer of tears in Billy's eyes.

Evan sighed as he followed his young friend outside. *I think someone has just gotten his first broken heart.*

They mounted and rode through Dickensville in silence. At one street, Evan saw Billy turn his head to the right, looking longingly in that direction. Then he turned frontwards again and concentrated on where they were going.

Billy fought against the crushing pain that made him feel as though his heart was sliced and bleeding. He wished that he hadn't come with Evan. He couldn't go home because his parents would question why he had come home so soon.

No, he had no choice but to go along with Evan, even though he didn't want to be around him and his bride-to-be when the woman he loved had just shredded his heart. He was able to hold it together until they were out on the road alone. Then the tears came and he let them flow unchecked.

Evan felt so badly for Billy. He knew what he was going through and it was a horrible thing. After a bit, when Billy's tears began to abate, Evan asked, "You wanna tell me what happened?"

Billy let out an angry laugh. "She said we can't be together because of my age and—" His voice cracked and he cleared his throat. "And because I'm an Indian."

Evan's heart broke anew for Billy. He knew that Billy was going to hear that a lot in his lifetime and it greatly pained the sheriff. "I'm so sorry, Billy. I know you love her."

"Evan, be glad that you're not an Indian. I hate it! I should just go live on a reservation and be done with it." Billy's shoulders shook as more sobs overtook him. "I don't belong anywhere! I was raised in a white community, but because of my Indian blood, I'm not good enough for anyone. I know nothing about any of 'my kind,' so I don't belong with them, either. If this is what the rest of my life is going to be like, what's the point of living? I might as well be dead."

Evan had never heard Billy talk like that before. He knew the pain he was in accounted for some of it, but he could also tell that Billy's life situation was contributing to his dark state of mind. He didn't want Billy to spiral down into depression.

"Billy, don't talk like that. Maybe it doesn't seem like it right now, but you'll meet the right woman for you."

"Evan, I love you, but you can take all that crap and shove it up your ass."

Taken aback, Evan didn't have a response to that.

"You have no idea what my life is like. I'm good enough to babysit, help with chores, or whatever, but I'm not good enough to court the girls in town. Maybe I should get one of them pregnant. Then they'd have to let me marry her," Billy continued.

"Now don't do anything crazy like that. That's not the answer."

"Then what is?" Billy yelled. "What do you do when you're not good enough for people because of your race?"

"You're good enough for me. You're good enough for your parents and Aunt Edna. For what it's worth, if I had a daughter your age, I'd let you court her."

Billy smiled a little as he brushed away tears. "Thanks."

"I don't see you as Indian or white or anything. You're just Billy, my friend and pain in the neck. And at the risk of you telling me to shove it again, you'll meet a woman who sees you the same way me and a lot of other people do."

"I appreciate what you're saying, but I don't believe that'll happen. No matter what I do, I'll always be just a stupid, dirty Injun to most people."

"Not everyone, Billy. You'll—"

"I don't want to talk about this anymore," Billy interjected.

Hearing the finality in Billy's voice, Evan said, "Ok. That's fine."

After that, they rode in silence. Although he tried to prevent them, every so often, tears fell from Billy's eyes. Evan pretended not to notice.

Chapter Six

Josie drank a few swallows of water from the canteen and then handed it to Lucky. He took a sip and replaced the cap.

"I'm thankful that at least some things in the galley were still usable. At least we have food and water. We should reach Jefferson by nightfall. We're gonna have to push hard, though. Are ya up to it?"

Josie nodded. "Yes. I don't want to be out here in the dark."

"Me, neither. Let's keep goin' then," he said.

Falling into step with Lucky, Josie said, "I can't believe this has happened and I can't believe that we weren't hurt like a lot of the others. I owe you my life, Lucky."

He grinned at her. "Never doubt the luck of the Irish. It's true and my name isn't Lucky for nothin'" He didn't mind playing up the more humorous notions that Americans had about his people. It sometimes helped him charm people into doing what he wanted or diffusing a tense situation.

Josie laughed. "Well, I can't thank you enough for lending your luck to me. I hope you get lucky in Echo Canyon with your silver mining."

"I have a good feelin' about it. So what made ya want to find a husband by mail?"

Josie heaved a sigh. "There are more women than men in Pullman so finding a husband is hard. And I'm not exactly what society dictates a woman should look like at the moment. I'm not petite and voluptuous."

Lucky's brows drew together. "I've always hated that. Trust me; there ain't nothin' wrong with your figure. You're a good-lookin' woman and I'm certain that your man will think so, too. He'd better, if he knows what's good for him. If he doesn't, I might just have to swoop in and steal your heart."

"I'll keep that in mind," Josie said, with a laugh.

As they walked along, Josie and Lucky developed a good friendship, getting to know each other and laughing when they traded teasing remarks. Lucky told her stories about his childhood in Ireland and how they had come to America. He was funny, considerate, and gentlemanly. All of it helped pass the time.

Billy stood outside the train depot with their wagon while Evan was inquiring about the train that was due in. He sighed, impatient to collect this woman and go back home. Although why he was in such a hurry to go back, he didn't know.

Evan came out and said, "Let's go. The clerk said that the train derailed up the line. Josie is in the next town back at a hotel. We'll go get her. She was able to send me a telegram. She's ok, thank God."

The thought that Josie could have been severely hurt or killed deeply affected him. Even though he hadn't met her yet, he felt that he knew her somewhat and to have lost her before she arrived would have greatly saddened him.

"What the heck happened?" Billy said as he climbed up on the wagon seat.

Evan said, "They're not sure yet. There was a bunch of people hurt and a few that died. I sent back a telegram letting her know we're coming."

"I'm glad she's ok. I feel bad for the rest of the passengers. The whole train derailed?"

"Yep. Strange things happen in life, that's for sure," Evan said.

"I'll say."

Evan wasted no time in getting on the road.

The next day, Evan and Billy reached Berkley, the town to which Josie and Lucky had walked. Pulling up in front of the Berkley Hotel, Evan ran inside. As he inquired what room Josie was in, he felt the first real jangle of nerves. He was about to meet the woman who he hoped would become his wife.

Upon finding that she was in room fifteen, he ran up the stairs and located the room. He straightened his clothes and tried to make sure his hair was neat. Raising his hand, he rapped and then waited.

The door opened to reveal a man, roughly Evan's height and build, but with blond hair and gray eyes.

"Hello. Can I help ya?" the man asked. He spoke with a heavy Irish accent.

Evan blinked once or twice and then said, "I think I must have the wrong room. I'm looking for Josie Bainbridge."

The man grinned at him. "Josie! Yer man is out here, lass! Pleasure to meet ya, Evan. Lucky Quinn, at your service."

Evan shook Lucky's hand, a bewildered expression on his face. "Are you sharing a room?"

Lucky laughed at that. "We're not. I was on the train with yer lady. I kept her safe for ya. There were a few unsavory characters on it and I wasn't gonna leave her to their mercy. Well, I'll let you get on with it. She's a pretty lass."

"Thanks," Evan said. "I'm glad she had some protection."

"My ma raised me right," Lucky said before going to his room.

Evan turned his head forward again to see a lovely blonde woman walking towards him. Lucky was right. Josie certainly was attractive in her pretty rose muslin dress with matching slippers. Her hair was styled in a chignon and its color reminded him of the golden wheat that grew in the summer. Her deep blue eyes caught the light as she looked at him a little shyly. He could see where the term "willowy" would certainly apply to her and he thought she was beautiful.

"Hello, Josie," Evan said.

Josie looked him over as she approached. The advertisement fit him, but really didn't do him justice, she thought. He was a ruggedly handsome man with a strong jaw and slightly crooked nose, most likely the result of some fight, she assumed. His eyes were a striking shade of green. He looked very strong and virile and Josie's heart thudded in her chest as she came to stand in front of him.

"Hello, Evan."

He smiled and Josie felt as though her bones were becoming soft. "It's really good to meet you, and I'm very relieved that you're safe and sound."

"It's nice to meet you, too. I owe that to Lucky. I have no doubt that he saved my life," Josie said.

Evan smiled despite the little jab of jealousy that pierced his stomach. "He seems like a nice fella."

"He is. This may be awkward, but he'd like to come with us since Echo Canyon was his destination, too," she said.

Arching a brow at her, Evan said, "He's going to Echo? How come?" The last thing he wanted was a strange man coming along while he tried to get to know Josie a little better. Billy was a different story.

"He's going to do some prospecting," she said.

Evan grinned. "Well, I wish him the best of luck. I haven't heard of anyone finding any gold or silver in Echo since I've been there, but you never know. It's ok if he comes along."

"Thank you. I feel like this is all some strange dream. It's certainly not how I envisioned meeting you," she said.

"Me, either, but you just deal with things as they come," Evan said. "Well, how about we get ready and leave. We should be able to reach Echo by nightfall if we go now."

"Oh, all right. I really don't have much; the railroad company will be sending my luggage to me. All I have is a small satchel," Josie said. She had bought her dress the day before yesterday at a local thrift store and a carpet bag along with it.

"What about Lucky?" Evan asked. "Is that his real name?"

"Yes, it is," Josie said with a smile.

"Ok."

"I think all he has is what he's wearing," Josie said.

Evan nodded. "I'll go see if he's ready."

"All right. I'll get my bag."

When they exited the hotel, Evan introduced Josie and Lucky to Billy. Josie wondered at the young man's rather lackluster greeting, but didn't say anything about it. He seemed pleasant enough, but not overly friendly. Billy rode in the back of the wagon with Lucky so that Josie could sit up on the seat with Evan.

As they started out, Evan's thigh brush Josie's and she felt the solid muscle of his leg. Her cheeks grew slightly warm from the contact.

"So other than the train derailing, how was your trip?" Evan asked, tongue-in-cheek.

She chuckled. "It was fine up until that point."

"I'm glad to hear that. I was really getting worried about you," Evan said.

Josie looked him in the eye and said, "I would never stand you up."

He said, "The thought had crossed my mind, but I knew better. Based on your letters, you didn't seem like the kind of person who'd do that."

"I'm glad you think so. I was afraid you'd leave, thinking that I wasn't going to come. That's why we sent off that wire right away," she said.

"It's a good thing you did," Evan said. "Your room will be ready when we get there." He turned around to look behind him. "Lucky, you can bunk on our sofa tonight if you want to. We don't have a hotel in Echo."

Lucky smiled at him. "That's right kindly of ya, Evan. I'll take ya up on it if you're sure it's not too much trouble."

"Not at all. I'll warn you about my Aunt Edna, though. She's liable to flirt with you," Evan said.

Lucky laughed and said, "Good. I haven't flirted with a good-lookin' woman outside of Josie in a while."

His wink put Evan's mind at ease that he was just joking. Josie also didn't seem like the kind of woman who would cheat on a man.

"Don't say I didn't warn you," Evan said. He turned a little farther in the seat and saw that Billy had no interest in their conversation. He sat looking out over the countryside, but Evan knew that he wasn't really paying attention to it, either. He pursed his lips and turned back around, worried about the boy.

Josie saw his expression and turned around to see the dejected expression on Billy's face, wondering what caused it.

Lucky also noticed and wondered about Billy's circumstances. It was obvious that he was heartbroken about something and he felt badly for the young man. He changed sides in the wagon bed so he was sitting by Billy.

He nudged his foot with his and asked, "What's her name?"

Billy looked at Lucky in surprise. "What?" He hadn't even noticed that Lucky had moved to sit close to him.

In a low voice, Lucky repeated his question.

Billy said, "No offense, but I don't know you and I don't want to talk about it with a stranger."

Lucky nodded understandingly. "Talkin' about women who break your heart is rough. I know from experience. Men are tough and strong, but all it takes to bring us down is a woman breakin' your heart."

Billy scowled and turned away. "Rough isn't the word for it."

"I've been there. Three times I've had my heart broken," Lucky said.

Billy looked at him. "Three? How did you stand it?"

"Drank, mostly," Lucky said with a laugh. "I moped for a while and then had to get on with life."

"I don't care much about getting on with life because my life will never change," Billy said.

"Aw, now, c'mon. Don't talk like that, lad. You're a nice lookin' fella. Some sweet young thing will come along. You'll see," Lucky said.

Billy's black eyes fixed on his in a hard stare. "It's different for me. I'm an Indian so no white woman wants to marry me. So unless my skin miraculously changes color, my life isn't going get much better."

"Ah, I see. So that's what happened. It's your race that she objected to," Lucky said.

"Yeah. That and she said I'm too young. She's a widow with two kids," Billy said.

Lucky watched the way Billy's face lit up at the mention of the children. "Ya like those kids, dontcha?"

"Yeah, I do. I told her that I'd take care of her and the kids, but she doesn't believe me. She doesn't believe *in* me," he said.

Lucky crossed his arms over his chest and said, "All right. Let's take a look at this from a practical point of view. Put aside yer feelings for a moment."

Billy didn't know why he was listening to Lucky, but he said, "Ok."

"So she's a widow. How old?"

"Twenty-three."

"How many kiddies?"

"Two."

"Do you work?" Lucky asked.

"Sort of. There really aren't any jobs available in Echo. I'm an artist and every other month, I take my stuff to Dickensville and sell it," Billy said.

"Ah, I see. So you don't have what ya could call regular employment. Well, ya can see where that would worry her. She's got two little mouths to feed and they're her first concern," Lucky said.

"I know that. I'm not stupid," Billy said.

"All right, then how do ya propose to take care of her if ya don't have enough pay comin' in?" Lucky asked.

"That's the problem. I don't have anything regular," Billy said.

"And if there's no chance of a job, you're sort of stuck. See, a woman in her position has a lot to consider when it comes to choosin' a man. She needs proof that ya can take care of her," Lucky said.

"She said that she and the kids would be outcasts if she married me. So it wouldn't matter if I was rich, she still wouldn't want me," Billy said.

"I've had my share of that kind of thing," Lucky said.

Billy gave him a doubtful look. "You're white. Why would you have that problem?"

"Because I'm Irish. A lot of people look at the Irish and all they see are drunks and stupid ones at that. They don't think I can be anything more than a manual laborer. So it's not exactly the same, but it's similar," Lucky said.

Billy's gaze turned down to the floor of the wagon. "At least you can get married or court someone. No one wants me to court their daughter."

Lucky nudged Billy's elbow. "So ya find a girl without a father. It's easier to convince a mother about these kinds of things than it is a father."

Billy laughed at his logic. "Well, all of the girls in Echo have fathers so that won't work, either."

"Hmm," Lucky said. "So what are ya gonna do about it?"

"Do? There's nothing to be done about it."

"There's where you're wrong, lad. Ya haven't even tried," Lucky said. "Ya have to at least try. Show everyone that you're just as good as they are, maybe better. Ya said you're an artist?"

"Yeah."

"So, ya need to work on that harder. Branch out a little. Have ya tried your hand at portraits? Ya know, with live people?" Lucky asked.

"No," Billy said.

"Well, I know people who've done that kind of thing and they make decent money," Lucky said.

Billy thought about that and he could see where something like that might work.

Lucky could see that the wheels were starting to turn in Billy's mind. "If ya truly love this woman and those kids, you'll do whatever it takes to make them happy and once ya do that, she won't be able to resist ya."

Billy looked into Lucky's eyes and smiled. "Thanks." For the first time since leaving Shelby's, he felt a little hopeful.

"That's what friends are for, lad," Lucky said and then moved away to leave Billy alone with his thoughts.

Chapter Seven

The travelers were beyond exhausted by the time they'd reached Echo. Evan had suggested that they stay overnight in Dickensville, but Billy had balked at that idea. Lucky and Josie also said they'd rather push onward. So it was around nine when they arrived at Evan's house.

"Well, here we are. Home sweet home," Evan said, glad to be back.

From what she could see in the dark, the medium-sized white house looked very nice. There was a front porch and two large maple trees stood on each end of the porch, giving shade in the summer.

No sooner had the wagon stopped, than Billy said goodnight and ran across the yard to his house. He didn't want to stick around for all of the introductions. He was genuinely happy for Evan, but his heart hurt too badly to act as though nothing was wrong.

Josie watched him go and asked, "Did I do something to offend him?"

Evan said, "No. He and his lady friend had a parting of the ways and he's really hurting over it."

Sympathy filled Josie and she said, "That's such a shame."

"Yeah, it is," Evan replied. "Well, c'mon. I see Aunt Edna's still up. You can meet her and then I'll take you to the boarding house. Mrs.

Hanover will help get you settled in."

Josie said, "All right. I'm looking forward to meeting her. I'm also nervous. I want her to approve of me."

Evan said, "She's going to like you, Josie. I know I do."

Josie's face became warm and she laughed. "Well, aren't you charming?"

Evan smiled in response to her comment. "I don't know how charming I am. I just tell the truth, which usually annoys people," he said, leading her up onto the front porch. He turned around to see that Lucky was still standing by the wagon. "You comin', Lucky?"

"In a minute. I'm just lookin' around a bit. Go on ahead."

Evan knew this was Lucky's way of letting the first meeting with his aunt be private. His liking of Lucky grew with his considerate gesture.

"Ok. Don't be too long," Evan said.

"I won't."

Josie followed Evan into a parlor that was cozy and cheerful. The fireplace was flanked by two wingback chairs that faced the rest of the room. A sofa stood on the opposite wall from the door and another chair had been placed by the window next to the front door. Pretty, colorful afghans were laid over the back of the sofa and a couple of the chairs. Josie wondered if Evan had made them. She was surprised to see an expensive looking Persian rug covering the floor.

In the chair on the left of the fireplace, an older woman, whom Josie judged to be in her later fifties or early sixties, sat with her head down, snoring softly.

Evan smiled fondly at the familiar sight. Going over to the chair, he crouched down like always and patted her knee lightly. "Hey, sleepyhead. Wake up."

Edna opened her eyes and looking into his green gaze. "Evan! You're home! Where have you been? I've been worried because you weren't back when you said you'd be," she said, embracing him.

"Sorry about that. There was a train accident."

Edna's blue eyes widened in alarm. "Oh no! How dreadful." She caught sight of Josie and said, "Oh, thank goodness you're ok. Well, introduce me, Evan."

He rose and she stood with him, albeit stiffly. For the millionth time, he wished there was something that would help her arthritis. Evan led her over to Josie and made the introductions.

Edna liked Josie right away, having a good feeling about the girl. "Well, you're quite the beauty," she told Josie, making her laugh.

"Thank you. I look terrible right now, I'm sure."

"Nope. You look just fine, dear. Trust me, I'd tell you if you were disheveled."

Evan chuckled. "She would, too. She's where I get that particular trait from."

"Why beat around the bush?" Edna responded.

Josie had been expecting to see a small, white-haired old lady, but Edna wasn't. She was probably five feet eight and wore her gray-streaked brown hair in a bun at the nape of her neck. Bright blue eyes looked her over and Josie had the distinct impression that Edna missed very little. Josie saw how stiffly Edna walked and felt badly for her.

Stepping over to the front door, Evan opened it and said, "Lucky! Come in here!"

Edna wondered who Lucky was. She found out the next moment when a very handsome man entered the house. The man had the devil in his eyes and Edna liked him on sight.

"Evan, you brought me a man!" she said. "How thoughtful of you."

The other three laughed.

Lucky stepped forward. "Aye, he did. 'Lucky,' Evan said, 'My lovely, beautiful aunt is in need of a fine man like yourself. Come on home with me.' So I, of course, couldn't refuse such an offer. And you're even more bonnie than he said ya were."

Edna put a hand to her chest and said, "And he's Irish to boot! Splendid. I just love Irishmen."

Lucky took her hand and kissed the back of it. "Well, then it's fortunate for me that I am one, isn't it? That way I can capture your heart that much quicker."

Edna laughed and said, "I think you have a piece of that Blarney Stone in your pocket."

Lucky grinned and said, "I just might. Ya never know."

"Lucky's going to sleep on the sofa tonight since there's no hotel. I'll help him find a place tomorrow," Evan told her.

Edna gave Lucky a saucy look and said, "I have a place for you right upstairs."

"Aunt Edna!" Evan objected.

Lucky laughed hard over that. "Ya shouldn't have said anything, lass. Now he's onto us."

Putting a hand over her mouth, Edna said, "How stupid of me."

Lucky winked and said, "Don't worry. We'll find time."

Evan groaned and motioned for everyone to sit down. "I'll make some coffee and you and Lucky can tell Aunt Edna about the train crash," he said to Josie.

Edna looked at them. "You were in it?"

Josie nodded and between her and Lucky they gave Edna a full recounting of the experience.

"What a miracle that you're sitting here right now and that you weren't hurt badly," Edna said, shaking her head. "I'd say you have some angels watching over you."

Josie nodded. "I'd say you're right," she replied, finishing the coffee Evan had given her.

Evan noticed how tired she looked and said, "Why don't I take you over to the Hanovers'? I'm sure you're ready to sleep."

"I am," Josie said, rising. "Mrs. Taft, it's a pleasure to be here and I'm so looking forward to us getting to know each other."

"Please, call me Edna," the other woman said. "I'm looking forward to it, too. Sleep well."

Lucky stood and gave Josie a hug. "Goodnight, lass. I'll see ya tomorrow."

"Goodnight, Lucky," Josie said, smiling at him.

Evan had to stifle another stab of jealousy. "I'll be back," he said.
"Goodnight, Edna," Josie said.
"Goodnight, dear."

"It's not far," Evan said as he helped Josie back up into the wagon.

"All right," Josie said. She was suddenly nervous about being alone with him—not because she didn't trust him, though. She just didn't know what to say.

Evan gave her a sidelong glance and said, "I saw you looking at the afghans and the answer to your question is 'yes.' I made them."

Josie let out a snort of laughter. "Was I that obvious?"

"No, but I'm a sheriff and I read most people really well."

"Well, they're beautiful. What made you start crocheting?" she asked, latching onto the subject to avoid an awkward silence.

As the team walked along, Evan said, "Well, I was probably about eight and I saw Aunt Edna working on an afghan. It looked interesting to me and I asked if I could try it. She didn't have the heart to tell me that only women usually did that sort of thing, so she gave me a ball of yarn and showed me how to make a chain and do a single stitch.

"I caught on quick and I've been doing it ever since. I've been teased about it over the years, but anyone who's ever been nasty about it has been taught not to repeat that mistake."

Josie heard the rough note enter his voice. "You don't impress me as the sort of man to take things like that lying down."

"I'm not. Crocheting is something that Aunt Edna and I enjoy doing together. She became a mother to me after my family passed away and there's nothing I won't do for her. Except bring her a man," Evan said, laughing as he thought about the way she and Lucky behaved with each other.

Josie laughed. "Lucky is quite a character. You'll have to get him to tell you about growing up in Ireland. He and his brothers were real hellions."

Evan said, "Lucky? No. I can't see that about him."

His sarcastic remark made Josie chuckle. Then she said, "I hope my guitar isn't damaged. I'm glad I marked all of my luggage really well."

Evan nodded. "Me, too. I'm anxious to hear you play."

"I'll be happy to play for you," she said as they went along.

Shortly, Evan pulled up in front of a large Victorian structure done in what looked like pink in the darkness. Lamplight poured from the front windows, illuminating the ground outside.

Evan helped Josie down from the wagon and picked up her satchel from the wagon bed. Josie walked up onto the wide porch of the boarding house and watched Evan knock on the door. As she looked at him, she found him incredibly handsome and she felt her pulse rise a little again as these thoughts crossed her mind.

The door was opened by a rather portly man with a bald head and bushy gray eyebrows.

"Ah, Evan, there you are, and I see you have your lady with you," he said in a very deep voice.

"Hi, Arthur. We're finally here. Sorry for the late hour," Evan said.

"Don't worry yourself about it. Come right on in," Arthur said. As Josie passed him, he said, "My, my, but Evan sure has himself a pretty girl."

Josie blushed and smiled. "Thank you."

"Josie Bainbridge, this is Arthur Hanover. He and the missus will take good care of you," Evan said.

Arthur chuckled. "I have to don't I? I don't want to make the sheriff angry at me."

Evan grinned. "That's right."

"Miss Josie, it's a pleasure to make your acquaintance," Arthur said.

Josie liked his kind expression and his lively dark eyes. "Likewise, Mr. Hanover."

"None of that. Arthur will suffice, young lady," he said with mock seriousness.

"Arthur, then," Josie said.

"Good," Arthur said.

A tall, thin woman came hurrying into the foyer from a large parlor.

"Oh, my goodness!" she said. "Miss Bainbridge, it's so nice that you're finally with us. I'm Gwen Hanover. What a pretty girl you are. I'm certain you'll be comfortable here."

"Dear, don't get yourself all excited," Arthur said, chuckling. "My wife is a little high strung now and again."

Gwen smiled at her husband's good-natured teasing. "Hush, Arthur. He's right, though. Oh, Evan! How good to see you. Was your trip all right?"

Briefly, they explained to the Hanovers what had occurred with Josie's train.

"Well, it's a relief that you're safe and sound. You must be exhausted. Let's get you settled," Gwen said.

Josie nodded, exhaustion weighing on her. "Yes. I'm very tired."

Evan said, "Sleep well, Josie. I'll come by tomorrow around ten and show you around, ok?"

"Ok. I'll see you then," she said with a smile.

He would have liked to have had a more private moment with her, but that was out of the question. "Goodnight, ladies," he said and then went out the front door.

Arthur followed him outside. "Evan, she's a beauty. You're going to have to make sure to lay claim to her very fast." Concern showed in Arthur's eyes. "I'd hate to see anything happen to her."

Evan's jaw clenched. "Arthur, I'll make it clear to everyone that Josie's mine and heaven help anyone who makes a false move towards her."

Arthur clapped him on the back and said, "Glad to hear it. You know we'll keep her safe here. Thad's been doing a good job while you've been gone, but you need a deputy."

"Don't I know it? If only we had the funds for that. Well, see you later," Evan said.

"Goodnight, Evan," Arthur said and went back inside.

Chapter Eight

Someone knocking on her door woke Josie the next morning. She raised her head from her pillow and looked at the clock on the bedside stand. It read eight o'clock.

"Josie? It's Gwen."

She threw the covers back and jumped out of bed. Going to the door, she only cracked it a couple of inches since she'd slept in only her chemise and she didn't have a robe.

"Good morning, dear," Gwen said. "I thought you might like some breakfast before Evan comes."

Josie's stomach growled and she realized that she was starving. "Yes. That would be great. I'll get dressed and be down shortly."

"All right. Just come to the kitchen. We only use the dining room when there are more boarders."

Josie smiled. "All right. Be right there."

Gwen nodded and left. Josie closed the door and looked around her room. It was large and airy. Two windows gave a nice view of the mountains even though they faced the front street. Green brocade drapes dressed the windows and a very pretty green and white braided rug covered the floor between the bed and bureau. A wingback chair stood in one corner with a small desk close to it.

Josie had been pleasantly surprised to find she had a private washroom. The convenience was very welcome. Quickly, she began to wash up and dress. She had no choice but to wear her dress from yesterday since she had no other clothing at the moment. Thinking about her limited funds, Josie hoped that her belongings from the train would come soon. She didn't have the money to keep buying clothes to wear.

Once she was ready, Josie descended the long staircase and really took in the appearance of the house, something she had been too tired to do the previous night. At that point, all she'd wanted was to go to bed.

The walls of the foyer were covered in a gold and white, textured wallpaper that was very pretty. The front door had an oval glass inlay that allowed those inside to see who was at the door. Josie turned right, looking into the very large parlor on the left side of the wide hallway. The furniture was done in various shades of browns and tan and looked expensive.

Going along the hallway, Josie paused briefly to look at the portraits and paintings that hung on the walls. They were artfully arranged in attractive groupings. Also on the left side of the hallway was a dining room in which a huge, beautiful cherry dining table and matching buffet and china cupboard all kept company together. Further on, to her right, was a formal drawing room, this done in cream and gold, with furniture of pinks and mauves. Straight ahead was what Josie surmised must be the kitchen, since she heard voices coming from the room.

Entering it, she discovered that it, too, was a big room. The table could easily seat eight and there were two ranges; a six-plate model and a smaller two-plate stove. Cupboards lined the walls and Josie could see the door of what most likely was a large pantry. The delicious aromas of bacon, coffee, and eggs hit her nostrils and her stomach growled again.

Arthur looked up from a book he'd been reading and smiled at her. "Well, good morning, Miss Josie," he said in his rumbling bass voice. "You look well-rested."

She smiled at him as she took a seat. "I am, thank you. Did you sleep well?"

He nodded and took a sip of his coffee. "Yes. Very well. I hope your room is to your liking."

"It's a very pretty room, and I appreciate the private washroom," Josie said.

"We thought you might. We normally like to give those rooms to our lady boarders so they don't have to use the common washroom," he said kindly.

"Thank you for being so considerate," she said.

"That's quite all right," Arthur said.

The kitchen door to the outside opened and a woman entered. Josie was surprised to see that she wore men's trousers and a simple, white button-down shirt over which she wore an apron. Josie judged the attractive woman to be somewhere around thirty, but she couldn't be sure.

Arthur said, "Josie, meet Phoebe Stevens, our cook and housekeeper extraordinaire. Phoebe, this is Josie Bainbridge, Evan's prospective bride."

Phoebe gave her a tight smile and said, "Nice to meet you."

"And the same to you," Josie said.

Phoebe tucked golden brown strands of hair that had come loose from the braid she wore behind her ears as she went to the stove. "What would you like to eat?" she asked Josie.

Josie wasn't used to other people cooking for her, so she felt a little awkward as she said, "Just some scrambled eggs and bacon is fine. I don't want to be any trouble."

"You're not," Phoebe said. "That's what I'm here for."

Josie said, "Thank you."

She watched Phoebe expertly crack eggs into a skillet and put some strips of bacon on a plate and sit it in the warmer. Her movements were efficient and it was easy to see that it was all second nature to her.

"Coffee?" Phoebe asked Josie.

"Yes, please."

Phoebe gave it to her and went back to cooking the eggs. Josie thought there was something sad about Phoebe.

Arthur said, "So your sheriff will be coming soon. Any idea what he has in store for you?"

Josie smiled. "None, other than he's going to show me around."

Phoebe said, "That'll take all of about five minutes. I hope he has some other way to occupy you for the day."

Arthur's eyebrows raised over that comment, but he refrained from saying anything. "I'm sure Evan will be able to adequately entertain you."

Josie just smiled as Phoebe sat a hot plate of food in front of her. Phoebe's eggs were the fluffiest and tastiest she'd ever eaten and it didn't take long for Josie to clean her plate. When she looked up, Arthur was watching her with an amused expression.

"I like to see a woman eat well," Arthur said.

Jose smiled. "I was starving. Phoebe, your eggs and bacon were delicious. Thank you."

"Thanks," Phoebe replied.

Arthur said, "Phoebe is a woman of few words, but many talents."

"Thanks, Arthur," Phoebe said with a grin. Josie could see that the two had a high regard for one another.

A knock sounded on the front door and Arthur rose, holding out his arms, which Phoebe stepped into. Josie watched in open-mouthed wonder as the two of them waltzed down the hallway to the front door. She heard a feminine laugh join Arthur's deep chuckle as Arthur opened the door. If she hadn't seen it with her own eyes, she wouldn't have believed that Arthur was so graceful or that the slightly masculine Phoebe was a beautiful dancer, either.

"Well, look what the cat dragged to our doorstep," Arthur said, his powerful voice ringing in the foyer.

Josie became nervous and smoothed down her skirt. She wanted to look nice for Evan and wished she wasn't wearing the same dress as yesterday. There wasn't anything she could do about it now, so she went to the front door.

Evan watched her approach and smiled over how pretty she looked. He knew that she was wearing the same dress as the day before, but he made no mention of it. It didn't matter to him what she wore. No clothing could hide how beautiful she was and he mentally thanked Jerry for coming up with the whole mail-order-bride idea.

"Good morning, everyone," he said. "You look pretty, Josie."

She smiled. "Good morning. Thank you." He certainly looked handsome in his jeans, black Western shirt, and black boots.

"We'll see you both later. Come, Phoebe. We have work to do," Arthur said.

Josie and Evan laughed as the two of them waltzed back down the hall to the kitchen.

"Do they always do that?" Josie asked.

Evan chuckled. "They do it a lot, anyhow. Gwen isn't a very good dancer and Arthur loves to dance. He's light on his feet for a big guy, too. So, he and Phoebe dance a lot, since she likes to dance, too."

"It's certainly not something you see every day."

"You do if you live here," Evan said, with a smile. "Are you ready?"

"Yes," Josie said and took the arm he offered her.

As he walked her to his buggy, she enjoyed the feel of his strong arm under her hand. Once they were settled, he took up the reins and asked, "Do you ride?"

"Yes. I enjoy it, too," she said.

"Good. It'll make it easier to get around since we don't have taxis here. I'll show you what I mean today," Evan said. "We'll have to get you a horse. Most likely Earnest has one for sale. I'll have to work at getting him down to a reasonable price.

He tried to ignore the way her thigh brushed his, but it was difficult. She also smelled good and his male senses stirred as he looked into her eyes.

"I don't have the money for a horse," Josie said. She didn't want to give away her financial circumstances, but she needed to let Evan know that she couldn't afford such a large purchase.

"Oh, don't worry. I'll make Earnest let you pay on time," he said.

Josie heard the hard tone in his voice. "Are you a bully?"

Evan laughed and Josie found herself smiling at the rich sound. "I am when I have to be. Sometimes it's the only way to get things done around here."

"Really? Doesn't the mayor help you?" Josie asked.

Again Evan laughed. "We don't have a mayor. The last mayor ran off with a bunch of the town's money and they haven't bothered with one since."

"There's no mayor? But who helps you?" Josie said.

"There are some things I need to explain to you. Echo is tiny compared to Pullman or compared with a lot of places in Montana, too. We don't have a lot of things. We have no mayor, no real town council, no doctor, and if things don't get turned around, Echo is in real danger of dying out." He pointed to a couple of stores that were empty. "This has been happening more and more. All of the mining operations went belly up because the gold and silver dried up. That's why I said what I did about Lucky's reasons for coming here. There are other places he could go and have a lot better luck at it."

Josie looked along Main Street as Evan kept Smitty at a walk. There were more businesses closed than open, she saw. "You said in your letters that things were bad, but I guess I didn't realize just how bad. It's a shame. It's a pretty town."

Evan nodded as they pulled up in front of the general store. "I know. It was built up really nice and then when the mining quit, things just went downhill from there. I thought you might need a few things and I'll introduce you to a few people at the same time."

Josie let him help her down and then entered the store. It was a little rough on the inside, but clean. As they walked around, Evan hoped that Josie wasn't going to bolt when she realized just how desperate things in

Echo were. He was trying to tell her slowly, but he knew she was going to find out rather quickly.

It soon became evident to Josie that the store had certainly seen better days. It was large, but there wasn't much stock on the shelves. She thought that it must be because with so many less people around, there wasn't much sense in carrying a lot of stock. The store would be at a loss and close for sure.

They encountered one of the owners of the store, Tansy Temple. Evan introduced Josie to the buxom redhead.

Tansy said, "I'm glad you made it ok. Gwen told me what happened with your train. How awful. My husband, Reggie, went to Dickensville this morning so he'll bring back a newspaper and hopefully there'll be something in it about the accident."

Josie frowned. "I hope my luggage gets here soon."

Evan knew how worried she had to be since her whole life was in those suitcases, but he knew that her guitar meant even more to her than the other things. "If it doesn't come tomorrow, I'll go to Dickensville and send out a wire to the railroad to see what's going on with the luggage from the train."

Josie nodded. "Thank you."

"Is there anything I can help you find?" Tansy asked, concern in her brown eyes.

"I need another dress until my things arrive," Josie said as she glanced shyly at Evan.

"I'll tell you what; why don't I go check in with Merle at the diner and I'll meet you at the buggy so you ladies can do whatever you need to?" Evan said.

"Ok. That sounds good," Josie said, grateful to him for understanding. There were just some things that a woman found hard to talk about in front of a man.

"Ok. Tansy, good to see you. Tell Reggie I was sorry to miss him. I'll be back soon, Josie," Evan said.

Tansy waited until Evan had left before saying, "Ok. I'll help you with a dress if you tell me all about how it feels to have landed the sheriff!" Giggling, she took Josie by the hand and pulled her along to the small section of women's clothing in the store.

The sensation of someone sitting down on his bed woke Billy. He thought it might be Jimmy or Amy, who were still staying with him and his folks. Billy had the feeling that they were going to have the two youngsters for good. Rolling over, he encountered a bare, broad, muscular, male back. It wasn't his father.

"Good morning, lad."

The voice sounded slightly muffled and he heard the sounds of chewing.

"Lucky?"

"Aye. Ya got a lot of paintings, Billy," Lucky said as he eyed them.

Billy yawned before saying, "Yeah. Why are you sitting on my bed?"

"Well, 'tis best place to look at 'em all," Lucky replied.

"No, I mean, why are you in my house, in my room, sitting on the bed?" Billy said, noticing the tattoos on Lucky's back.

"Evan told me where your door is and so I came in. It's time you were up anyhow," Lucky said. "We got work to do."

"Work? What work?" Billy asked as he sat up and studied Lucky's tattoos.

Lucky finished whatever it was he'd been eating and turned around to see Billy looking at the tattoos. "Like 'em?"

Billy nodded. On one shoulder blade was a rendering of a griffin poised to strike, while on the other, a black bull was ready to charge. Both creatures faced each other. His eyes moved over them. They were exquisitely done and he was envious of their quality. He'd have liked to have met the person who'd created them.

"Who did them? They're like nothing I've ever seen," Billy said.

Lucky said, "They were done by a fella I knew in Canada. He was talented for sure, but from what I see here, you're not far off."

Billy scoffed at his remark. "I'm nowhere close to this guy."

"I'm tellin' ya the truth," Lucky said.

"Why don't you have a shirt on?"

Lucky chuckled. "Edna told me I wasn't allowed to yet."

Billy laughed. "She does the same thing to me, but I hate wearing shirts anyway."

"She's a lusty one, she is. I can just imagine what she was like with Evan's uncle before he passed," Lucky said.

"I don't want to think about that," Billy said. "So what's all this about work?"

"I'm gonna pay ya to guide me to where I'm goin' and we're gonna talk more about sellin' your work here," Lucky said. "Sort of partners, I guess. Ya need to have a place in town to show this stuff. It's not catchin' anyone's eye hidden away here," Lucky said.

"Get up. I have to go to the outhouse," Billy said.

Lucky rose and moved to the side, still looking at the paintings. "All right, but we'll talk more about this when ya get back."

As he hurried out the door, Billy could have groaned. The last thing he wanted to do today was talk to people. He wasn't in the mood. Still, if Lucky was going to pay him, it would be stupid to turn down the money. With his parents having two more mouths to feed since taking in Jimmy and Amy, they could use the cash.

On his way back, Billy stopped as he suddenly understood what Lucky had been saying to him the previous day. If it was going to be hard on his family to take care of two young kids, how much harder must it be for a single woman to raise her children on her own? He took a detour and walked out through the woods a little, sitting on a fallen tree trunk.

It was painful, but he forced himself to realize that Shelby had done what she had to in order to provide for her kids. There was no way she could take a chance on him when two little lives depended on her. She'd sacrificed her own happiness for her children, something that all good mothers did.

Although it did little to heal the hurt inside, he wasn't so angry at her. His heritage was another matter. Until now, he'd always liked his last name, but it certainly didn't help his cause. Briefly he thought about taking his parents' last name, but it wouldn't change his race, so there was no sense in doing that.

Frustration and anger set in again as he walked back to his house. By the time he arrived there, his mood was foul. He was dismayed to find that Lucky was still there.

"I thought ya fell in," he said. "Get dressed and I'll do the same. I want to at least find it today so I know where I'm goin' from now on," Lucky said impatiently.

Billy said, "I'm not sure you've noticed, but I'm a grown man and I don't like you trying to order me around. I haven't eaten yet. I'd like to have something in my stomach before hiking up there."

Lucky said, "I'm sorry, Billy. I wasn't thinkin'. I have a one-track mind sometimes. Just meet me over at Evan's when you're ready."

Billy relented when he saw genuine regret in Lucky's expression. "It's ok. Give me fifteen minutes."

"Right." Lucky left out the outside door, whistling as he went.

Billy didn't want to deal with his cheerful mother when he felt anything but. Jimmy was most likely off with one of his friends, but Amy would be home with his mother, so he'd have her to deal with, too. However, Billy knew if he acted strangely, his mother would only ask a bunch of questions he didn't want to answer. With a sigh, he put on a brave face and went into the kitchen.

Phoebe's words about there not being a lot in Echo for Josie to be occupied with proved to be dead wrong. Evan showed her all of the businesses that were still in operation and then took her out to the Earnest ranch to see about buying a horse.

The Earnest ranch was a sad affair, Josie saw. The house had certainly seen better days and the huge barn was no better.

She noticed Evan's jaw tighten as he looked at the place and saw anger in his eyes.

"What's wrong?" she asked.

Evan hadn't realized that his feelings had shown on his face. "It's a long story. I'll tell you on the way back. Right now, we'll concentrate on buying you a horse."

She became anxious as they drew closer to the barn. A squat bulldog came trotting out of it, barking hoarsely at them.

"Hi, Barkley," Evan said, smiling down at the dog.

Barkley's stubby tail wagged so fast that it was hardly visible and he panted loudly with happiness. Josie smiled as she stepped down from the buggy without waiting for Evan. Barkley trotted around to inspect her.

"Hi, there," she said, petting his smooth, brindle coat. "He's a handsome dog."

Evan said, "Yeah, I like him a lot better than I do his owner."

"Is this Mr. Earnest unpleasant?" Josie asked.

"You could say that," Evan responded as they headed for the barn.

Josie put a hand on his arm, stopping him. "Then why bring me here?"

"So you can meet him while I'm with you instead of in town while you're alone. This way you'll know what he looks like and what he's like so you can avoid him like the plague. He's the proverbial snake in the grass, but he's the only one around who has any horses worth buying," Evan said.

Josie got a glimpse of what Evan was like as a lawman and she thought she was glad to be on Evan's side. "All right."

"Josie, I'm not going to let anything happen to you," Evan said.

She nodded and gave him a little smile. Apparently satisfied, Evan continued on his way, leading her inside the barn. Going through to the barn floor, Evan hollered, "Earnest! You in here?"

"No," said a voice from behind them.

Evan turned around and smiled at Travis Desmond, Pauline's

father. Pauline looked nothing like her father in that Travis had light brown hair and a lighter shade of brown eyes.

"Hi, Travis. I'd like you to meet Josie Bainbridge. Josie, this is Travis Desmond, a good friend of mine."

Travis gave Josie a friendly smile and shook her hand. "Nice to meet you, ma'am. Glad to have you here in Echo."

"It's nice to be here," she said.

"Is your boss around?" Evan asked.

Travis' smile disappeared. "Yeah. In the house. He hardly ever comes out here, you know that. Why do you want to bother yourself with him, anyhow?"

Evan frowned. "I'm looking to buy Josie a horse. Does he have any that he'd be willing to part with?"

Travis thought over their current horse stock and he knew that Marvin Earnest would try to cheat Josie out of a good horse if he could. "There's one horse that would be good for her, but you'd better let me go talk to him about it first. Meet me out back at the pasture."

Evan nodded. "Ok. C'mon, Josie."

Travis headed in the other direction, intent on screwing Earnest out of a good horse if he could. It wasn't their best horse, but it was a good first beginner horse.

As they waited for Travis to return, Josie's trepidation about meeting this Earnest mounted.

Evan smiled at her in a reassuring way, and said, "Josie, relax. It'll be ok. I'm right here."

The only response she made was to nod.

"Well, Sheriff Taft, Travis tells me that you're looking to buy a horse."

Both Evan and Josie turned at the sound of the smooth voice. Josie thought that she had never seen such a contradiction in a piece of property and its owner. She had been expecting a slovenly, older, ugly man, but Marvin Earnest was none of those things. His attire was spotless, the elegant three-piece suit fitting his nice physique to perfection.

His hair, a very rich, golden blond, was neatly styled. He looked to be somewhere in his early thirties; much younger than she'd anticipated. Sky blue eyes zeroed in on Josie and his gaze sharpened. "My word, Evan. She's quite the beauty," Marvin said.

Although the man was beautiful, Josie could see the cruelty of his character in his face and eyes. Instinctively, she moved slightly closer to Evan.

Evan smiled tightly. "Yeah, she is. Josie, this is Marvin Earnest. Marvin, Josie Bainbridge, my bride-to-be."

Josie felt a little jolt of surprise over his introduction, but she had the distinct impression that Evan was being territorial for a reason.

"A pleasure to meet you, Miss Bainbridge," Marvin said. "So you are in need of a steed."

"Yes. It's very nice to meet you, too," she lied. She knew that she'd better be nice to him if she wanted a horse at a price she could afford.

Marvin's smile seemed genuine on the surface, but there was a coldness beneath it. He turned to Travis and the smile disappeared. "Well, get the horse you told me would best suit Miss Bainbridge. I don't pay you to just stand around," he snapped.

Travis' expression darkened and it seemed as though he was about to say something, but changed his mind. Putting his thumb and forefinger in his mouth, he let out a piercing whistle. Nickers and whinnies sounded along with hoof beats as six horses came into sight over a rise in the pasture.

Soon they crowded around the fence, trying to get to Travis, who nickered back at them. Josie smiled at how accurate his imitation sounded. Travis singled out the horse he'd had in mind; he'd only told Marvin that it wasn't the best-quality animal in order to get him to part with it for a decent price. It was a good thing that Marvin had no knowledge of good confirmation.

"This is the one you want, Josie," he said as the dark bay gelding nudged his pocket, looking for a treat.

Stepping over to the horse, Josie pet its sleek neck and smiled as the horse sniffed her hands.

"His name is Captain. He's not the fastest horse, but he's solid and has good stable manners," Travis said.

"He seems very nice," Josie said.

Evan caught Travis' wink, but didn't let on. "Ok, Earnest, let's talk price. Since Josie's new in town and is working on find a job, she'll need to pay on time. We'll settle on a total price and then figure out an amount for her to pay you each week."

Marvin's eyebrows rose. "On time? I need to turn a profit now, not later, Sheriff."

Evan stepped a little closer to Marvin. Just the sight of the man was enough to enrage him and Evan felt his temper rise immediately. He clamped down on it and said, "I understand, but something every week is better than nothing."

"Fine. Two hundred and I'll expect ten dollars per week," Marvin said, dropping all pretense of pleasantness.

Evan said, "That horse ain't worth more than one fifty and make it five a week. She's not made of money, Earnest."

Earnest looked at Travis, who shook his head a little. "Let's split the difference and say one seventy-five and I'll let it go at five dollars a week. That's my final offer."

Evan looked at Josie, who nodded at him. "Done. She'll need the halter and lead rope for now. I'll get it back to you."

Marvin said, "As a show of generosity, you can keep it, Josie."

Josie smiled and said, "Thank you, but I wouldn't want to take advantage that way. You're being very kind as it is."

This time, his smile was genuine. "I insist."

"Ok," Josie said. "Thank you." She didn't want the halter and lead rope and decided to give it back to Travis as soon as she could.

She opened her purse and took out five dollars. As she handed it to Marvin, she made sure that their hands never touched.

He took the money and said, "Thank you. Come into the house so we can write up the agreement."

Evan bristled. "Look, we don't need to do that." He didn't want to spend any more time in Marvin's company than absolutely necessary. "We're all witnesses to the agreement."

Marvin smiled calmly. "If I don't do it properly, my accountant won't be happy. If you want the horse, you'll come in so we can get it done. The sooner we begin, the sooner we'll be done."

After grinding his teeth together for a few moments, Evan said, "Fine. Don't take all day. We've got things to do."

"So do I," Marvin said. "Follow me."

Travis said, "I'll tie Captain to your buggy, Evan."

"Thanks," Evan said, sending his friend a sympathetic look.

Travis nodded and moved towards the pasture again.

Again Josie was surprised—this time about how nice the inside of Marvin's house looked. It was done in attractive colors with beautiful drapes and carpets. Everything was clean and orderly, too. Marvin led them to an oak-paneled office where a large desk stood in the center of the big room. Two floor-to-ceiling windows let in plenty of sunlight.

"Sit, please," Marvin said as he sat down at his desk and opened a drawer.

Josie chose the chair closest to the door. She felt like a mouse at the mercy of a very lethal cat and she wanted to be able to run if necessary.

Silence pervaded the room as Marvin wrote up the agreement and then started to hand it to Josie. Evan tried to intercept it, but Marvin jerked it out of his reach.

"The horse is Josie's, so this goes to her," Marvin said.

Josie took it from his hand and looked it over. "You're charging me interest?"

"Well, it's the same as a bank loan, in a sense, and there's always interest on a loan," Marvin said reasonably.

"Now, look here, Earnest," Evan said. "That wasn't part of the deal and you know it. One seventy-five, no interest. That was the deal. Five dollars a week. That's it. Now either you honor it or we're leaving without the horse and you can shove your agreement where the sun don't shine."

Marvin looked into Evan's stormy green eyes and felt a small sense of satisfaction for being able to get under his skin. He smiled wryly and took the agreement back from Josie, ripping it up. "Fine." Quickly, he wrote up the new agreement, which Evan snatched out of his hand.

The sheriff read it and, seeing that everything was in order, he handed it to Josie for her to sign while Marvin wrote up a duplicate copy. Evan checked that one over, too, wanting to make sure that Marvin hadn't tried to pull a fast one. Josie signed that one, as well.

Evan stood up. "Let's go, Josie."

Marvin looked at her and said, "It's nice doing business with you, Josie. I look forward to seeing you around town."

Josie gave him a small smile and said, "Thank you," before following Evan from the room.

Chapter Nine

As they drove back into town, Captain trailing behind the buggy, Evan was silent as he brought his temper under control. He took a couple of deep breaths and then said, "I'm sorry about that, but you needed to understand what kind of man Earnest is so that you're not fooled by his cultured gentleman's act. He's a bastard of the highest form and I'd like to put a bullet between his eyes. If I ever have a reason to, I will."

Josie was shocked by the level of hate she heard in Evan's voice and saw in his eyes as he looked at her. "What did he do to make you hate him like that?"

He looked away and snorted sarcastically. "What hasn't he done? He treats his employees like dirt and keeps them under his thumb because he knows that they need their jobs so badly that they'll put up with him just to keep food on the table. That's the only reason Travis stays. If he wasn't married with a daughter, he'd have quit a long time ago."

Josie said, "I can see that he's not a nice man. It's in his eyes."

"He's evil. Pure evil, Josie, so you stay away from him at all costs. I'll bring your payments to him. I don't want you coming out here alone because you can't count on Travis or any of the other ranch hands being around," Evan said. "Do you promise not to come here alone?"

Josie was scared by this point. "I promise. Isn't there anyone else we can get a horse from?"

"I already checked around and no one else has any for sale. That's the problem with Earnest. He has money and he uses it against people."

"If he has money, why doesn't he fix up his ranch? It looks horrible."

Evan said, "He only spends what he absolutely has to on the outside stuff so that he has money for clothing and to keep the interior nice. He's crazy, Josie."

"What do you mean?"

"See, his family used to be extremely wealthy, but then the mining dried up and there went some of their fortune. They were very vain people from what my friend Spike tells me. They sent Earnest away to some fancy boarding school and he grew up with all of the advantages most people never have.

He idolized his father and when he died, Earnest wanted to keep the place exactly like it was, as sort of a shrine. But the money kept dwindling and so he let certain things go so he could keep the shrine. Sometimes it's like he's in denial that his family is gone and his old way of life, too. Like I said, he's crazy."

"Is he dangerous?"

"Yes. Don't ever let yourself be alone with him if at all possible," Evan's gaze bore into hers. "Women are not safe with him."

Josie looked at her new horse and then back at Evan. "Take it back. I don't want it."

Evan took her hand. "Josie, I won't let anything happen to you. You need a horse and this is the only way to get one. I'm not trying to scare you, but you need to understand the circumstances. You're not alone, though. We'll deal with things together, ok?"

Josie looked into his eyes and saw the promise in them and heard it in his voice. His touch made her feel safe and she relaxed. She squeezed his hand back, liking how strong and solid it felt in hers.

She nodded. "Ok. I trust you or else I wouldn't have come here."

"It'll be all right," he said, not ready to release her hand.

It had been a long time since he'd held a woman's hand and it felt very nice. He looked into her eyes again and then at her mouth. It looked soft and he wanted to kiss her. It was too soon, though, and he reined in the impulse, covering his desire with a smile.

"I'll take you to see the sheriff's office when we get back," Evan said.

Josie smiled. "I've never seen a sheriff's office. I've been excited to see it."

"I'm glad that you've never needed to see one before, but it's not very exciting," Evan said.

"I'll be the judge of that," Josie said in a teasing manner. "After all, I'm riding along with the sheriff and that's pretty exciting."

He grinned at her. "It is? Wow. I'm flattered. It's exciting for me to be riding with such a pretty lady. Until I picked you up, I hadn't done that in a while."

"There you go charming me again," Josie said.

"Is it working?" he asked.

She laughed. "Yes."

Evan loved the sound of her laugh. "Good, then I'll keep doing it."

Josie smiled. "Well, don't expect me to keep flattering you. It'll go to your head if I do."

"You're probably right about that," Evan said. "I'll tell you what. Only flatter me twice a day so that doesn't happen. I mean, if you really think it's necessary to do it more than that, it's ok, but twice a day should be fine."

She gave him an impish grin and asked, "What makes you think I'm going to find two things to flatter you about in a day, let alone more?"

Evan's expression became one of mock hurt. "Hmm. Just for that, I'm not going to kiss you."

She gasped. "Who said you were kissing me, anyway?"

"No one, but I was thinking about it," he said.

Josie said, "You'll just have to keep on thinking about it, because that's not going to happen."

"No?" He chuckled. "The problem with thinking about something a lot is that it makes you want to do it all the more, but if you do what it is you've been thinking about, chances are you'll get it out of your system."

His rambling logic made her laugh. "I'm not sure that's true."

"How about we put it to the test?" Evan asked.

Josie supposed it might have been left over exhaustion, relief to get away from Marvin, or combination of both, that made her feel slightly reckless. Besides, it seemed like forever since a man had wanted to kiss her.

"I don't know. Do you think an experiment like that is a good idea?" she asked, batting her eyelashes at him.

Evan was pleasantly surprised by her flirting. "I think it's an excellent idea."

"Ok, but only on the cheek," she said, her blue eyes dancing.

Evan countered with, "How about we start with your cheek and see what happens after that?"

"I guess that would be all right," she said, still smiling.

"Ok."

Evan put his arm around her lightly, inhaling her scent before closing the distance to her cheek. She completely surprised him by turning her head at the last second so that their lips met in a brief kiss. Both of them felt a shockwave ripple through their bodies.

Josie couldn't believe she'd done that and by the stunned expression on Evan's face, she could tell he couldn't, either. His intense shock was comical and she couldn't keep from giggling.

"I changed my mind. I hope that was ok."

He let out a laugh and said, "Yeah. Fine with me. You're tricky; I can see I'm going to have to keep my eye on you."

"Just your eye?" she blurted and clapped a hand over her mouth.

Evan burst into loud guffaws of laughter.

"I can't believe I said that! I must still be tired from all the traveling. Maybe I should have a nap or something," Josie said. Her cheeks were bright red with embarrassment.

Figuring he'd better put some distance between them or he was going to give her a real kiss, Evan straightened up. He took her hand again, though. "Don't apologize. I'm not complaining."

"I'm not a loose woman. I don't want you to think that," she said.

He squeezed her hand a little tighter. "I know that. One little kiss doesn't make you a loose woman, Josie. We were just having a little fun, that's all. Nothing wrong with that."

Grateful to hear him say that, she said, "Good. You never know. It might happen again sometime."

"I sure hope so," Evan said.

They laughed together over that and turned the conversation to other things, but all the while they drove back to Echo in the June sunshine, they held hands, neither one of them willing to let go.

"You're not a real Indian, ya know."

Billy flipped his sweat soaked hair out of his face and said, "What? Yes, I am."

He and Lucky were climbing up a rather steep part of the trail to one of the abandoned mines and the sun was hot. Both men were sweating heavily by this point.

"You're not. Have ya ever shot a bow and arrows?"

"No," Billy said.

"Can ya build a fire with just a couple of sticks?"

"Well, no—"

"Do ya know any Indian medicine, or all about the stars, or how to scalp someone?" Lucky continued.

"No! I would never scalp someone," Billy said. He didn't do well with a lot of blood.

"Have you ever seen a tipi?"

"No."

"Do ya know anything about any of their religions?" Lucky asked.

Billy thought about that. "Isn't there some Wacky Tacky guy or something?"

Lucky's laughter was long and loud and Billy joined him.

"I don't think ya want to call Him that if you ever do meet any Indians, lad. They won't take kindly to it," Lucky said. "What tribe are ya from, er, well, your parents, anyway?"

"Uh, Ma and Pa say I'm Nez Perce, Cheyenne, and Lakota. And I have some white blood in there somewhere, but about the only way you can tell that is by my hair color," Billy said.

"I see. Well, all the tribes have a slightly different name for Him, but they all mean Great Spirit in one way or another. The Lakota call Him Wakan Tanka—"

"I was close!" Billy interjected.

Lucky chuckled. "I'm not sure they'd agree. Anyway, my point is that ya might be of Indian descent, but you're not an Indian in any other sense of the word."

"I guess that's true," Billy said after pondering it for a moment.

"So how do your parents know all this about ya?"

Billy frowned. "What do you mean?"

Lucky rolled his eyes. "Where did they get ya, lad? An orphanage?"

Billy stopped so abruptly that Lucky ran into him, knocking him forward a little.

"What're ya doin'?" Lucky asked in irritation.

Turning around to face Lucky, Billy said, "I have no idea where they got me. I just always assumed it was an orphanage, but they've never said."

"Haven't ya ever asked?" Lucky looked at Billy in disbelief.

"No. They're my parents and I hardly ever think about it. At least I didn't until this past year," Billy said.

"When all the stuff with girls started happenin'?" Lucky asked, as he caught his breath.

"Yeah. No one ever brought up the issue of me being an Indian until then. I always played with the other kids and no one ever made much of it. Not until I asked Mindy Emerson's pa if I could take her for dinner one night."

When Billy stopped talking, Lucky asked, "What happened?"

"He told me no and when I asked why, he said that he really liked me, but that he wouldn't let her be courted by an Indian," Billy said.

"Ah, I see. That was the start of it all, then," Lucky said.

Billy turned back around and started climbing again. "Yeah."

"Well, young Billy, you know what you and I are gonna do?" Lucky asked.

"What?" Billy asked.

"We're gonna prove 'em all wrong about us," Lucky said.

"We? Because we're going to be partners, right?" Billy said.

Lucky could tell that he didn't believe him. "That's right."

They reached where they were going and Billy stopped. "We're here. This is the entrance to the mine."

Coming up beside the boy, Lucky took a look out over the rim of the opposite side of the canyon from where Echo was situated. He took a map from the back pocket of his pants and unfolded it. "Now, s'pose ya tell me if this map is accurate."

Billy took it and looked it over and matched it against what was in front of him. "Yep, that's it."

Letting out a pleased laugh, Lucky said, "Billy, ya see that red outline there around all those acres?"

"Yeah. So?"

"Turn towards me."

Billy did and his eyes met Lucky's happy gray ones. "What?"

"You're lookin' at the owner."

"You're kidding," Billy said. "You own all this?"

"That I do. See there was an old fella that I met in Denver a little while back. He was selling this land and no one wanted it. So I kept listening and finally one day, I asked him about it and why he was selling it. He told me that there used to be a mine up here, but it'd gone dry long ago. His askin' price was too good to pass up and so I bought it. I sank a lot of my money into it," Lucky said.

Billy looked at him like he was insane. "Why the hell would you do that? This land is worthless, Lucky."

"It's not, Billy. Look around ya. What do ya see?"

"Rocky, grassy, land that's not good for anything," Billy responded.

"Now, lad, what would you do with land like that? Think about it," he said.

"You can't farm it and you can't put cattle on it, either. There's not enough grass to support steer."

Lucky put a sweaty arm around Billy's shoulders and said, "Think a smaller animal."

It suddenly came to Billy. "Sheep! You're gonna start a sheep ranch?"

Clapping Billy hard on the back, Lucky said, "I am! It's perfect for sheep. They eat anythin' and everythin' that a cow or a steer won't. Goats, too. Now, if ya help me get this going, we'll be partners. It'll be a sixty forty split, since I'm the one who put up the money, but you're the one who knows the area and can help me quietly get what we need. Is it a deal?"

"I didn't think you were serious. You really want to make me your partner? Why?" Billy asked.

"I told ya, we have more in common than ya think. People have these preconceived notions about us. Well, we're gonna prove 'em all wrong. By the time we're done, we're gonna have so much money that those fathers who wouldn't let ya see their lasses will be begging you to marry 'em, and I'll have the satisfaction of showing everyone what a 'dumb' Irishman can do. Is it a deal or not?"

Billy looked at the hand that Lucky held out to him and slapped his palm into it. They shook hands and then laughed.

"Where do we start?" Billy said. "We need sheep."

"I've got them comin' into Dickensville in two weeks along with a trained sheep dog. Ya think we can rig up a large holding pen by then? We're gonna have to drive 'em here from Dickensville. Do ya know a back way to get in here? I don't want to bring 'em through town."

Billy grinned. "Lucky, you picked the right partner. I might not be a real Indian, but I know Echo and the whole county like the back of my hand. We'll map out a route tonight."

"Excellent. Now, look, we gotta keep this quiet, so only tell maybe Evan. He can help us with some things, I imagine," Lucky said.

"What about my parents?"

"Not even them. They might accidentally let it slip around those little ones and ya know how kids are. 'Tis best to keep it between just us three for now," Lucky said. "Once we get things in place and going well for a couple of months, then we'll tell them. If it doesn't start to pan out, I don't want to look like an idiot. We're just gonna tell everyone that we're mining, but that it's not getting' us anywhere. Understand?"

Billy smiled at his ingenious plan. "Yeah. Ok."

"Good. And look at that; a stream, by God. The Blessed Father is smiling on us for sure," Lucky said. "Well, c'mon and let's go back."

"Ok," Billy said. "We can go this way. It'll be easier."

"Why on Earth didn't you bring us this way then?" Lucky said as he followed Billy.

"Because you said you wanted to see the mine, not the land below it," Billy said.

"Oh, right. I did, didn't I?"

They laughed together as they walked side by side down the trail, making more plans as they went.

Chapter Ten

When they arrived back in Echo, Josie was ecstatic to find that her luggage had arrived along with her guitar while they'd been gone. Evan followed her upstairs, wanting to make sure her possessions were intact.

Josie went to her guitar case first. It looked slightly banged up, but not as bad as she had feared. Opening the case, she was overjoyed to see that the instrument was undamaged. Picking it up, she sat on her chair and readied the guitar on her lap.

Choosing a chord, she began strumming and the pretty sound filled the room. Evan sat down on the bed and listened intently. The only instrument played in Echo was the piano at church. The song she played was very pretty and Evan was instantly enthralled.

Josie got caught up in playing, as she always did. Music was a balm to her and she missed it when she couldn't play every day. The song she played was a love ballad and she began singing.

The hair rose on the back of Evan's neck and goose bumps spread along his arms. Her sweet, soprano voice washed over him and he intently watched her perform. Josie's hands moved gracefully as she changed chords and strummed. She closed her eyes as she sang and it amazed Evan that she could play accurately without looking.

She was lost in the song and her voice was infused with emotion, lending a haunting quality to the song. Evan was surprised to feel tears prick the backs of his eyes. He had to blink hard to keep them from falling. By the time the song was over, he was back in control of himself.

The guitar music faded away as Josie finished. She opened her eyes as Evan clapped. He wasn't the only one listening, they found. There was more clapping from the doorway. Arthur, Gwen, and Phoebe stood applauding Josie's impromptu performance.

Blushing, Josie laughed. She hadn't been aware that anyone else had joined them.

Arthur said, "It seems as though we have a talented musician in our midst. That was wonderful, dear."

Gwen chimed in as they all entered her room. "He's right. You have such a pretty voice, too."

"Yeah, I liked it, too," Phoebe said, giving Josie a little smile.

Evan was surprised that Josie had gotten that much out of Phoebe and knew that it was the music that had inspired it. Phoebe wasn't a talker, as a rule, and when she did, it was usually because something had really moved her.

"Thank you very much. I hadn't planned on doing that, but when I get my guitar in my hands, well, I can't seem to help myself," Josie said.

Evan smiled. "Don't apologize. We're glad that's the case. We certainly benefited from it. Will you come play for Aunt Edna tonight? I'll cook and you can play."

Arthur chuckled. "You don't want to pass that up, Josie. Evan is a very good cook."

Josie said, "Yes, I'd like that."

Rising, Evan said, "Well, I'll leave you to unpack and get settled in more. We'll see the office tomorrow. I'll have Billy come back to get you later on, ok?"

Josie nodded. "All right. Thank you for your help today."

"You're welcome. Just remember what I said," Evan replied.

Arthur said, "I had Levi take your horse around to our stable. That way you didn't have to worry about it this time."

"Thanks," Josie said.

Gwen tsked. "I'm just sorry that you had to deal with Earnest, the vile man."

Phoebe's expression darkened at the mention of him and she strode out of the room.

"Oh, dear," Gwen said. "I shouldn't have said that. I'd better go talk to her."

Josie watched the older lady leave the room and then turned to Evan with questions in her eyes.

Evan said, "Phoebe had some unpleasant dealings with Earnest a while back."

"Oh," Josie said.

"She's never been the same since," Arthur said. "I'll go see if I can help Gwen with Phoebe. Thank you again for the song and I look forward to hearing more of your beautiful music."

Once he'd left, Evan said, "Josie, things will be fine. No one is trying to scare you. It's just good for you to understand about Earnest so you don't make the mistake of trusting him. That's all."

Josie decided she needed to be brave. She couldn't act like a scared rabbit all the time. She had a life to live and she wasn't going to let anyone stop her from doing it.

Giving Evan a smile, she said, "I know. Don't worry about me. Besides, there's a rather handsome sheriff I know who will keep me safe."

"I think that's twice you've flattered me today," Evan said with a grin.

Josie said, "Well, it looks like I've reached my limit then."

He winked at her and said, "We'll see. Happy unpacking."

"Goodbye," Josie said.

As Evan walked from the room, Josie felt like fanning herself from the heart the sight of his fine physique from the rear view created within her. When her door shut, she blew out a breath and looked at her luggage. Working on putting her things away would keep her mind off how virile Evan looked. She hoped.

When Billy and Josie arrived at the Taft house, delicious aromas reached their noses even from outside.

Billy inhaled deeply and said, "Evan made his meatloaf. Wait till you taste it. You're in for a treat."

Josie dismounted Captain and said, "I can't wait. I'm starving."

Billy said, "I'll take Captain to the barn with Smitty. They can get to know each other since Captain will be around from now on."

"Thanks, Billy," Josie said. She put a hand on Billy's arm. "I know this is really none of my business, but I'm sorry for what you're going through and if I can ever be of help to you, let me know."

Her concern was touching and Billy nodded. "Thanks. That's very nice of you."

"You're welcome."

He gave her a small smile and then led the horses away.

Josie went up on the porch and knocked.

"C'mon in!" she heard Edna shout.

Going in, she saw that Edna was working on a needlepoint project. "Hello, Edna. How are you?"

"Fat, ragged, and sassy," Edna said and laughed.

Josie laughed with her. "I'm glad to hear it, but the 'fat' part isn't true."

"You're so kind," Edna said. "How are you settling in?"

"Fine. Everyone at the boarding house is so nice and helpful."

Edna nodded. "Yes, they're good people."

"They are. I'll go see if there's anything I can do to help."

"All right. I'm sure your man will be glad to see you."

Josie blushed as the older lady chuckled. Going into the kitchen, she found Evan checking the meatloaf. He wore an apron over his jeans and blue denim shirt.

"Well, you look very domestic," she told him.

Evan smiled at her. "Thanks. I do all right at it."

"It smells like you do more than all right. Billy was praising your meatloaf. I can't wait to eat it," Josie said.

Evan looked at her and thought she looked very pretty in her blue gingham dress. Hunger flooded him, but it had nothing to do with food. He wanted to kiss her so badly that it was all he could think about for a few moments.

It seemed as though he wasn't the only one thinking about it. Josie's eyes met his and a strong awareness passed between them. Josie felt daring as she approached Evan. Standing up on tiptoe, she kissed his pleasantly stubble roughened cheek. He smelled of man and some other scent that was intoxicating.

Her soft lips on his cheek almost did him in. Somehow he kept from grabbing her and crushing her mouth with his. He smiled and asked, "What was that for?"

Josie said, "Just saying hello."

Evan arched a brow at her. "No tricks this time?"

"Do you want there to be?"

Giving her a smile, he said, "You don't know how badly I'd like there to be."

"I might have an idea," she said.

Evan said, "I think we might have to do something about that later on."

"I think you're right," she agreed and then took a big breath. "In the meantime, what can I do to help you?"

Evan thought about it. "Set the table? I have everything else under control."

"Ok. Where are your plates and such? I need to learn where things are."

Pointing to a section of cupboards, Evan said, "There's where we keep the plates, and the silverware is right here in this drawer."

Josie began looking around the kitchen. There was a nice six-plate cook stove, a large sink with a pump, and plenty of counter space. The walls were white-washed and the cabinets were made from cherry wood, giving the room a very warm, homey feel. In addition to the cook stove, there was an old fashioned fireplace with a metal arm for holding large pots. There was no fire in it right now, but she could imagine how handy it was for making soups and such. All in all, it was a very nice kitchen and Josie knew she would enjoy cooking in it.

Turning her attention to setting the table, she thought about what a nice man Evan was. She liked how close he was with Edna and how much he cared about her wellbeing. It was also evident that, for the most part, he seemed to be well-liked by the citizens of Echo.

Evan turned away from the stove and watched Josie set the table. Her movements were efficient and graceful and he saw again how nimble her fingers were as she placed the silverware next to the plates. He imagined what it would feel like to have her pretty hands on his body and a wave of desire flowed along his veins.

Facing the stove again, Evan got a grip on himself, but it was difficult. He'd been a while without a woman and Josie was very beautiful. He was going to have to be careful around her, he could see.

When Billy and Lucky came in the front door, Evan was very grateful for the distraction.

"Edna, love!" Lucky said. "Here I am."

Edna looked at his bare upper body and laughed. "You remembered."

Lucky sent her a wicked grin and said, "Of course I did. Ya said this was the price for coming to dinner."

She laughed even harder when he bent down and made a muscle. "Feel that," he said.

Edna wasn't going to pass up his offer. She squeezed his hard bicep. "My goodness, Lucky. What a fine specimen of a man, you are."

With a wink, Lucky said, "I'm glad ya approve."

Billy, who was also shirtless said, "Look at his tattoos. The guy who did them is really talented."

"You have tattoos?" Edna asked.

"I do," Lucky confirmed. He turned around and knelt so she could get a good look at them.

Edna was as impressed with them as Billy had been. "I don't really approve of tattoos as a rule, but I have to admit that they're beautiful. What do they mean?"

"Well, the griffin is a symbol of strength and protection. The bull stands for strong will and determination."

"I can see all of that about you," Edna said. "You don't strike me as the kind of man to back down from difficulty."

"I'm not," Lucky said as he stood up again.

Evan came out of the kitchen and saw the two shirtless men. "At it again, Aunt Edna?"

She gave him a mischievous grin. "They don't seem to mind."

"You two aren't sitting at the table like that," Evan told them. "Get your shirts on."

Billy said, "Ok," and put on the shirt he'd brought with him. Lucky did the same.

"Is that better?" Lucky asked.

"Yeah," Evan said. "We're just about ready. Come on out."

Edna held out her hands to Lucky. "Help an old woman up?"

He smiled and assisted her in standing. Then he tucked her hand into the crook of his elbow and patted it. "Come with me. I'll escort ya there safely."

Evan said, "We're only going to the kitchen."

"Hush, Evan," Edna said. "Let me have my fun."

With an eye roll, Evan turned around and went back to the kitchen.

"Your nephew doesn't have much imagination, does he?" Lucky asked.

Edna smiled. "Depends on what he's doing."

Billy said, "When it comes to crocheting, he has a great imagination. He can make just about anything."

"What's that? He does what?" Lucky asked as they reached the kitchen. He'd walked slowly so Edna stayed steady on her feet. In gentlemanly fashion, he helped seat her. "Josie! You're a sight for sore eyes. How was your day?"

Josie smiled as Lucky kissed her cheek. "It was a good. Evan helped me get a horse and I was so happy that our luggage came. My guitar is fine."

"Praise be," Lucky said.

She helped Evan carry food to the table and then was pleased when Evan held her chair for her. Once everyone was seated, Edna said a short blessing, and they all began passing plates and bowls. Billy tore into the meatloaf like he hadn't eaten for days.

Lucky looked at him with disapproval. "Hey there, boyo. Slow down before ya choke."

"He always eats like that," Edna said with an indulgent chuckle.

Billy swallowed and smiled at her. "Sorry. We were hiking all over today and I'm really hungry."

Josie said, "You should have had a snack, Billy."

"No way. Not when Evan's making his meatloaf. It's worth waiting for," he replied.

"You're right about that," Josie said. "It's delicious, Evan."

That she was enjoying his cooking made Evan feel good. "Thanks. It's my Uncle Reb's recipe."

Edna said, "It's a good thing he knew how to cook, because I'm terrible at it. I've tried and tried, but I just can't seem to master it. Except for cookies. I make very good cookies, which makes no sense. Do you cook, Josie?"

She nodded. "Oh, yes. I enjoy it. I didn't do it much since it was just me, though."

Evan said, "I know what you mean. When I lived alone, I didn't cook much at home. I still ate meals with Uncle Reb and Aunt Edna a lot."

"Yes. He took great pity on us. That way Reb didn't have to cook all the time," Aunt Edna said.

Evan smiled at her, but refrained from commenting.

Billy said, "I've never learned how only because Ma won't let me in the kitchen to do it. She's fussier than Evan is about the house, especially the kitchen."

The look Evan shot him was anything but pleased. Billy shrugged. "It's true. It's not a bad thing you're a good housekeeper. At least when you and Josie get married, she won't have to pick up after you all the time."

Evan's expression turned darker and Lucky said, "Lad, if I were you, I'd shut my trap right about now."

Edna said, "So where were you traipsing around at today?"

"Up at the old silver mine," Lucky said. "I had Billy show me where it's at."

"Did you find anything interesting?" Edna asked.

"I didn't," Lucky said.

He and Billy exchanged a long look. Lucky arched a questioning eyebrow at the boy who frowned as though considering something before nodding.

The other three watched them with curiosity.

"Something you boys would like to share?" Evan asked.

Lucky gave each of them a fierce look. "All right, it's like this, what I'm about to say can't leave this room. Do ye promise? If ye can't then I won't say nothin'."

The grave expression on his face told the others how serious this was to him—and apparently to Billy, too.

Evan said, "I promise."

Josie looked at Lucky and said, "I promise."

Edna said, "I promise, but it's going to cost you."

Lucky and Billy laughed. "You tell 'em," Billy said and went back to shoveling food into his mouth.

Lucky shook his head and then told them about his sheep farming idea.

Josie said, "I'm confused. You said you wanted to do some prospecting for silver."

"I did say that and sorry for the lie, lass, but it was necessary. That's what I want everyone to think, but that's not what we're up to," Lucky said.

Evan frowned. "Why do you want it to be so secret?"

Lucky said, "Contrary to what many people think, I'm not dumb just because I come from Ireland. I did research on Echo Canyon before I came here, ya see. I already knew it was dying out. Everybody around here has cattle farms and most of them aren't doin' good."

"Right," Evan said. "I still don't understand."

"If they know I'm working on farming sheep and it could be more profitable than cattle, several things might happen. One, they might try to stop me before I really get goin'. Two, they're gonna start their own operation and then I'll have to compete with them right away. Lastly, a combination of the two."

Edna saw what he meant. "They'll try to thwart you because they feel threatened."

"Right. I'm after not letting that happen," Lucky said.

"You're what?" Billy asked, coming up for air.

"After not lettin' that happen," Lucky said as though Billy were stupid.

Billy had to run it through his mind a moment. "Oh, you mean you're not gonna let that happen."

"Right. So that's why I want everyone to think I'm just mining up there, but I'm not having any luck at it," he said and chuckled.

Evan took a bite of potatoes and chewed thoughtfully. "How are you getting them here?"

"They're comin' in to Dickensville and we're gonna drive them here. I bought a trained sheep dog to help," Lucky said.

"What makes you an expert on sheep?" Evan asked.

"It's what we did in Ireland until our ma and da passed, God rest them. Things got too hard after that and most of my brothers and sisters didn't want to carry on. It was just me and my sister Corrine and it was too much for just us two," Lucky said. "We had to sell off the place and split the money with the rest since it was in the will. That's when I decided to come to America and several decided to come with me."

"Where are they now?" Edna asked.

"Corinne's married and living in California. Duncan is God-only-knows where. Ian is in Toronto, and Becky's still in New York. My brother, Mick, didn't survive the trip over."

"Oh, Lucky, I'm so sorry," Josie said.

Lucky nodded. "Thanks. He was only older than me by a year. Looked nothin' like me. Ginger lad, he was."

Billy's brows puckered. "You mean he was careful?"

"What? He was like a bull in a china shop," Lucky said.

"But you said he was ginger," Billy said.

The others burst into laughter, but the boy couldn't figure out why they were laughing. Lucky put an arm around Billy and shook him a little. "I can see you're gonna be a lot of fun. I meant that he was a redhead. Like ginger, the spice."

Billy laughed at his gaff and said, "I need a translator around you, I think."

"Nah. You'll catch on," Lucky said.

When the hilarity died down, Evan said, "You're gonna have to drive those sheep a long way to get here."

Billy said, "No, we won't. We're gonna bring them up over Creasy's Pass and cut the distance in half."

Evan considered that for a moment. "How many sheep?"

"Ten ewes and a ram," Lucky said.

"And the two of you and a sheep dog are going to bring them?"

"We are," Lucky confirmed.

Billy said, "It should only take two days to get them here coming that route."

"There's something you haven't thought of. Part of that pass comes through Earnest's land," Evan said.

"So? He'll never even know we came across it since we'll wait until nightfall to bring them," Billy said.

"You've got fences and a bull to contend with."

"We'll use the gates and I can keep the bull busy with some turnips," Billy said.

"Those gates are going to make noise and alert the dogs," Evan said.

"That's why I'll get some scraps from somewhere in Dickensville and feed them with them."

"Your sheep dog is going to object to the other dogs and cause a ruckus," Evan countered. "Besides, that's trespassing, Billy."

Billy grinned. "Not if someone gives me permission to pass through."

"Earnest isn't going to do that," Evan said.

"No, but Travis will," Billy said.

Lucky jumped into the conversation. "Wait a minute. We don't need to be involving anyone else here. Who's Travis?"

"He's a good friend of mine. He works for the guy we bought Josie's horse from. I still don't see what you mean about Travis," Evan said.

"Travis is Earnest's foreman, so if Travis gives us permission to cross, we can cross without trespassing and you won't have to worry about enforcing that particular law," Billy said.

Evan sighed. "That's really bending the law to the point of breaking it, Billy."

"C'mon, Evan! Don't you see how good this could be for Echo? If we make a go of this, we could hire some people and help them out, too," Billy said. "Can't you just look the other way just this once?"

Evan knew dang well that even if Travis gave his permission, it was still trespassing, but he weighed this knowledge against the satisfaction of pulling one over on Earnest and helping out the town. His first instinct was to consider the greater good, but his uncle's teachings wouldn't quite let him do it.

"No, Billy, I can't. If I do and someone finds out, Earnest will have his lawyer come after you and have me removed as sheriff. Then what?

No, you're gonna have to find another way to get around having to come into town," Evan said.

Disappointment and anger burned inside Billy, but he held his silence by stuffing a last piece of meatloaf into his mouth.

Edna said, "Evan, go into your room and shut the door."

"Why?"

"Because I don't want you to hear what I'm about to say. Call it plausible deniability if you want."

"Are you going to talk about breaking the law?" Evan asked.

"I'm not talking about anything until you leave the room," Edna said. "Reb used to do the same thing. If he didn't want to know what someone was up to, he just left so that he couldn't say he knew anything about it."

"He did?" Evan asked.

"I'm surprised he didn't teach you that. He should have," Edna said with a chuckle. "He used it often enough. Of course, times were a little different back then. Now, go on. Get out."

Evan thought about the greater good again and thought that if his uncle would have left the room, then maybe it wouldn't hurt for him to do the same. The risk-taker part of him rose and he said, "I think I need to take a short walk. Why don't you come with me, Josie?"

Josie started. "Oh. Yes. Of course."

Rising, she followed Evan outside even though she wanted to know what kind of plan the others were going to cook up.

"What do you think they're going to do?" Josie asked as they walked along the short lane towards the main road.

Evan smiled and said, "I don't know and I don't want to know, so if they tell you, don't tell me."

"Ok. I won't. Isn't Lucky funny? I love the way he talks," Josie said. "I don't think he knows what the 'th' sound is. Everything is 'tink' or 'dat' or 'dis.' He is a little confusing, but I'm sure he thinks the same of us Americans, too."

"I'll bet he does. Actually, from what I understand, the Irish don't use the 'th' sound. I knew an Irish family as a kid and when I mentioned it to them, they laughed at me and told me that the Irish hate that sound. I knew them for about three years and I got used to the way they talk. You also won't hear him say 'yes' or 'no' hardly."

"Really? How come?" Josie asked.

"It's not in their vocabulary. The old Gaelic translation never had 'yes' or 'no' in it. He'll say 'right' or 'I will' or 'I won't', but not 'yes' or 'no'."

"I'll have to pay attention to that. Come to think of it, I don't think he did say 'yes' or 'no' since I met him," Josie said. "But how does it work?"

"Well, say I ask you if you'll let me kiss you," Evan said. "Instead of saying 'yes' or 'no', you would say 'I will' or 'I won't'."

"Ok. Ask me," Josie said.

Evan just looked at her.

"For educational purposes, of course," Josie said, smiling.

"Oh, yes, purely for educational purposes. All right, then. Josie, will you let me kiss you?"

There in the dark, Josie found that more than anything, she wanted Evan to kiss her. "I will."

"You will?" Evan asked. "Are you being serious?"

"I am," she said. "Will you kiss me?"

Evan came very close to her and put his arms around her waist. "I will."

Her breath coming a little quicker at the hungry look in his moonlit eyes, Josie put her hands on his biceps. The hard muscles underneath her palms flexed a little at her touch and she liked knowing that she affected Evan that way. As his lips settled firmly over hers, she closed her eyes and gave herself up to the experience.

Gradually Evan deepened the kiss, giving them both a chance to get used to each other a little. The problem was that with each passing moment, he liked kissing Josie more and more and he didn't want to stop. Holding her in his arms felt like heaven and no wine or dessert could have tasted sweeter than her lips.

By their own accord, Josie's hands had found their way up over Evan's shoulders. She was thoroughly caught up in his kiss and objecting to him holding her tighter didn't occur to her. His lips were soft and insistent and she wanted more. After a few more moments, however, she felt rational thought return a little and she began drawing back from him.

Evan felt the change in her and did the same. When they parted, he smiled down at her, even as his body raged with passion. Josie smiled back and the sight of her curving lips only made him want to kiss her again. Instead of doing that, though, he asked, "Well, Miss Josie, will you let me kiss you like that again sometime?"

She laughed and put her forehead against his chest. "I will."

"Thank God," Evan said, which made both of them laugh. "I wonder if it's safe to go back inside because I'm not sure it's safe to stay out here."

Josie looked back up at him. "I think you're right. I'll go check and let you know if they're done."

"Good idea," Evan said, and watched her head back to the house.

Chapter Eleven

Looking out over the rolling, somewhat wild terrain before them, Evan and Josie watched the sheep peacefully grazing on the lush vegetation. The tricolored collie, whom Lucky had dubbed Lily, kept a watchful vigil over her fluffy charges. Evan didn't know and he didn't want to know how Lucky and Billy had gotten the herd there, although he knew it somehow involved Travis since the man was now in the sheep-raising business with the other two men.

It was three weeks after Josie and Lucky had arrived in Echo and already Evan was attached to the woman at his side. Evan had been involved with women before and he knew that things were different with Josie than the others. She was a mixture of sweet, smart, and talented. Evan had been amused to find that she also had a feisty side and he liked it very much. That she was beautiful didn't hurt, either.

Watching her profile as she looked at the sheep, Evan thought that he'd never get tired of looking at her. The problem was that he wasn't the only one looking at her. There were many of the single men around town who watched her, Evan knew. Some had introduced themselves to her and while she'd been polite, she'd never done anything to give them the idea she'd be interested in them.

Evan had gone out of his way to make it clear that she was his and that no one had better cause her any trouble. He was helped out in this respect by Lucky and Billy, who often traveled around with her, thereby giving her protection. The sheriff was grateful for this, especially because there had been crimes that needed dealt with that had kept him quite busy.

Josie enjoyed spending time with the men and their friendships had become solidified. However, she didn't want to have to depend on them and she sometimes found it annoying. Since starting their sheep business, Billy and Lucky didn't have as much time to do this, and Josie found it a relief to be able to move around on her own.

Turning to say something to Evan, Josie found him staring at her. "What?" she asked.

His smile made her stomach feel fluttery like it did much of the time. "You're beautiful."

"Stop that," she said. His compliments always pleased her, but they also made her blush. She hoped that someday she'd get over that part. It only bothered her because she wasn't used to having men tell her such things.

"I can't help it. I say what I think, remember?" Evan asked.

"Yes. You're like Edna that way," she said. "I still can't believe the way you talk to each other at the end of the day. Chitchatting while you're going up the stairs. It's very strange and yet very sweet."

Evan chuckled. "You're just lucky that I don't make you take off your shirt every time you come in the house like she does with Lucky and Billy."

"I'm very thankful for that," she said.

"I wouldn't mind it, though," Evan said, grinning.

Josie let out a laugh and swatted him. "Shame on you."

"You like it and you know it," Evan countered.

"I don't know what you're talking about," Josie said in a haughty tone.

"I could remind you."

Josie's blood ran a little faster at that thought. Evan's kisses caused a yearning inside her unlike anything she'd ever felt and there were times when she didn't want to stop there. She knew that he felt the same way and although it was wicked, she sometimes wished that he wouldn't.

"No. I remember just fine. I don't want to have an audience," Josie said, meaning Lucky and Billy, who were talking on the other side of the pasture.

"Oh, I don't think they'll mind," Evan teased her.

She giggled. "No, but I will."

"C'mon, just one little kiss before I have to go back to work," Evan said.

"No!"

Evan smiled. "Just one little peck."

Josie couldn't resist his coaxing and said, "All right. Just one."

He hadn't expected her to agree, but Evan wasn't going to complain that she had. He tipped her chin up and gave her a soft, brief kiss. "There. See? I behaved myself and now I can go off a happy man," he said.

She smiled into his eyes and said, "I think you're far from happy."

He grinned back and said, "You're right, but I'll settle for as happy as I'm going to get for now."

"Me, too. I'll see you tonight?" she asked hopefully.

Evan was always pleased that she wanted to be together in the evenings. "Of course. I'm not sure what time I'll be home, though, so go ahead and eat with Aunt Edna if I'm not home by the time supper's ready."

Josie fought against the disappointment she felt. She was going to have to get used to this if she was going to be Evan's wife. "Ok. I'll keep a plate for you."

"Thanks. Have a good day with our pals," Evan said. He hated like the devil to leave her, but he had to.

She nodded. "I will. You never know what they're going to get up to."

"I know," Evan said. "See you tonight."

"'Bye," she said.

Watching him walk away, Josie's eyes roamed over his broad shoulders, slim hips, and strong legs. He was the kind of man every woman dreamed of and Josie knew she was lucky to have found a man like him. But did she love him? Did he love her? She didn't know yet, but she craved seeing him every day and she didn't want to leave him at night when it was time for her to go home.

She'd also grown close to Edna and enjoyed spending time with her very much. She smiled to herself as she thought about how Lucky and Billy had taken to automatically entering the house without their shirts on. Then she thought about how she'd seen more of their bodies than she had Evan's and her blood heated again.

It was a strange thing. Although she noted Billy and Lucky's male beauty, she wasn't attracted to them—seeing them did nothing for her. She'd seen men shirtless in Pullman since there were various carpenters and other such workmen around, so it wasn't as if she'd never seen a man's bare torso before. Lily barked, disrupting her train of thought, and she was grateful for the distraction.

Looking up, she saw Travis coming across the pasture. She gave him a wave. "Hi. How are you?"

He smiled and said, "Good. I'm on my lunch break and thought I'd come see how things were going."

She said, "There's nothing exciting going on. Just sheep grazing."

"I see that. It's a good thing. I can't wait until we start turning profits and I can tell Earnest to shove it," Travis said, the hate for his employer coming through clearly in his voice.

Josie had encountered the man alone twice and she'd felt her skin crawl both times. She'd exchanged pleasantries with him and then gotten away from him as soon as possible, Evan's warning about him in the back of her mind the whole time. The mention of him made her shiver.

"I don't understand how a human being can be so vile. I don't know how you can work for him. Why has he gotten away with whatever things he's supposedly done?" she asked.

"Because he has enough money and clout to pay off the judge in Dickensville whenever some allegation is lodged against him. He could afford to fix his place up, but he won't because it would take away from keeping the Shrine in good condition," Travis said. "Every time I think about quitting, I picture Jenny and Pauline. I work for them, to take care of them."

Josie understood Travis' deep devotion to his wife and child. He was a good man, and she thought again that she also looked forward to the day when Travis could get out from under Earnest's thumb.

Travis waved to Lucky and Billy and said, "Well, I have to go face the music now."

"What do you mean?" Josie asked, her brows drawn down.

"Uh, well, I sort of let it slip about the sheep," Travis said.

"What?" Josie's eyes went wide.

Travis said, "I accidentally mentioned it to Ross, the butcher. I was mad at Earnest and blowing off steam when I went in to get some pork chops. I'm just glad that no one else was in there."

"Oh, no. Will he say anything?" Josie asked.

"No. In fact, he wants in on the operation. I'm here to set up a meeting for tonight," Travis said. "Wish me luck that they don't tear my head off."

"Good luck," Josie said, feelings of both sympathy and trepidation gripping her.

Travis took a deep breath, squared his shoulders, and began walking towards his business partners.

Sitting in the back of Ross Ryder's butcher shop, Lucky, Billy, and Travis looked at the roll of money Ross had just plunked down on the table at which they sat.

"Good God, how much did ya just say was there?" Lucky asked.

Ross, a brute of a man, said, "Five hundred. I'm willing to give it to you to buy my way in to what you're doing."

"Why?" Billy asked. "I mean, I didn't know you had this kind of money."

"No one does," Ross said. "And I'm counting on you to keep your mouths shut about it the way you're counting on me to keep mine shut about your farm."

Lucky crossed his arms over his chest and said, "Sure and I understand that, but answer Billy's question. Why?"

Ross said, "Look, Earnest's cattle farm is about the only other cattle ranch around here besides the Terranova's that's making any money. That's great, but they're still sending the cattle off to market, which limits my business. I need a meat source in order to stay in business. I have some cattle and people bring me some of theirs, but it's not gonna keep me in business forever. If we can make a go of this, I'll have my share of the sheep to butcher and we can help each other there, too."

Travis nodded. "I see your point. Not only will you have an alternate meat to butcher and sell, but we'll already have someone to butcher the meat we want to keep here and sell that, too."

Lucky said, "I think that could work. What do ya want done with this money?"

Ross leaned on the table and it creaked under his weight. "Buy more sheep. The more we have the better. You oughta be able to buy quite a lot with that."

"They'll have to be good quality and it would be good to have a second ram so we don't inbreed. We're gonna have to keep careful records of that," Lucky said.

Ross said, "Fine. You know what you're doing. I don't know anything about raising sheep, only how to kill and butcher them."

"It's not only the butchering I'm interested in, Ross," Lucky said. "There's wool to be had, too. We have other ways to make money from them, so we're not just gonna kill them all or we won't have a herd. I'm after buying some goats at some point, too. We can sell their milk and make cheese, too."

Rubbing his chin thoughtfully, Ross said, "We could sell some of that stuff in here, too. You know, sort of draw in more customers than just people wanting meat. You need somewhere to sell it out of and I have the place."

Billy grinned, getting more excited. "This could really work, but Travis has to keep his mouth shut from now on."

Travis bristled at his critical remark. "It was an accident."

"Even so, lad, ya have to stay quiet. We can't have people hornin' in on our business and blabbing to everyone about it," Lucky said.

"I know," Travis said. "I swear I won't say anything to anyone else."

Ross nodded, his blue eyes serious as he said, "When will you get the sheep?"

Lucky said, "I'll go to Dickensville tomorrow and start buying. You'll have to go with me to drive 'em home, Billy."

"But who's gonna watch the sheep?" Billy asked.

Travis shook his head. "I can't. I have to work."

Ross said, "I can't, either. I have to open the shop."

Travis and Ross looked at each other and a silent communication passed between them.

"Do you think he would?" Travis asked.

"I don't know. Would he do a good job?" Ross replied.

Travis said, "He's a trained veterinarian, so I would think so."

"Do you know where he's at now?" Ross asked.

"I might. He's usually out at the Devils' Knot about this time of year," Travis said.

"Who are ye talkin' about?" Lucky asked.

In unison, Ross and Travis said, "Winslow."

Billy groaned and laid his head on the table. "Not Winslow."

"He's our best bet," Ross said. "He barely talks, he can always use the money, and when he's on the job, he's reliable."

"Who the hell is Winslow?" Lucky asked, not liking being left out of the loop.

Travis said, "He's a fella we grew up with. He's Chinese, but his parents gave him what they thought was an American first name. His name is Winslow Wu."

Lucky laughed at that. "Well, how's that for a name? Winslow Wu. Sort of has a nice ring to it. So we can pay him to watch the sheep?"

Travis said, "Provided you can find him. He should be at the Devil's Knot, Billy. You better find him tonight and set it up with him. If you swear him to secrecy, he won't say anything."

Billy straightened up and pushed his hair away from his eyes. "Ok. It's the only way. I don't trust anyone else to not run their mouth about it. Whatever we do, we can't let Spike get wind of this. I love Spike, but we all know he can't keep a secret to save his life."

Lucky looked at Billy and said, "That's good to know. I'll keep that in mind."

Billy stood up. "Let's go before it gets any later. We'll want to be on the road early."

"All right then," Lucky said as he tucked Ross' money into his pocket. "Lead the way, Billy."

The Devil's Knot was a rock formation on the opposite side of the canyon from where the sheep farming venture was located. Centuries ago the rocks had been formed by the river that used to flow through that particular part of the canyon and the huge monolith did indeed resemble a knot.

The devil part came from the way the wind hit a series of caves in the canyon wall and made loud wailing sounds as though something from Hell was on the loose. It was not a good place to stay in the winter because the caves offered little protection from the driving snow and rain. However, in the summer the place afforded one relief from the intense heat that could plague that particular part of Montana during the hot season.

Winslow Wu lay right out in the open on the lush carpet of grass, watching the stars wink down at him. It was the way he preferred to sleep at night. The breeze was gentle and the caves only softly moaned every so often. Unlike other people, the sounds of the caves didn't bother him. In fact, he found them comforting.

The half-moon cast a fairly good light on the ground and Winslow both saw and heard the two men coming. They were talking and Winslow listened intently, not giving away his location just yet. He recognized Billy Two Moons, but he didn't know the Irishman with him.

"Where do you think he is?" Lucky asked.

"It's hard to tell. He has a cave over here that he uses," Billy said.

Lucky asked, "Why doesn't he live in a house?"

"I don't know. He likes to move around depending on the season."

"What's that noise?"

Billy chuckled. "It's just the wind blowing through the caves. It sounds scary, though."

"I'll say. I could believe the place is haunted. It feels like it," Lucky said.

Winslow decided to alert them to where he was. "Oh, boys! I'm over here."

Billy and Lucky both jumped, not expecting the voice to come from close by.

"Winslow! You gave me a heart attack!" Billy complained as they came closer.

Not bothering to sit up, Winslow said, "That wouldn't be any fun."

Billy smiled down at him. "Yeah. I know you like playing pranks. Lucky Quinn, this is Winslow Wu."

"Pleased to meet you," Lucky said as he looked down at Winslow.

Winslow extended a hand to Lucky, still not sitting up. Lucky bent down and shook it.

"Likewise," Winslow said.

Lucky took in Winslow's appearance. Short cropped black hair stood up slightly on his head. He judged Winslow to be somewhere in the neighborhood of five foot ten—tall for a Chinaman, he thought. There was no question that Winslow was a very strong man, given his muscular build. He wore pants but no shirt, and his powerful chest was bare. His black eyes glittered in the moonlight and Lucky saw his keen intelligence reflected in them.

"So what can I do for you?" Winslow asked.

"Well, we've come to ask a favor, but we'll pay ya," Lucky replied.

"Then you have a job for me," Winslow said.

"We have," Lucky said. "We're starting a sheep farm, but we don't want a lot of people to know about it."

"But it seems like more and more people do," Billy interjected.

Winslow became concerned. "Don't let Earnest get wind of it. He won't take kindly to it."

Lucky thought it was strange to hear a Chinaman who spoke English fluently with no Chinese accent. He was curious as to how that had happened. "We know. Ross, the butcher, is coming in with us, and Travis Desmond, too."

Winslow said, "I don't have anything to invest in it, but it sounds like a good idea."

Billy said, "We don't need you to invest anything. We're going to Dickensville tomorrow to buy more sheep. We only have ten ewes and one ram. Ross gave us money to buy more to get a really good herd going."

"Ok," Winslow said. "That sounds like a good plan. So where do I fit in?"

"We need ya to watch the herd while we're gone," Lucky said. "Billy said you're discreet. We'll pay ya well."

Winslow's sharp brain began working and he was quiet for several moments.

"Will you do it?" Billy asked.

"Wait a minute," Winslow said. "I'm thinking."

Both of the other men stayed silent. After a time, Winslow said, "I'll do it, but I want something in return."

"Which is?" Lucky asked.

Winslow stood up in a swift movement, making the other men move back quickly. "I'll not only watch them tomorrow, I'll watch them all the time. My payment will be a cabin built somewhere on the property and you'll have an almost twenty-four hour veterinarian and shepherd. I'll take building supplies in exchange for my services."

Lucky's eyebrows rose. "Ya want to live there?"

"I thought you liked to roam around," Billy chimed in.

"Only because I didn't have anywhere permanent to live that I would like," Winslow said. "I don't want to live in town, but I've never had enough money to build a place. People only use my services on occasion, but I don't make much money that way. But this would be perfect for all of us. I get a place to live and you get a professional to help keep the sheep healthy and to assist at lambing time."

"Glory be," Lucky said. "It's a deal."

Winslow shook hands with both of the other men as he grinned.

Billy said, "Wow. You're actually pretty good-looking when you smile. I don't think I've ever seen you do it before."

Winslow said, "I only smile when I have something to smile about."

"This is the most I've ever heard you talk, too."

"Same reason," Winslow said.

"Well, that don't matter to me," Lucky said. "At least that way, ya won't mind living around sheep since they won't talk back to ya anyway."

Winslow laughed over his remark and Billy watched in fascination since he'd never heard Winslow laugh, either.

"I'll get my stuff and you can tell me where your hidden sheep are. I'll go now so I'm there already."

Billy said, "Thanks. That means Lucky doesn't have to sleep with the sheep again."

Lucky said, "I don't really mind, but it will feel good to sleep in a bed again. I'm willing to do whatever it takes to make this work. You couldn't do it because it would bring up too many questions."

They followed Winslow to the cave he'd been using for shelter and storage for what few possessions he had. He lit a lantern so he could see to pack his bag. It only took a matter of minutes until he was ready.

"All set," he said and started walking, leaving the other two men behind for a moment or two.

Lucky said, "You're a fast walker ya are, Winslow."

"You can just call me 'Win'," he said.

Billy said, "We can? Since when?"

"Since we became business associates," Winslow said. "Only people close to me get to call me that. Evan does."

"He does? I didn't know you were close," Billy said.

"Think about it. Evan's close with a lot of people," Win said. "That's one of the things that makes him a good sheriff. He cares about people."

"Yeah, but he doesn't always talk a whole lot, either," Billy said.

"Unlike a certain Indian kid I know who rarely ever shuts up," Win said.

"Hey! There's no need to insult me," Billy said. "Besides, I'm not even really an Indian."

Win stopped and looked up at him. "Of course you are."

"No, I'm not," Billy said, outlining all the reasons Lucky had told him he wasn't.

"Doesn't matter. I don't drink tea like my parents or eat a lot of the things they ate. I don't practice their religion or any religion for that matter, but I'm still Chinese. You can't escape your heritage, Billy, just because you don't necessarily act like your ancestors. Embrace your heritage and be proud of it. I am," Win said, and started walking again.

Lucky kept pace with him and asked, "Ya don't practice any religion?"

"Nope. I don't believe in a supreme being, no matter what his or her name is," Winslow said.

"*Her* name?" Lucky said.

"I find all kinds of religion fascinating, but I don't subscribe to any of them. There are many religions who worship a female deity. Catholics worship Mary, don't they?"

"They do, but not as a supreme being," Lucky said. "She's sort of like a Spirit Helper is in Cheyenne or Lakota circles."

"I don't believe in those, either," Win said.

"So ya don't have faith in anything?" Lucky asked, his disbelief showing on his face even in the dim lighting.

"I have faith in what I can accomplish and in a few people, but that's it. There's never been any divine spirit or being who's ever helped me. I watched my parents be treated like dogs, only fit to help in the mines or cooking or cleaning for people. I saw my father die from the sickness he got from all the mine dust in his lungs and then later my mother because she'd simply worked herself to death," Win said. "I have faith in how cruel people can be towards one another and how petty, selfish, and naïve they are, too."

Lucky's frown was disapproving. "I'm sorry about your family, I am, but there are a lot of things at work that we can't see."

"To what purpose?" Win asked. "If these beings do exist, and I don't believe they do, why do they care about us? What could their reason possibly be?"

Billy jumped into the conversation. "Ok, can we argue about this later? Let's just get where we're going and call it a night, huh?" He could tell that things were going to get heated between the two men, but only because Lucky was starting to become offended. Win, while being emphatic about what he was saying, was keeping his voice at an even tone.

Lucky said, "You're right, lad. It doesn't matter what you or I believe as long as we can get along, Win. So, I think it best that we not talk about that particular subject much."

Win smiled. "That's probably a good idea. We'll stick to talking about sheep and women."

Now Billy frowned. "Can we not talk about that, either?"

"Uh oh. Did one of your little girlfriends get tired of waiting around for you to fall in love with them?" Win asked.

"What do you know about that?" Billy said.

"I know a lot of things people don't know I do," Win said. "I hear gossip as much as everyone else does, Billy, and you'd better watch your step there. There are a couple of those girls who really think they have a chance with you."

Billy snorted. "I haven't seen any of them in almost a month and don't worry, I already know they don't. Their parents do not approve of me as a possible suitor."

Win laughed. "Me, either. Who wants their daughter, sister, or whomever to marry a Chinaman? So, I'm going to wait and see how this works out for Evan and I might go ahead and do the same thing. In the meantime, there are a few women in other towns I see when I need to scratch that particular itch."

"Prostitutes?" Lucky asked.

"I guess if you want to call them that. You sound like that's a bad thing," Win said. "Don't tell me you've never been with one."

"I haven't. I was a virgin until I got married," Lucky said.

Billy shouted, "What? You were married? Why didn't you tell me that before now?"

Lucky cursed and said, "Because I don't like to talk about it."

Win stopped walking again. "What happened?"

"Yeah. What happened?" Billy asked.

Lucky passed a hand over his face and said, "Me and my big mouth. I was married to a Cheyenne maiden, the most beautiful woman God ever made and now I'm not. That's all I'm sayin' about it."

"You were married to an Indian?" Billy asked, fascinated. "Wait! That's how you know all that stuff about them, isn't it?"

"It is," Lucky said in a tense voice. "After I bought this land from that old timer, I was heading along one of the trails when out of nowhere comes a bunch of Pawnees. I thought my goose was cooked, I did. I prayed the hardest I could, keeping my eyes closed the whole time. I hear more yellin' and there's all this fightin' going on around me. I just stayed on my knees in a ball the whole time."

Win was as caught up in the story as Billy. "Then what?"

"Well, it got quiet and someone pokes me on the shoulder and says, 'You can get up.' So I did. I wasn't sure I was alive so I asked if I was and the whole huge group of Cheyenne warriors laughed at me. Most of them seemed to understand English and those that did told the others what I'd said. I told them I was just passing through, but they wanted me to come back to their camp with them. I'll always be grateful to the Lord for making me say yes," Lucky said.

"That's where you met your wife," Billy said.

"I did. Such a sweet thing, she was, and still is as far as I know," Lucky said, a lump forming in his throat.

"Where is she?" Win asked.

"The military rounded us up and forced us to go to a reservation. The only problem was, they wouldn't let me go with her because I'm white. I fought like hell, but there were too many soldiers holding me. She saw and ran back to me, tellin' me that she was divorcing me and that I needed to go live my life if I ever loved her," Lucky said. He took a steadying breath. "She was pregnant, about five months or so. Not only did I lose my wife, but my child. I don't even know if it's a boy or a girl."

"They wouldn't let you see her or at least the baby?" Billy asked, his heart aching for Lucky.

Lucky shook his head. "I hounded them for over a month and I even tried to bribe a couple of the guards to bring her to see me, but they wouldn't. No one in and no one out, is what they told me. I had no important friends to help me, so there was no way for me to get to her. So I finally had to face the fact that I was never gonna see her again or get to see our baby. I'm doin' what she wanted me to and livin' my life. Now, that's the last I'm gonna say about it. It's too hard to think about and I hope you lads can respect that."

Billy and Win both murmured words of assent and the three men went on their way.

Out of nowhere, Lucky said, "Win, I can't believe ya went to see prostitutes."

The other men laughed and Lucky joined in, glad to lighten the mood again.

Chapter Twelve

Josie sat in Evan's parlor, working on a quilt square while Edna read and Evan crocheted. Looking at him, she smiled to herself over the sight of a handsome, virile man making a pink baby bootie. It was both touching and amusing. There were some people who might not find their courtship exciting, but not Josie. She found it very exciting to get glimpses of what their married life might be like together and spending this kind of time with Evan and Edna did that for her.

The more time she spent there, the more she loved it and she wanted to make it a permanent arrangement. She was getting used to the fact that Evan sometimes wouldn't arrive home until late. She didn't mind making supper for her and Edna, either. Sometimes Lucky and Billy ate with them. There were also times when she, Edna, and Evan went over to the Deckers' for supper.

Arlene wasn't the only woman in town with whom Josie was becoming friendly. She'd met Jerry's wife, Sonya, and she and Tansy met in town for coffee sometimes when Tansy didn't have to be at the store. Josie would have liked to have gotten to know Phoebe better, but although the woman was friendly enough, she seemed intent on keeping most people at arm's length.

Evan shifted his weight in his chair and re-crossed his ankles on the ottoman in front of him. He'd dropped a stitch somewhere and it had thrown the last row off. It wasn't something he often did and it aggravated him when it happened. His concentration wasn't quite where it should be and that had to do with the pretty blonde sitting opposite him.

There were times when he didn't think he could stand seeing her home at night and yet nothing would keep him from doing it. It was getting harder and harder to be parted from her and he knew that he couldn't keep on like this. Yes, his libido was a part of that, but it was Josie herself that he missed when he couldn't be with her.

He felt badly that there wasn't much around Echo to do, but she never complained about being bored. She'd picked up some sewing work and a couple of cleaning jobs, so she was making some money. Evan was proud of how self-sufficient she was and how resourceful she could be. And hearing her play guitar and sing was a magical experience for him.

An idea began forming in Evan's mind and he was quite pleased with himself for thinking of it. He decided that it was time to really start romancing Josie and showing her exactly how much he cared for her. They had fun doing simple things like cooking together and taking walks, but he wanted to do something special for her.

Josie looked at the clock on the mantel and saw that it was getting late. She sighed, drawing the attention of both Edna and Evan.

"What's the matter, dear?" Edna asked, even though she suspected the nature of the problem.

Smiling, Josie said, "Oh, nothing. I should go since I have to be up early in the morning to go to clean for Vince. I'd rather do it before it gets too hot; he's always up early and won't mind."

Edna said, "Yes, it's the time of year for ninety-degree weather."

Evan said, "I hope it cools down a little at some point. We need rain, too."

Josie put away her things in the basket she'd been leaving at Evan's house and then stood up. Going over to Edna, she kissed the older woman's cheek and said, "Goodnight. Try to behave yourself."

"What's the fun in that?" Edna said with a chuckle.

Josie smiled as Evan stood up.

"I'll be back soon," Evan said to his aunt.

"Don't hurry on my account," Edna said. "I'm not going anywhere."

"With you, you never know," Evan said.

Edna just grinned as they left the house.

Josie felt Evan take her hand, but she pulled hers away from his and put distance between them.

"What's the matter?" he asked.

"Nothing," she said in a teasing voice.

He smiled. "Are you playing hard to get?"

"Maybe," she said as they walked towards the barn.

"Why are you being naughty?" he asked.

She giggled. "Sometimes we women just like making our men work a little harder for our affections."

"You do, huh? So you want me to work harder?" Evan said. "What is it you'd like me to do?"

"Catch me!" Josie said.

Picking up her skirts, she ran for the barn, leaving Evan behind in surprise. That was another thing he loved about Josie. There were times when she did something completely unexpected. He gave chase, catching her just inside the barn door. She squealed quietly as he wrapped his arms around her and tickled her.

Her knees went weak with the laughter his tickling caused, but Evan held her upright. He relented after a few moments and they laughed together. Their horses nickered as though laughing along with them.

Evan still held her and he said, "You're a bad woman, Josie Bainbridge. I might have to lock you up."

"Only if you're in the cell with me," she said, looking into his brilliant green eyes.

"Hmm. It might get sort of crowded in there," Evan said.

Josie said, "I won't mind. Will you?"

"No. Will you?" Evan asked, as he held her a little tighter.

"I just said I wouldn't," she said.

He laughed. "You did, didn't you? My mind turns to mush when I hold you like this and you're all I can think about."

She reached up to brush a lock of ink-hued hair away from his forehead. "You need a haircut again."

"You've been spending too much time with Aunt Edna. She's always after me about it," he said. "So that's your response to what I just said?"

"I'm trying to distract myself from the way I feel when you hold me," Josie said.

Evan's heartbeat started trotting along. "And how is that?"

"Warm and a little breathless," she said. She ran a hand over his jaw. "You are so handsome, but I know you know that. I'm sure you've had women tell you that before."

His bashful smile told her she was right.

"I can't believe you've never been in love before," she said to him. "It's unimaginable to me that some other woman didn't want to marry you."

Evan suddenly felt as though an icy cold wave of water had just washed over him and he froze as memories assaulted him. "Let's get you home before it gets later," he said, dropping his arms from around her waist.

Josie was shocked into silence at such an abrupt change in Evan. "Did I say something wrong? I didn't mean to offend you. I was complimenting you."

He tried to smile at her. "No. You didn't do or say anything wrong, Josie. It's my problem, not yours."

She gripped his arm as he turned away from her. "I'd say it *is* my problem, Evan. One second you're warm and affectionate with me and then the next, you turn away from me. What was it about my comment that made you do that?"

"Josie, I know that you're concerned, but it has nothing to do with you and I don't want to burden you with it," he said.

Josie didn't loosen her hold on him. "Evan, I don't know how serious you are about me, but I am very serious about you and if we are going to be married at some point, you need to understand that I expect you to tell me about your life. You haven't done that with me so far."

Evan's brows puckered. "Yes, I have. You know all about my life."

"No, I don't. There are things that you won't tell me. I know that your parents and sisters passed away when you were young, but you won't tell me how and neither will anyone else," Josie said.

"What difference does it make?" Evan asked. "It won't bring them back and you can't do anything about it."

She saw the pain in his eyes and heard it in the slightly rough timber of his voice. "I could help you find some peace, Evan."

"I have peace about it as long as I don't talk about it," he said angrily. "The reason no one will tell you about it is because there's only one other person besides Aunt Edna who knows about it and that's the way I want it to stay."

Josie's eyes widened and she felt stung. "So even if we get married, you wouldn't tell me? Your wife?"

Evan's defense mechanisms kicked in and he said, "I don't know because you're not my wife yet."

The ice in his voice was foreign to Josie and she said, "Yet? I won't marry a man who won't talk to me about everything. I've told you everything about my life," Josie said. "It's not fair for you not to reciprocate."

Evan bit off the angry words that were on the tip of his tongue before he could say them. It wasn't Josie's fault about his family and she was right; he should tell her, but he just couldn't. At least not yet. Closing his eyes, his jaw clenched as he reined in the bitterness and pain.

"I'm sorry, Josie. I shouldn't have said those things to you. I … it's just—I know I shouldn't ask, but can you just give me a little more time about all that?"

The raw emotion in his voice softened Josie's heart and she knew that whatever had happened must have been horrible for him. "Yes. I'll wait for a while longer."

Suddenly, Evan took her in his arms again, holding her tightly, needing her nearness to help quiet his turbulent feelings. "Thank you. I'm so sorry."

She felt his shoulders tremble slightly and her heart filled with sympathy for him. Never would she guess by his generally good-natured personality that something terrible was lodged inside him. "It's all right, Evan. It's ok." She pulled back slightly so she could look him in the eye. "I'll be patient a while longer," she said.

He took her face in his hands and said, "You shouldn't have to be, but I'm grateful that you're so understanding. I shouldn't have gotten angry. I'm sorry."

"I think I surprised you somehow. I didn't mean to," she said.

"I know. It's not your fault," Evan said and kissed her softly.

Josie's scent alone was a comfort to him. The feel of her in his arms was also soothing and he felt his nerves calming.

Stroking her silky hair, he said, "I promise I'll tell you all about my family. You deserve to know and it's only right that you do. I'll answer your original question, though."

Josie stared into his eyes and said, "All right."

Evan also hadn't opened this door in quite a while and it was painful. However, it was necessary.

"The reason I hate Earnest so much is because he's responsible for my ex-fiancée leaving me."

A jolt of surprise stabbed Josie. "You were engaged?"

"Yes. I was already engaged when we came to Echo. I didn't know Earnest very well and he seemed like a nice guy. He can be very convincing at that sort of thing. Even though people warned me about him, I became friends with him.

"You did? I can't imagine that. He's so sinister," Josie said.

"I was an idiot. What happened is my fault because I wouldn't listen to anyone about him. Louise and Earnest started to get closer, but I never thought that it was anything but platonic. Neither of them gave any hint around me that their relationship was anything but a friendship, sort of like you and Lucky. They developed feelings for each other—well, Louise cared for him, but he didn't really care about her. He doesn't care about anyone but himself. It was just the thrill of the chase for him. He just wanted to see how much he could hurt and humiliate me."

Anger on Evan's behalf grew inside Josie. "No wonder you said he was evil."

He let out a mirthless laugh. "That's not the worst of it."

Josie kept her arms around him. "Ok. Go on."

"Louise and I hadn't been intimate yet. They were sleeping with each other the whole time that Louise and I were planning our wedding," Evan said, feeling the shame and fury again as he talked about it.

"It doesn't sound like she was any better than he was," Josie said. "I don't understand how she could do such a thing."

Evan said, "Me, neither. He got her pregnant, but he didn't want the baby. He forced her to have an abortion. I only found out about it because she had to go to Billings to have it done and she was gone for a few days. She has family there and she'd told me she was going to see them. When she came back, I knew something was very wrong. She was in a lot of pain and looked sick. That's when she told me everything. She'd only come back to get her stuff and leave again."

Horrified, Josie could only stare at Evan. No wonder he'd reacted the way he had when she'd brought up the subject of other women.

"I confronted Earnest about all of it and he just laughed at me, knowing full well that there wasn't a damn thing I could do about it. I hit him a couple of times, and it was a good thing that Thad was with me to pull me off him. If I'd been alone, I would have killed him," Evan said. "It's still hard for me not to shoot him. That's why I said what I did to you about pulling a trigger on him if I ever get a chance."

"Now I understand why you hate him so much—I hate him on your behalf," Josie said.

Evan held her closer. "That's why I'm so afraid of you being alone around him. Not because I don't trust you, because I do. It's him I don't trust and I know that if he can, he'll get to me through you."

"If he's so dangerous, can't you just arrest him or something?" she asked.

"The problem is that so far no one will testify against him or when they do, he pays off the judge. Also, he's good about doing things that aren't necessarily illegal. Stealing someone's fiancée and getting her pregnant is morally wrong on so many levels, but it's not illegal. As for the abortion, he said that she didn't have to go through with it, but she knew he didn't want the child, so she got rid of it," Evan said.

"He truly is evil. Evan, I promise you here and now that I will never, ever cheat on you," Josie said. "I also promise to never be alone with him if at all possible."

He smiled and kissed her again. "Thank you. I'll keep you safe, don't worry. He doesn't come to town a whole lot, which is a good thing."

Josie shivered. "I'm glad of that."

Evan was surprised to feel a sense of relief in telling her about Louise. It had been hard, but it seemed as though it had also helped. Looking into Josie's eyes, Evan felt a shift in the vicinity of his heart. Something blossomed inside that he recognized as love. Had he been holding his feelings back because of what had happened with Louise? Had he needed reassurance and to unburden himself before he could start to fully let Josie in?

Tears stung his eyes as he continued to stare into hers. Then he pressed a kiss to her lips, trying to convey what he felt for her. He was always amazed at how soft her lips were and how good she tasted. When she wrapped her arms around his neck and leaned further against him, Evan let out a soft groan and kissed her harder.

Flames of passion created a fever inside of Josie. There was a difference in Evan's kissing, but she couldn't figure out what it was. Reason left her and she surrendered herself to the powerful sensations he evoked in her. There was a feeling of freedom in Evan's embrace, as though a barrier had been broken through and Josie felt closer to him than she had before now.

When he started to pull away from her, Josie made a sound of protest and held him tighter. After a few moments, she felt him give in and he held her tightly again. She didn't want this new closeness to end and her emotions began spinning out of her control.

Knowing that if their frenzied embrace continued that there would soon be no turning back, Evan forcefully extracted himself from Josie even though it was the last thing he wanted. Both of them were breathing hard.

"I gotta take you home before I can't," Evan said.

Josie felt like a boat adrift at the loss of his arms holding her. It took her several moments to get her bearings. She saw the same need in his expression and knew that he was right. Although loathe to, she stepped back from him, allowing herself the space to get her erratic breathing under control along with her thoughts.

She couldn't believe how close they'd come to making love. It both scared and excited her, but she'd been raised to believe that intimacy before marriage was wrong. She wasn't naïve, however, and knew that people engaged in relations before then. Evan's former fiancée fell into that category. She couldn't imagine anyone being able to win her away from Evan.

As she watched his chest rise and fall and the way he raked a hand distractedly through his inky hair, Josie wanted to belong to him in every way possible. She wanted him to *know* that she belonged to him.

"Come home with me," Josie said.

Evan nodded. "I am. I'll get your horse."

She could tell that he hadn't caught her meaning. "Stay with me."

He'd turned away from her, but he froze in place as her statement sank in. Slowly, he turned back around. Coming back to her, he looked at her intently. "Please understand that I want that so bad it hurts, but I can't."

"Why?" Her eyes held his.

"Because the Hanovers will know and I don't want that. They'll either see me come in or leave and I don't want anyone to know our business. Besides, we really shouldn't without being married. And if the Hanovers don't see me, Lucky will. It's none of his business, either," Evan said, regret tinging his voice.

Josie gritted her teeth to prevent bitter words from coming out of it. Silently she nodded and moved past him, going to Captain. She hadn't bothered with a saddle since she was only going a short distance. She released the lead rope from his bridle and started backing him out of the barn.

Watching Josie, Evan seriously considered changing his mind, but knew he couldn't do that to her. He wouldn't do anything to ruin her reputation, and if someone found out that they were sleeping together, it would certainly do that. It was just too risky, and he didn't want them to have that kind of fear in the backs of their minds during such an intimate time. So, even though he knew that Josie was far from pleased, he stayed resolute about the situation.

As he led Smitty from the barn, Josie said, "Evan, I can see myself home. It's not far and I'm a grown woman. I don't need you to always go with me. Goodnight."

He didn't even get a chance to respond before she put her heels to Captain and trotted away. Evan was torn between going after her and leaving her have some space. She was right about it not being far and her being a grown woman, still his protective streak screamed at him to follow her. She'd hear him, though and get angry.

Against his better judgement, he left her go, putting Smitty back in his stall and going on to bed.

Chapter Thirteen

It turned out that Evan had nothing to worry about. Josie had made it a little more than halfway home when she ran into Lucky.

"Good evening, Josie, my lovely lass," he greeted her. "What's on?"

Her mood was sour and she took it out on Lucky since he was the first person she'd come across. "On what?"

Lucky raised a brow at her waspish tone, but simply said, "Sorry about that. How are you?" There were times when he desperately missed his homeland and the way he was used to speaking.

"Simply splendid," she said, sounding anything but.

"I see. Guess what?" he asked, trying to distract her from whatever had made her so morose.

"I don't want to guess. Just tell me," Josie said.

Lucky almost chuckled at her churlish tone. "Well, Billy and I are leavin' in the morning to go get more sheep. Ross, the butcher, is goin' in with us and gave us money to buy them."

"Great," Josie said, not caring one little bit.

"Not only that, but we now have a Chinese fella named Winslow Wu watching the herd for us. He's an animal doctor and he's gonna build a place out there and watch them full-time for us."

That did pique her interest. "A Chinese man name Winslow?"

Lucky laughed. "Right. I don't know why his parents named him that, but that's his name. He says his close friends call him 'Win', so that's what I'll call him from now on. Win Wu. He's a nice enough lad. He has some strange ideas, but other than that, I like him."

"Good."

Lucky looked heavenward a moment and then asked, "Josie, what's troublin' ya?"

Josie said, "Nothing I want to talk about."

"Come now. Let me help ya," Lucky said.

"It's not something you can help me with. No one can," she said.

"Is it somethin' to do with Evan?"

"Yes," she said.

"All right. Did ye have a fight?"

"Sort of."

"Mmm. What did he do?" Lucky asked.

"Nothing."

"What did he say?"

"Something."

Again Lucky had to stifle laughter. "So you're mad at him for doing nothing, but sayin' something. Do I have that right?"

"Yes."

"What's the 'nothin' he didn't do?"

"It's personal."

"Oh."

"You men are all the same," she blurted out.

Good Lord help me now. It's never good when a woman starts out that way. Lucky knew this well since he had so many sisters. "How so?" *Best to tread lightly.*

"You just do things and then when things are going along you stop and act like it's ok to and as though it's only your decision. First you make us not be able to think and then you act reasonably. It's not fair," Josie said.

Lucky was thoroughly confused by this point. "Well, I know us men ain't always easy," he said.

"No, you're certainly not," she agreed. "And you seem to think that we can't take care of ourselves. I can ride home on my own. I'm doing just fine."

Lucky didn't dare point out that he was riding along with her. "That ya are."

"I don't need to be watched like some child. I can go where I want, when I want, and I can go alone if I want," she said.

"Exactly right. Do ya want to be alone?"

"No. You're fine. It's almost the same thing."

Lucky actually had to bite his tongue to stop the mirth from erupting. "Oh. Right. So ya just don't want to be with Evan then?"

"Oh, I want to be, but that's not going to happen," she said angrily.

Right at that moment, Lucky suddenly wished that he hadn't happened upon Josie or that the ground would crack right open so he could drop in and escape. Every possible response he thought of would only make things worse, he felt, but he also knew that staying silent wasn't an option, either.

"Mmm hmm," was the only thing he could come up with that might be safe.

"Would you care?" she asked.

"About what exactly?"

"About it happening?" she asked.

"I, uh, it's none of my business, really," Lucky said.

"But you wouldn't say anything to anyone if we did."

"If we did what?"

"Not you and me, we, me and Evan, we."

"Aw, for cryin' out loud, Josie! Will ya talk so I can understand ya?" Lucky replied.

"Never mind, Lucky. You men never listen and you never understand, even when we've told you what was going on," Josie said.

Her statement made perfect sense in her mind, but Lucky was

incredibly confused by it. He rode with her as far as the Hanovers' place, and then kept going, feeling the need of a few pints and some friendly conversation at Spike's after the evening he'd put in.

"Honey, I'm home! Did you miss me?" Thad asked loudly as he entered the sheriff's office the next morning.

Evan laughed in spite of his bad mood. "I sure did. You've been gone a long time."

"Yeah, he was a wily one, but I like the chase as much as bringing down my prey. And, I made quite a tidy sum, too," Thad said as he sat down in an empty chair. "I just thought I'd stop in and see what's been happening before I go get a bath and then collapse into a comfortable bed."

"I'd say a bath was definitely in order," Evan said, grinning. "You smell like hell."

Thad said, "I know. It's bad when you can smell yourself. How's your lady?"

"Mad at me," Evan said with a frown.

"Uh oh. You probably told her that she put something in the wrong place, didn't you? I always told you that your fussiness was going to get you in trouble," Thad said.

Evan couldn't help his need for orderliness as much as he tried to fight it. He'd gotten that from Edna. She might not be able to cook, but she was a heck of a housekeeper.

"No, it's not that. Like everyone else, she finds it funny," Evan said.

Thad chuckled. "I'm sure she'll appreciate it once you're married. You have asked her, haven't you?"

The sheriff shook his head. "Not yet, but I'm going to. I have to get a ring."

"Ok. So why's she mad at you?" Thad asked as he took off his hat. "Jesus, I stink to high heaven." He put the hat back on because it helped keep the stink contained.

"I'll say. Next time you're on the road that long, do me a favor and bathe before you come to see me, ok?" Evan said, moving away from Thad.

Thad laughed. "I'll do that. So, answer my question."

"I'd rather not. It'll get straightened out," Evan said. "Please go get a bath. My eyes are burning. Come to our house for dinner tonight so you can meet Josie."

Thad had left town before Josie had arrived and had yet to lay eyes on her. "Ok. Good luck with whatever it is. It's usually just easier to tell women you're wrong and apologize so you can get back to normal."

"That might be how you handle it, but not me. Get out of here," Evan said, holding his nose.

Thad chuckled and exited the building. He didn't bother mounting up again since it wasn't far to the store. He led his black stallion, Killer, along behind him. When Thad was out on the road, he didn't care much about hygiene, but when he arrived back in town, he always got cleaned up right away and then engaged in some other pleasant activities. Humming to himself, Thad smiled in anticipation as he walked down the dusty street.

Josie looked over some scented soaps that Tansy had just stocked the day before while she waited for her friend to find the material that she had ordered. Tansy had gone into the back, leaving Josie to peruse the other merchandise. She would holler for the shopkeeper if someone came in.

Picking up two different soaps, she then placed them in her basket. Turning around, she let out a gasp and dropped her basket.

Marvin's sensual mouth curved in a smile. "Well, Miss Bainbridge, how nice to see you. It's been a while." He bent and picked up her basket and the soaps, holding the basket out to her.

"Y-yes. Nice to see you, Mr. Earnest. Thank you." She took the basket even though touching something that the vile man had handled made her skin crawl. "I'll send Evan with my payment at the end of the week as usual. In fact, I'll have a little extra for you."

"I wasn't worried about it, Josie," Marvin said, noticing the way her pupils dilated and the way her breathing had accelerated. Making others fear him in one way or another was something he enjoyed immensely. "Please call me by my first name," he said, making it understood that it was not a request.

"Ok."

"Say it," he said with a pleasant smile.

"Marvin," Josie hastily complied.

"Very good. So, doing some shopping, are we?" he inquired in the same pleasant tone.

She actually conjured up a genuine smile. "Well, since I have a basket and I'm standing in a store, I guess that would be the natural conclusion."

The laugh that came from him was also genuine. "That was a rather stupid question, wasn't it?"

Josie couldn't help the fascination she felt as his face transformed from cold and scary to warm and friendly in a matter of seconds. She found herself smiling despite her fear. "You said it, not me."

"So I did. You're looking well. You really should come out to see the rest of my humble abode," he said. "I'll give you the grand tour."

Just that quick, he was back to playing the cat and Josie knew full well that she was the mouse. "That's a very generous offer, Mr.— Marvin, I mean. I must decline since it would be improper of me to go to a gentleman's home unescorted."

"You go to Evan's house," Marvin countered.

"Yes, but Edna is always there," she rejoined.

"Yes. Dear Edna. How is her arthritis these days?" he asked.

Again, Josie couldn't believe that she heard actual concern in his voice. "Some days are better than others."

Marvin nodded. "I've always liked Edna. She's a good person and a lot of fun. I miss her. Tell her I said hello."

"I will," Josie said, relieved that he was turning away.

Suddenly he swung back around, almost colliding with her. It knocked her slightly off balance and he reached out to steady her. "Think about coming for that tour. Bring whomever you'd like to come with you. Maybe your big Irish friend? Say you'll think about it."

Josie was trapped and, short of screaming, there was only one way to make him go away. Just as she was about to reply, the sound of a revolver cocking behind Marvin kept any sound from exiting her mouth.

"Get your filthy hands off her, Earnest," a rough voice said from in back of Marvin. "Or, on second thought, go ahead. I'd love nothing more than to celebrate my latest success by blowing your brains out all over that wall."

Josie watched Marvin's face go through a series of emotions that started with fury, changed to fear, and then into a mask of confidence. Slowly, Marvin removed his hand from her arm and said, "Mr. McIntyre. How nice that you're back in town again." Marvin turned around to find that Thad was pointing the gun directly at his forehead from only about two feet away.

"Shut your slimy, lying mouth, Earnest and get the hell out of here. I'm just itching to pull this trigger on you and, unlike Evan, I wouldn't be subjected to a lot of questions about it," Thad said.

Marvin said evenly, "Your hatred of me is amusing as always, Thad, but it's misplaced. I was doing nothing more than keeping Miss Bainbridge from ending up on the floor. However, I do think it prudent to be on my way and come back at a later time to do my shopping. Good day to you, Josie."

Thad growled in response and the sound was scary to Josie. Once Marvin had gone, Thad put away his gun and turned back to Josie.

"You ok?" he asked her.

"Yes, thank you," she said, wondering if she had traded one danger for another.

"Well, Josie, this wasn't the way I'd meant to meet you, but it's nice to anyway," Thad said. "I'm Thad. I'm sure Evan's told you about me."

It clicked in her fear riddled mind who Thad was and she relaxed, her shoulders slumping. "Yes, Thad, he has." She started to shake as everything Evan had told her about Earnest came roaring back. "It's nice …" Tears welled in her eyes and spilled over, making it impossible for her to continue.

"Shh," Thad said and put an arm around her. "It's ok, Josie. You're safe. Nothing's gonna happen to you. He left."

She nodded, but couldn't stop crying. "He, I—he's so evil!"

Thad said, "Yeah, he is, but he'd never really try anything in the middle of the day like this. I was hoping I'd get to shoot him. If he ever corners you like that again and I come along, scream or something so I can do it."

The humor of his remark made her sob change to a laugh. Thad shook her slightly and laughed with her.

Looking up into Thad's dark eyes, Josie said, "Thank you, Thad, both for rescuing me and for keeping me from panicking."

"That's what friends are for. Now, I mean it, if you can ever give me the opportunity to murder that bastard, be a friend to me and do it," Thad said.

She laughed and said, "Ok. I'll do that."

"Good. Now, I'm going to move away from you before my stench knocks you out. I'm pretty rank. I just came to get my favorite soap so I can go get a bath and make myself presentable again. I'm coming for dinner tonight, so make something good, ok?" Thad said. He kissed the side of her head and then went over to the shelf that held all the soaps.

Josie smiled. "There are some new ones. I like this lilac scent."

He grinned over at her. She was a very pretty woman. Evan needed to marry her soon, he thought to himself. Especially with Earnest sniffing around. He didn't want history to repeat itself. "I think I'll just stick with the sandalwood, but thanks for the recommendation."

She laughed as Tansy came out of the back.

"Good Lord! I'm sorry that took so long. It got put in the wrong place," she said and then covered her nose with her hand. "Thad! Just take the soap and go. You can pay me later. Oh my God!"

Thad picked up two bars, winked at Josie and said, "Hello to you, too, Tansy. Nice to see you."

"Out!" Tansy hollered.

Chuckling, Thad walked to the counter and laid some money down before leaving.

"I love that man, but I hate it whenever he comes back to town from being away so long. He always smells worse than ten skunks," Tansy declared.

"He's quite the character," Josie said.

"Yes, he is," Tansy agreed as she looked at Josie. "Are you feeling ok? You look pale."

Josie saw no reason to alarm her friend so she decided against telling her about the episode with Earnest. "I'm fine. I think it's the heat or something. Well, I'd better pay you for my things and get going. I have some sewing I want to finish before this evening."

"Sure," Tansy said. She didn't quite believe Josie, but she didn't press the issue. "How's your handsome man today?"

Josie smiled, but it was forced. "I haven't seen him yet today, but I'm sure I will at some point."

Tansy said, "Yes, he's usually able to find you. That's part of what makes him such a good sheriff. He's very good at tracking people down."

"That's what I understand," Josie said as she paid Tansy. "Have a good day."

"I will. Come by for tea later if you get a chance," Tansy said.

"Ok," Josie said with a smile.

Tansy watched Josie with concern as her new friend walked away. She knew that something was bothering Josie, but she didn't know what. With a sigh, Tansy went back to stocking shelves.

Chapter Fourteen

"I don't know why you don't wait to do that until I'm outta the tub," Thad said. "It'd be a lot easier for you." He sat in a large claw-foot tub, one of the luxuries of the boarding house. It was out back in a bath house that Arthur had built several years back. He'd had a separate water pump and sink installed in it and there was also a cook stove for heating the bath water. When Thad was out on the road, he always dreamt of two things; Phoebe and that bath tub.

Phoebe chuckled and said, "Because I like the view from here."

"It's a good thing for me you do," Thad said as Phoebe turned his head this way and that as she cut his hair. "Why don't you come with me tonight? You'd have fun."

Phoebe pursed her lips as she trimmed along his left ear. "No, thanks. I'm not much for get-togethers."

Thad would have really liked it if Phoebe would go with him, but he'd known she wouldn't before he'd asked. He couldn't figure out why a woman her age wanted to be with a man old enough to be her father, but he wasn't complaining. Their relationship was simple and casual, the way Thad liked it.

However, there were times when he wanted to go out and do things, but Phoebe refused. He couldn't figure out why, though. She'd said one time that she didn't want to run into Earnest, but he'd repeatedly told her that he'd keep her safe. It hadn't made any difference to her. He felt bad that Phoebe hardly ever went anywhere. It wasn't natural for a thirty-one-year-old woman to stay home all the time.

Finished with the left side of his hair, Phoebe moved over to the right side and settled on her knees again. "Your hair grew fast."

"It usually does. Why do you think I let you cut it whenever you want to? It's easier to keep that way."

Phoebe smiled and said, "That and the last time you were in town I didn't get a chance to do it. I didn't get a chance to do much of anything because you were hardly here before you had to go again."

He grinned at her. "Well, what you did was plenty and kept me going until now."

Phoebe laughed at him. "I'd say we were both due for a longer visit, though, wouldn't you?"

"Most definitely," Thad said. His eyes roamed over her naked form. She always cut his hair this way; on her knees and completely bare. "Hurry up and finish that."

"Almost done. So tell me how you caught this one," she said as she ran a hand through his wet hair, checking to see if she needed to do any more trimming.

"That's a long story. That's why I was gone so long," he said.

Deciding that his hair was perfect, she put her scissors aside and ran a hand over his newly shaven jaw. "You are such a handsome man when you're all cleaned up."

Thad gave her a doubtful look. "You mean for an old fart."

Phoebe looked into his dark eyes. "No, I mean you're a good-looking man, regardless of your age. Why don't you believe me about that?"

"Ok, ok. Don't get riled up. Thanks," Thad said, not wanting to get into the whole age difference subject again. "Are you gonna get in here or not?"

"Do you think there's enough room?" she asked. This was part of their usual ritual and she loved it.

"C'mon, girl. We'll make it work," he said with a wolfish smile.

Phoebe laughed and proceeded to slip into the tub with him.

When Thad entered Evan's house that evening, Josie almost didn't recognize him. Instead of his salt and pepper hair brushing his shoulders, it was now short and very nicely combed. His strong jaw was shaved and he wore black pants, a red shirt, and a black vest. Thad looked very dapper and Josie saw what a handsome man he really was.

He caught her look of surprise and laughed. "Yep. It's the same man, Josie."

"I didn't … I mean …" Josie forced herself to stop stammering and said, "You look quite dashing."

"Thanks, honey," he said, with a pat on her shoulder. "There's my girl," he said to Edna.

Edna laughed and held out her arms to him. "It's high time you got your rear end back in town."

He hugged her and sat down in one of the other chairs. "So what kind of juicy gossip do you have for me this time?"

"After dinner, Thaddeus," she said.

He smiled. "How about during dinner?"

Edna gave him a sly look. "I might be persuaded for the right enticement."

"I'm not taking my shirt off, Edna," he said. "It took too long to get dressed and I don't wanna wrinkle my shirt."

"Spoil sport," she said. "Are Lucky and Billy coming?" she asked Josie.

"Oh! I forgot to tell you all," she said.

Evan came out of the kitchen and looked at Thad. "Thank God you got a bath. I don't know that you ever smelled as bad as you did this time."

Thad said, "There's a reason for that, but we'll get into that later."

Evan nodded. "What did you forget to tell us, honey?"

"I met up with Lucky last night on the way home and he said that Ross went in on their sheep farming with them. He gave them a bunch of money to go buy more sheep. He also said that some Chinese man called Winslow is going to watch the sheep full-time now," Josie said.

Evan groaned. "Win is watching the sheep? How did Ross get wind of it? What are they gonna do, tell the whole town?"

"Travis accidentally mentioned it to Ross," Josie said.

"Oh, boy," Evan said. "Travis better keep his lips shut from now on."

Thad kept looking back and forth between them. "What are we talking about here? Who's Lucky?"

Quickly they filled him in on the events surrounding Josie's arrival and the business venture that Lucky and Billy had started together.

"Billy? You mean Billy next door? What does he know about sheep?" Thad asked.

Evan said, "Nothing, but Lucky does. His family raised sheep back in Ireland."

"Oh, ok. So they're trying to keep this a secret?"

"Yeah, so Earnest doesn't find out and do something to sabotage their business."

Thad said, "Well, they got the perfect man to watch the herd. No one knows protection better than Win. Unless I have a gun, there's no way I'd want to fight him and I'm not afraid of anyone. He's a different story, though."

"Why?" Josie asked.

"I've never seen anyone move as fast as he does and he's an expert with almost any weapon. He can also make a weapon out of things you would never even think of using for that purpose," Thad said.

Evan nodded. "I was crocheting at the bar one night and some guy was giving him trouble. Before I knew it, he'd hit the guy and taken my yarn. He used it to strangle the guy. Once the guy passed out, he took it from around his neck and gave it back to me. He asked me if I was going to have to lock him up and I said no. He was justified in what he did and there was no real harm done to the guy, so I didn't see a problem with it."

Josie said, "Yarn as a weapon. I'd have like to have seen that."

"It was something to see, all right. If I ever did have to lock him up, I'd probably have to shoot him to get him there, too. I'm glad he's one of the good guys," Evan said.

"Me, too. I'm curious to meet him," Josie said.

Edna said, "He's a handsome man and he knows how to come in here, too." She winked and they laughed.

Josie said, "Well, let's eat since our sheep herders won't be here. I don't want the pork chops to dry out."

Thad helped Edna to the table and they began their meal.

"I thought Irish people were good singers," Billy said as they drew close to their land.

Lucky looked over at him in the rapidly dwindling light. "Are ya sayin' that my singing isn't good?"

"Let me put it this way; I've heard cows that sing better than you do," Billy retorted.

Lucky snapped, "Well, if ya can do any better, have at it."

Billy smiled to himself and said, "Ok. Ready?"

"I am," Lucky said, with a nod.

He was shocked when Billy started singing *Maggie Murphy's Home*. Billy's voice was somewhere in the baritone area and was so unexpectedly beautiful that between it and the words of the song, Lucky was brought to tears.

"On Sunday night 'tis my delight and pleasure, don't you see,
Meeting all the girls and the boys that work down-town with me.
There's an organ in the parlor to give the house a tone,

And you're welcome every evening at Maggie Murphy's home," Billy
sang. He kept going, having no idea of the effect he was having on his
friend.

By the time Billy finished the song, Lucky was a wreck, tears flowing
freely down his face. He took out a handkerchief and blew his nose
loudly.

"Are you crying?" Billy asked, his dark eyes wide.

"Aye." Lucky wasn't ashamed to admit when something touched
him that way. "That was beautiful, lad. I never woulda guessed that ya
had a voice like that. And that song, well, it gets to me, it does. Thank ya
for singin' it for me."

"You're welcome. I didn't mean to make you cry," Billy said. He'd
never thought his voice was anything special, but apparently it was.

"'Tis all right. Don't be sorry. You're a talented man. Ya paint, ya
sing, ya—" He broke off, suddenly listening intently. "Be quiet, Billy."

They rode behind the thirty sheep while the second collie they'd
bought to help them get the sheep home, ranged ahead. Lucky had heard
the dog growl and knowing that a well-trained dog wouldn't do so
needlessly, he was instantly on the alert. Quickly, he dismounted and
threw his reins to Billy.

He saw a figure move up ahead and crept towards it, moving silently
the way his Cheyenne friends had taught him during his time with their
tribe. Slipping his knife from the scabbard on his calf, Lucky crouched as
he neared whoever it was near them. His big shoulders bunched, ready
for battle should it be necessary.

"Lucky, it's just me," Win said. "I'm impressed. If I hadn't already
been aware of you, I'd have never known you were sneaking up on me.
You never made a sound."

Letting his breath out in relief, Lucky said, "I'm glad it's you and not
someone else since I'd have to kill them to keep their mouth shut."

Win laughed. "I knew which way you were coming and kept a watch
to make sure that no one was around here. How many did you get? It
looks like a lot."

"Thirty and another dog. That's what tipped me off. Him growlin'. He's a good one and stayed with the herd, I see," Lucky said, replacing his knife.

Win saw the gleam of the blade in the moonlight. "You any good with that thing?"

Lucky smiled. "I'll show ya sometime."

"Looking forward to it," Win said as they neared Billy.

"Boy am I glad it's just you," the younger man said. "How's the rest of them?"

Win said, "Fine. No problems. I came down here to help you get them the rest of the way home. I left the dog with them."

Billy nodded. "Let's get on with it. I'm bushed."

Once the new sheep were safely joined with the original herd and the dogs introduced to one another, Billy and Lucky spread their bedrolls out near Win and lay down.

Lucky groaned loudly as he relaxed his body. "It's good to be back home, such that it is. Billy, where do your parents think ya are?"

"Right where I am. I told them I was going to camp out tonight. I do it every so often, so they didn't think anything of it. I figured I should be here to help if something went wrong," Billy said.

A soft snore emanated from Lucky's open mouth and Billy chuckled. "I wonder if he always falls asleep that fast."

Win laughed. "I don't know, but I hope he didn't fall asleep on his wife like that. She might have been offended."

Billy smiled and then sobered. "Win, I feel so bad for him. I mean to just be forced away from your wife like that and her pregnant besides? It's a wonder he didn't go insane from it."

Win had thought much the same thing over the past couple of days. "He's a strong man. That's all I can say about that. It's not right that they're rounding people up like cattle. They've been doing it for decades. Both your people and mine have been pushed and shoved around and we haven't been able to do much about it in the end. That's why I lived the way I did until now. No one could tell me where to go or what to do."

Billy said, "Why didn't you move somewhere else? I mean, you could have gone anywhere with your education."

Win rolled over and looked up at the stars. "You'd think so, but I have the same problem you do. If your skin isn't white, it makes it hard to get work, even if you're educated like I am. Hell, even Lucky has problems. I know how some people treat the Irish and that's not right, either."

Propped up on an elbow, Billy looked over at Lucky, who slept peacefully, and felt a wave of sympathy flow through him for the suffering he'd seen. Billy realized that Lucky had had a much harder life than him and yet he'd kept on going despite the heartache dealt to him on a number of occasions.

If Lucky could endure losing his brother, wife, and child, then Billy could get over his broken heart and move on. Lying down, he made up his mind to put Shelby behind him and look to the future.

"Go ahead and sleep, Billy. I'll take first watch and wake you after a while," Win said.

Yawning, Billy said, "Ok. Thanks."

It wasn't long until Win heard Billy's breathing slow down into a regular rhythm as well. The sheep had started to settle down, some lying down to sleep. While the dogs had lain down on either side of the herd, they were still alert and would be ready for action at a moment's notice. Win was content to lie there quietly and contemplate his future.

The starlight was brilliant that night as Evan rode with Josie to the boarding house. Looking over at her, he saw her smile. "Penny for your thoughts."

"I was just thinking about the stories you were all telling tonight. I can't believe that you chase after people the way you do," she said.

"It's how I was trained, both by Uncle Reb and by Thad. And watching the two of them together when we were after someone was like watching a ballet. They'd worked with each other so long that they knew what each other were thinking and just what to do. It was an amazing thing," he responded.

Josie rode a little closer and said, "It sounds like you and Thad are alike in that respect."

"I guess you're right. We've known each other long enough that we have a system of our own worked out," Evan said.

"Do you miss going out on the road with him?"

"Sometimes. It's exciting to chase down someone, knowing that when you can get them locked up that they won't be able to hurt anyone again. And the challenge of it pulls you in and it's all you can focus on sometimes." Evan looked over at her. "But I only go now if it's necessary. It's pretty hard for me to since I'm the only law enforcement here. If the wrong people get wind of the fact that I'm going to be out of town, it would give them incentive to cause trouble," Evan said.

"I can imagine," she said.

"Speaking of which, I won't be in town tomorrow because I have some business to take care of in Dickensville. I need to send off a couple of wires and check in with the sheriff there to see if there's anything I need to be on the lookout for. If Thad's in town, I usually go once a week. He'll cover for me while I'm gone, so if you need anything, he'll be able to help you."

"All right. I'll feel safe with him around," she said and then gave Evan a sly look. "But I won't kiss him."

Evan chuckled. "You'd better not. And not even on the cheek. I know how tricky you are about that."

She laughed. "You should have seen the look on your face."

"You sure as heck surprised me. I like how fun you are," Evan said.

Josie said, "I don't think I'm all that fun."

"You're wrong."

"Evan, I'd like to talk about something that I feel needs more addressing," Josie said.

Evan said, "Ok. Shoot."

"It's about last night." Josie gathered her courage.

Stopping his horse, Evan gave her his full attention. "What about it?"

Josie pulled Captain over next to Smitty and looked up at him. "I know that it was wrong of me in a way to ask you to stay and make love before we're married, but I need you to really understand what I was thinking and feeling."

Evan said, "I've been wondering about it, but I wasn't sure if I should bring it up or not. I feel bad about us having a disagreement like that. I know we talked about it a little earlier today when you came to tell me about Earnest, but it still felt like we needed to talk about it more."

"I know. After the things you told me about Louise, I thought you might wonder if I would do the same thing to you. I wanted you to know that I could never do that and that I wanted to show you that I belong to you in all ways," Josie said.

"Josie, you didn't have to do that for me to know that about you," Evan said. "I know you're not a cheater. I don't want you to be intimate with me because you want to prove something to me."

Josie swallowed hard and said, "That's not the only reason. When you hold me and kiss me, I can't think straight and I don't want to. All I know is how good you make me feel and that I don't want to stop. And I wanted to be close to you like that because my feelings for you have been growing stronger and stronger. I've fallen in love with you, Evan, and if I didn't feel that way about you, I would've never asked you to stay with me."

Evan couldn't believe what he was hearing. He looked into her eyes and even in the dark, he could see it there. How had he missed it? "I understand now why you were so hurt. You felt like I rejected you. Honey, if I had known, I—"

"Would have done the same thing," she said with a smile.

He sighed. "Yes. You're right. As much as I want you, I won't make love to you until we're married."

Josie smiled again. "I know it's the right thing to do."

"Right," Evan said. "And yet ..."

"And yet ..." she said in agreement with his silent reply. "And yet you've been with other women."

There was no use denying it. "Yeah."

She cocked her head at him. "I think the double standard is what's aggravating me. It's all right for men to sleep with women before they're married, but not for women to sleep with men before getting married. Who are these men sleeping with? Women, right?"

"Um, yeah," Evan said, not sure how to proceed.

Looking him right in the eye, Josie said, "Why is it up to *you* to decide? Don't I get a say in the matter?"

His eyebrows rose. "So you're saying that you don't want to wait until we're married?"

"I'm saying I'd at least like to be consulted on the matter. I'd like to be consulted about everything. I don't want to be told what the best thing to do is. I'd like to be appreciated for my intelligence and for my opinion to be respected or at least recognized in the first place," Josie said.

"I *do* appreciate your intelligence and your opinion *does* matter to me," Evan said. "I didn't know that you would want to do that before marriage."

"Ask me if I do," she challenged him.

"Ok. Do you want to make love with me before we're married?" Evan asked, his confusion growing.

Josie smiled. "Thank you. The answer is yes, very much, but I won't."

Evan didn't know whether to be disappointed or relieved. Some of both, he supposed. "Me, too." He felt perturbed, but couldn't say exactly why. "And for the record, I love you, too."

Josie's mouth fell open and stayed that way for several moments before she said, "You're just saying that because I did."

"Yes, but only because I mean it. That's not something I just toss around," he said in an irritated manner.

Her own temper rose. "Well, I would hope not. It would be cruel to tell me you love me if you didn't mean it!"

"Well, I'm sayin' it because I mean it, ok? I love you!" he said loudly.

"Good, because I love you, too!" she shouted back.

They stared at each other for a minute and then started laughing. Evan moved Smitty over so that their legs touched. He leaned towards her and kissed her. It was the wrong thing to do because it created a wave of desire inside that made him feel shaky. Never had a woman made him feel the things Josie did. As he kissed her, Evan knew that he needed to get Josie to the altar very soon because he didn't know how much longer he could hold back.

It was so hard, but Josie pulled away from him. "Don't do that, Evan. I want you to kiss me, but when you do, it makes it so hard to stick to my beliefs about what we just discussed."

"I know. Me, too. Sorry. You need to get home or we're going to be in trouble," Evan said.

Josie nodded and tapped Captain with her heels. As they got underway again, Evan began laughing at their predicament and Josie joined in. Josie held out her hand to her sheriff and he took it. Hand in hand they rode to the Hanovers', rejoicing in their newfound love.

Chapter Fifteen

When Evan arrived home from Dickensville the next night, he was tired, but relieved that there were no major criminal issues reported to him. He was pleased that things were quiet around Echo. He'd sent out a couple of wires about some law enforcement business and he'd also done some shopping.

Riding up to his house, he saw that it was dark. It was late and he knew that Edna would have gone to bed by that time. As he was putting Smitty in his stall, he heard someone come in the barn. Turning, he saw Billy striding towards him.

"Hey, Sheriff," Billy said. "How'd you make out today?"

"Fine. Nothing exciting to report, which doesn't bother me a bit," he said.

"Gives you more time to romance your lady," Billy said, smiling.

After giving Smitty a nice supper and a couple of goodnight pats, Evan said, "You're right. And I intend to do just that."

"Good. She's quite a woman."

"I know," Evan said. Being sensitive to the fact that Billy might still be smarting over Shelby, he changed the subject. "How're the new sheep?"

Billy walked with Evan to his house. "Great. They're settling in and the new dog Lucky bought is a good one, too. With the left over money from the sheep, we're gonna build Win a nice cabin. I can't believe our luck that we have a veterinarian watching our sheep."

Evan let out a laugh. "Lucky will say that it's because of him."

"No. He actually credits God with everything, which annoys the heck out of Win," Billy said.

"I can imagine," Evan said. "Win doesn't believe in anything he can't see, smell, feel, hear, or taste."

"Why is that?" Billy asked as they sat down on the back porch.

Evan sighed, as he took off his hat and sat it to the side. "I'd rather Win tell you himself. He tends not to like it when people talk about him. I *will* tell you that he's had a very hard life and that he lost faith long ago that any sort of god was watching out for him—or anyone else, for that matter."

"I can understand that," Billy said. "I sometimes feel that way."

Evan said, "Me, too, every so often."

"I don't know how Lucky can believe the way he does after everything he's been through," Billy said. "He lost his brother, his wife, and his baby. Did you know that?"

"Lucky had a wife and child? No, I didn't," Evan said.

"Crap. I shouldn't have said anything," Billy said. "Long story short, he was married to a Cheyenne woman and she was a few months along when they were forced onto a reservation. They wouldn't let Lucky go with them. Right before the military dragged him away, she divorced him and told him to go live his life. He doesn't even know if the baby was a boy or a girl."

Evan's jaw flexed as he fought strong emotion. "Damn. You're right. That's a hard row to hoe, all right."

"It makes what I'm going through look like a cakewalk," Billy said.

"I haven't brought it up to you in a while because I didn't want to make you feel bad or anything."

"I'm fine, I guess. I think it would be easier if I didn't know that the things she said that day were lies. They were rotten, but I know that's not how she really felt," Billy said. "But I can see where she's coming from. I mean, we've got Amy and Jimmy to take care of now, and even with both of my folks working, it's tough. She's a single woman with two kids. I can't offer her any sort of security."

"I know this might not help a whole lot, but that's a very mature way of looking at it," Evan said.

"Thanks. So, I'm gonna work hard at this sheep business and start selling more of my art. Lucky said I should do portraits for people. I think I'll try it and see how it goes. There's not much I can do with the sheep right now, so I guess I'll go back to painting. One way or another, I'm gonna make people see that I'm not just some dumb Indian kid," Billy said.

"And would one of those people be Shelby?" Evan asked.

Billy shook his head. "No. That's over. There's no sense hoping for anything to work out there since who knows how long it's gonna take to make all of this successful. No, it's better if she finds someone else who can take care of them. That sure isn't me. I want it to be, but it's not, so it's best to let it go."

"Again, that's a good way to look at it. Sometimes the thing we think we want the most isn't the thing we actually need," Evan said.

"I guess so," Billy said in the tone of voice that always told Evan he was done with a subject.

"Well, I'm heading to bed," he said. "Don't be up too late."

Billy said, "I will be. I have work to do. Goodnight, Sheriff."

"Goodnight, Billy."

A floorboard creaked, alerting him that someone was in his bedroom. He heard the rustling of clothing and rolled over onto his back. As the woman disrobed, he watched her with hunger. Slowly she walked over to the bed, moving seductively, the moonlight catching the contours of her body.

Smiling, he said, "It's about time you came to see me."

"It's not always the right time," Phoebe said, sitting down on the bed.

She ran a hand over Marvin's strong shoulder and down his arm. A startled cry escaped her when he yanked her against him.

"That's better," Marvin said. "How's your old man?"

Phoebe said, "Who?"

He grabbed her neck and squeezed slightly. "McIntyre. Don't play dumb, Phoebe. I know that you're involved with him."

She knew better than to deny it. She should have known that Marvin would find out. He always did, but she didn't know how. It was one of the things she liked about Marvin—his power. It excited her and she craved it, yearned for his sadistic traits and actions as much as she did Thad's goodness and fun personality.

Phoebe didn't understand how it was that she could love two men who were so different, but she did. As Marvin stared into her eyes, she smiled slightly. "Jealous?"

He shook her a little. "Yes and you knew I would be. Whore!"

Phoebe laughed at his insult because she could hear the love and amusement underneath it. "You're one to talk. Don't think I don't know that you have a couple of women who take care of you."

"That's only because you make me wait so long," he said, turning gentle. Running a hand over her golden brown hair, he asked, "Why do you torment me so when I love you so much?"

She took his hand and kissed his palm. "Because you like it so much."

"Do you love me?" Marvin asked and it was almost a plea for reassurance.

Phoebe nodded. "You know I do."

"Then why won't you be mine alone?" Marvin asked, his eyes traveling over her.

"Because you're the dark and he's the light and I need both," Phoebe said. "I know you don't understand. How can you when I don't understand it myself?"

Marvin smiled. "So you want me to be good?"

With a laugh, she pushed him over. "You wouldn't even know where to start in order to be good. It's not in you, but I wouldn't have you any other way."

Pulling her on top of him, he kissed her hard and then set her away from him a little. "Are you sure about that?"

Phoebe became mesmerized by the dark look that overtook his beautiful features. The sheer evil in his eyes held her spellbound. It was exactly what she needed. "Yes. I'm sure."

With a malevolent smile, Marvin set about showing her just how bad he could be.

A week later, Evan surprised Josie by showing up at the Hanovers' early in the morning. She'd just been heading down to breakfast when there was a knock at her door. Pulling it open, she was greeted by that devastating smile of his that never failed to make her heart thump against her ribs.

"Good morning, sweetness," he said.

Her brows rose. "Sweetness?"

He nodded and gave her a lingering kiss hello. "Because that's how you taste."

A loud, surprised laugh escaped her. She knew she was blushing, but couldn't help it. "Shh. You shouldn't say things like that."

He leaned in closer to her. "Don't pretend you don't like it when I do."

"I didn't say I didn't," Josie said. "I just don't want anyone to hear."

"Don't worry. They won't. Lucky is already over at the Deckers' house and Thad is at the office. He's filling in for me today," Evan said.

"Oh. Are you going out of town again?" she asked, disappointed at the thought.

"Yep. With you. I'm here to steal you away for the day," he said, his green eyes glinting with good humor.

A pleased smile spread over her face. "You are? Where are we going?"

"Dickensville. I thought it was high time that I showed you around there properly. I'm sure you'd like to get out of Echo and see something different," Evan said.

Excitement gripped Josie. "What should I wear? Do I need to change? Are we coming back tonight or do I need to pack a bag?"

"We'll be back tonight. I don't want to take advantage of Thad on such short notice," he said. "And you look perfect, just like always."

She giggled. "I think you've been around Lucky too much. You've picked up kissing the Blarney stone."

"Nope. Just tellin' the truth," Evan said, loving the happy look on her face.

"Sure," Josie said. "Are we taking the wagon or buggy?"

Evan said, "Neither. We'll make faster time on horseback. That way we'll have more time to spend there. So shake a leg, woman."

"Humph. We go from compliments to bossing me around," Josie said, collecting her reticule.

She couldn't resist stopping in front of the mirror. She was glad that she was wearing one of her better dresses. If she had been going to clean for someone that day, she would have worn the dress she reserved for that, but since she'd only been going to sew, she'd dressed up a little more.

"You look beautiful, sweetness. Let's go," Evan said.

As she turned to him, Josie was so excited that she felt like skipping. She didn't, of course. After locking her door, she grabbed his arm, shook it a little, and laughed.

"We're going to have so much fun," she said.

He grinned and said, "That's the plan."

Unable to contain her enthusiasm any longer, she trotted down the hall away from him. "What are you still standing there for?" she teased. "Hurry up!"

Shaking his head a little, Evan followed her down the staircase and into the kitchen. Phoebe was just putting some sausage into a frying pan.

"Hi, Phoebe," Evan greeted her. "How are you?"

She gave him a small smile. "Fine, and you, Sheriff?"

"Good, thanks," he said. "Josie and I are going to be out of town today, but Thad is on duty for me in case anyone needs anything. Will you let Gwen and Arthur know?"

"Sure thing," Phoebe said and turned back to the stove.

Evan smiled. "I'm sure he'll be along for lunch. I know how much he likes your cooking."

That isn't all he likes, a naughty little voice inside her head said. "I wouldn't doubt it."

"All right, well, we'll see you," Evan said.

Josie had already gone outside to the stable. Evan caught up with her and said, "Here, I'll saddle Captain for you."

She smiled at his gentlemanly behavior and stood aside. She was perfectly capable of doing it, but she knew that Evan like doing things like that for her. Watching him, she liked the way he made everything look so effortless. His powerful arms lifted the saddle over Captain's back with ease and she couldn't help thinking about how it felt to be held in them. Everything about the man attracted her and Josie had a hard time not watching him.

To distract herself, she said, "Phoebe is an unusual person."

"How do you mean?" Evan asked as he pulled the girth tight and buckled it in place.

"I've been here for almost two months and I still don't really know anything about her other than she cooks and cleans very well. She's very standoffish."

"Yeah, she can be, but she's got her reasons," Evan said, thoughts of Earnest seeping into his mind.

As though reading his thoughts, Josie asked, "It has something to do with Earnest, doesn't it?"

The look of loathing on Evan's face when he turned around made Josie wish she could take back her question. She could have kicked herself.

"Yeah, it does," he said.

Josie held up a hand. "That's all I need to know. I don't want to hear any more. I just want to get going and enjoy the day with you. That's all I care about."

Evan smiled at her excited tone. "Good. Mount up, cowgirl."

"Yes, sir!" Josie said and did as she'd been ordered.

As they got close to Dickensville, the road traffic increased and Evan took Josie onto a smaller side road to have more private time with her. It wasn't much of a detour and it was worth it the little bit of extra time it took to get to their destination to have her to himself a little longer.

Her smile always captivated him and he kept making her laugh just so he could see it. It gave him such pleasure to see her carefree, playful side and to be able to indulge in some silly behavior himself for a change. After a particularly smart remark from her, Evan chased after her, both of them laughing as their horses ran along.

When they slowed their mounts, Evan caught Captain's reins and dismounted from Smitty's back. A love greater than he'd ever known filled his heart and he needed to hold her, to feel her in his arms. He led the horses off the road into a copse of trees there.

She looked at him curiously when he held his arms out to her. "What's going on?"

"Just come here," he said, motioning her closer with his hands.

Wondering what game he was up to, she let him lift her from her horse. "What's wrong?"

"Nothing," Evan said, taking her face in his hands after helping her down. "I love you so much, Josie. I can't believe my luck that you answered Aunt Edna's ad. You're feisty, sweet, smart, and beautiful all rolled into one woman and I'm not going to let you get away. Will you make me even happier than you already do by becoming my wife?"

Josie's breath left her on a surprised sigh and her eyes grew larger as she looked at him. His expression was one of utter seriousness and his green eyes held an intense light along with a little anxiety. She'd been hoping that he would ask her someday soon, but he'd completely caught her off guard and she couldn't speak for a few moments.

Then she raised her hand to his handsome face and said, "Evan, I love you, too, and I would be very proud to be your wife. Yes, I'll marry you."

Evan laughed with relief and joy and then remembered that the ring he'd bought was in his saddle bag. He held up an index finger and hurried around the other side of Smitty while Josie laughed at him. Running back to her, he opened the ring box and plucked the ring from it. Taking Josie's left hand, Evan first kissed the back of it and then put the ring on her finger.

Gazing at the beautiful ring, Josie couldn't believe that the day had finally come for her to be proposed to instead of another one of her friends. She also couldn't believe that she'd found such an amazing man. When she raised her eyes to Evan's again, they were brimming with happy tears. "It's gorgeous, Evan. Thank you."

Slipping his arms around her waist again, he asked, "So you like it?"

"I love it, but not as much as I love you," she said.

Evan claimed her lips in a kiss that was sweet and sensual at the same time. Josie felt a heat begin inside her that wasn't caused by the sun. It happened every time Evan kissed her and this time was no different. Just as on the night they'd declared their love for one another, there was a new feel to his kiss. Josie understood that he was staking his claim on her and it was a thrilling experience.

Josie's hands slid across his chest and up over his shoulders. Everything about him was strong, masculine, and arousing. What woman wouldn't become passionate in Evan's arms? His hair was soft against her fingers when she ran them through the black strands that curled down over the collar of his shirt.

As his hands roamed over her back, Josie moaned and gripped him tighter, needing to be closer to him. His corresponding growl heightened her excitement even further. Quickly, she began undoing the buttons of his shirt until it was halfway undone. She moved her fingers over his hot, bare skin. She had only seen Evan without a shirt just once, but the image had been burned into her mind. But touching him was a heady experience and she felt slightly dizzy as she did so.

Then, realizing what she'd done, she felt suddenly shy about her brazen behavior. With incredible difficulty, she forced herself away from Evan. "I'm sorry," she said in a shaky voice. "I shouldn't have done that."

Evan was off-kilter from her sudden abandonment and a confused frown settled onto his handsome features. "Huh? Sorry? About what?"

Josie motioned towards his undone shirt. "That."

Looking down, Evan saw his partly exposed chest. His mind fogged with passion, he asked, "Why is you sorry? Is there something wrong with me?"

Now she was confused. "What? No. There's nothing wrong with you. That's the problem. You're so virile and handsome that I can't keep my hands off you. I shouldn't have unbuttoned your shirt like that."

"Oh, is that all?" he asked, still befuddled.

His remark struck her as very funny and she began laughing. He caught on and let out a laugh of his own. "Shut up, Josie. I can't think at the moment."

"I can tell," she said.

"It's not funny," Evan said, even though he grinned. "You shoulda finished the job. I mean it's almost undone anyhow."

"No, no," she protested. "I did quite enough. Button it back up and then we should get going. I don't trust myself."

Frustrated more than he'd ever been in his life, Evan blew out a breath and began doing just that. "Me, neither," he said, shooting her a smile. "But I'm not sorry."

"Me, neither," she said, coming closer to him again.

He grabbed her, gave her a sound kiss, and then said, "Good. Get on your horse."

"Yes, Sheriff Taft," she said.

Once they were both mounted, Evan said, "Let's go have some fun, my bride-to-be."

Chapter Sixteen

Billy retched as the metallic smell of blood hit his nostrils. "Oh, Lord," he said and backed up from the sheep that Win had just killed.

The Chinese man laughed. "Boy, you really can tell that you're not a real Indian. Other than your looks and the way you can walk silently when you want to, you have no other Indian traits."

"Of course I don't. I've never even met another Indian, so how am I supposed to act like one?" Billy asked.

Lucky said, "You have to get used to this, Billy. It's all part of the business."

"Ross isn't killing them," Billy said.

"No, he's choppin' 'em up," Lucky replied and calmly slit the throat of the sheep he easily held in his powerful grip.

Billy doubled over and lost his lunch. When his sickness subsided, he walked down to the stream. Lying on his stomach, he stuck his head completely under the water to cool off. Raising his head again, he rinsed out his mouth and just laid there as water dripped from his long hair back into the stream.

Staring down into the water, he wondered what on Earth he was going to be able to do in order to help with the sheep farm. He couldn't kill them because he couldn't stomach the blood. Lucky was going to teach him how to shear the sheep, but that was only done once a year or so. Win was there for the everyday care of the livestock. He would help out at lambing time, but again that wasn't an all-the-time thing.

As the water flowed by him, Billy saw something glitter on the bottom of the streambed. Thinking it was a quartz stone he could add to his collection, Billy reached his hand down to the object and retrieved it. He sat up to inspect it. Soon, he concluded that it wasn't quartz, and he knew exactly what it was. Getting up, he went back to his friends.

"Hey, guys, can you come here?" he asked, stopping a safe distance from the sheep carcasses.

"We're in the middle of something here," Win said.

"I think you're gonna want to see this," Billy said.

"Why's that?" Lucky asked.

"I think I just found a piece of gold."

Lucky and Win stopped skinning the sheep and looked at each other. As if by design, they dropped what they were doing at the exact same second and hurried over to Billy.

Win held out his hand and Lucky didn't object. He'd seen gold before, but he felt that Win was better qualified to verify if it was the real thing or not since he'd done some mining with his father when he was younger. Billy dropped it into Win's palm and backed off again since both of the other men's hands and arms were covered in sheep's blood.

"Billy, do you have a penny?" Win asked.

"Uh, yeah." Billy fished one out of the pocket of his pants and hastily gave it to Win while Lucky smiled at him. "Shut up, Lucky."

Win chuckled and rubbed the penny with the nugget. He grinned when it left behind a dull yellow streak on the penny. The nugget was worn and rounded and when he pushed his thumbnail into it hard, it left behind a faint dent. "Stay where you are, Lucky." He walked over very close to the Irishman, using his shadow to block the sun. Even in the shade, the nugget shone. "Billy, you certainly did find gold."

Billy and Lucky both let out yells.

"I thought this was a silver mine," Lucky said.

"Sometimes both metals are found in the same area," Win said. "Now don't go getting all excited, fellas. There may not be much here. I don't want you to get your hopes up."

"Ok," Billy said. "I'll go back and look for more."

Win nodded. "That's fine, but try not to disturb things too much until I can go back to the Devil's Knot. I have a few mining things there that we can use."

Billy smiled. "I may not be able to kill sheep, but I can find gold. I'd say that's a big help to us."

"I'd say you're right," Lucky said. "Even if we don't find a big vein or anything, if we find a steady supply of it, we can use it to invest in more sheep and such. Besides, if it gets out that we found gold, we're gonna be fightin' off a slew of people trying to mine it."

"Yeah. I've seen it too many times," Win said. "I think that's a smart way to look at it."

Billy agreed. "I don't want anyone coming in here after it, either. Ok, I'll let you get back to your sheep killing and I'll go make us rich."

Lucky chuckled as he walked away and Win joined him.

The newly engaged couple had a fantastic day together, doing anything and everything that came to mind. Evan had taken her to meet Sheriff Stratton, who had teased Josie about getting mixed up with a man like Evan. They'd had a nice little visit and then Evan had taken Josie to the main street of Dickensville, which was lined with all kinds of shops.

They'd spent time in many of them and Evan bought Josie a few things despite her protests. They also snuck in kisses every chance they got, which added to their fun. Josie bought Evan a whimsical set of cufflinks in the shape of a sheriff's badge. They had lunch in place that served fancy French food and amused each other by trying to pronounce the dishes on the menu.

As the sun began dropping lower in the sky, they started for home and arrived a little after dark. They were tired but happy as they rode up to Evan's house. Leaving the horses tied to the hitching post, the hurried inside to give Edna the good news.

She was reading a book when they entered the parlor. Looking up at them, she saw them beaming. "Well, hello, you two. Did you have a good time?"

Josie said, "We did! It was an amazing day."

"It sure was," Evan said. "We have some good news."

Edna's eyes brightened with anticipation. "Oh? What is it?"

"Josie and I are engaged," Evan said, the expression on his face the happiest that Edna had ever seen.

She let out a cry of joy and began rising from her chair. She held out her arms to Josie, who stepped into them readily.

"Oh, you sweet girl! I'm so happy that you're becoming a part of our family," Edna said, hugging her tightly. "I knew the moment I met you that you were perfect for Evan."

Josie couldn't contain the tears of happiness as they welled up in her eyes. "Thank you so much. I promise to be a good wife to him."

"I know you will, honey. You're a wonderful woman and he's lucky to have you," Edna said. She kissed Josie's cheek and released her. Turning to Evan, she said, "Asking Josie to marry you is the smartest thing you've ever done."

Evan embraced her, chuckling. "I think so, too."

She held him close and began quietly crying. "I'm so happy for you, Evan. You don't know how much I've prayed for you to find someone special and settle down. All I've ever wanted for you was to be happy."

"I am. Thank you for everything you've done for me and all the love you've shown me all these years," Evan said. "I don't know what I would have done without you and Uncle Reb."

After kissing him, Edna pulled back from him and said, "You've been the biggest joy in our life. I only wish ..."

Evan nodded. "Me, too."

Edna said, "Well, we need to have a toast. Get out the good stuff, Evan."

He smiled and went out to the kitchen. Retrieving three glasses and the bottle of good scotch they kept on hand, Evan brought them into the living room. He poured each of them a little and handed the ladies their drink.

Edna held up hers and said, "May you have all the joy and love that Reb and I had for so many years and may it grow stronger with each passing day."

"I'll drink to that," Evan said.

"Me, too," Josie said.

They clinked their glasses together and drank down the scotch. Josie coughed a little and Evan patted her back as he and Edna laughed. Shortly afterwards, Evan rode home with Josie. Their goodnight kiss was lingering and they parted reluctantly.

Lucky sank down into the tub in the bath house with a sigh of contentment as the warm water rose around him. Although it was yet another warm night, the bath felt good to him. Not only had they sheared and butchered a few sheep that day, they'd trekked to the Devil's Knot and brought back Win's mining equipment and spent quite a bit of time panning. Their yield had been small, but encouraging, and all three men were happy with it.

Although he'd bathed well in the stream, the warmer water would help soothe his sore muscles. A massage would have been wonderful, but there was no one around to do that for him. His wife, *Avasa*, whose name meant "home," had done such things for him. Not a day went by that he didn't see her beautiful face or hear her sweet voice in his mind.

From the very first moment he'd caught a glimpse of her, he'd been smitten with her. The war party that had saved him from the Pawnees had extended him their protection and friendship immediately, although Lucky couldn't fathom why that should be. All he had known was that he was alive and that the men around him were friendly.

A few of them spoke English and he was able to tell them that he was traveling around looking for work.

One of them, *Minninnewah*, Wild Wind in English, said to him, "We have work for you. It will be hard, but rewarding."

"What kind of work would ye have for me to do?" he asked. He'd never heard of Indians needing a white man to do work for them before.

Wild Wind had said, "You will see."

The braves' dark eyes had held no maliciousness, only laughter, and Lucky had understood that he was being teased in some manner.

As they'd reached the Cheyenne camp, it wasn't long until Lucky had glimpsed Avasa for the first time.

"Dear God, who is that beautiful creature?" he'd asked to himself.

Wild Wind's keen ears had heard him. "That is Avasa. She is very pretty, yes?"

"As an angel," Lucky had responded, turning in his saddle to look at the maiden.

"Her husband thinks so, too," Wild Wind said.

Immediately, Lucky had turned back around, embarrassed to have been gawking at a married woman like that. "He's a lucky man."

Wild Wind had laughed. "I am teasing. She is not married."

Without thinking, Lucky struck out, his fist connecting with Wild Wind's upper arm. The other men with them laughed at Wild Wind's shocked expression.

"What's the matter with ya?" Lucky had yelled, drawing the attention of many people. "Ya don't tell a man that about a woman if she really isn't."

Wild Wind had laughed and said, "You are very loud and you look like an angry bear. Your Cheyenne name will be *Pe'pe'éstá Náhkôhehóváhne*—Yelling Bear."

"Now, wait a minute. I don't want another name. Lucky is just fine for me."

"We will see how lucky you are at your work," Wild Wind had told him.

The two men had already begun to form a bond that would never be broken.

Loud knocking on the bath house door made Lucky jerk upright in the tub. He'd been so lost in his memories that the sound scared him more than it might have at another time.

It made his tone of voice sharp as he shouted, "Who the hell is it?"

"It's me, Lucky," he heard Josie say. "Can I come in?"

"No! I'm naked for cryin' out loud! What's wrong?" he asked.

"Nothing! Come to my room when you're done. I have something to tell you," she said.

Lucky thought she sounded happy. "All right. I won't be long," he said, relaxing back in the tub as his heart began settling down again. As his thoughts began returning to their previous course, he cut them off, not wanting to go back there again.

Quickly he rose from the tub, dried off, and dressed. He got rid of the dirty bath water and made sure the tub was clean for whomever would use it next. This was something that Arthur demanded from his tenants and Lucky was happy to comply if it meant he got to use the luxury. Once everything was shipshape, he took the lantern he'd brought with him and headed up to the house.

He was quiet as he moved through it, jogging lightly up the stairs, and rounding the corner into the long corridor. He saw that Josie's door was open and that light poured through the doorway out into the hallway. Stopping at the doorway, he rapped lightly on the doorjamb.

Josie motioned him inside and he shut the door. He barely had time to put down his lantern until she was hugging him, jumping up and down a little.

He laughed. "What's all this, then?"

She backed away and held up her left hand as an answer.

Lucky saw the engagement ring and grinned at her. "So he stole ya away from me, did he?"

"Yes! He asked me today on the way over to Dickensville! Isn't it beautiful?" she asked as she bobbed up and down again.

Lucky took her by the shoulders and pulled her over closer to the lamp that was lit on her bureau. "Let me look at it properly." He turned it this way and that and then said, "It'll do."

Josie became offended and pulled her hand from his. "It'll do? I should say it will. It's a beautiful ring! It must have cost him quite a bit, too. So he wasn't cheap about it." Catching the amused gleam in Lucky's eyes, she swatted him. "Shame on you!"

He laughed. "Sorry. Couldn't help myself. You're right. It's a beautiful ring, lass, and I couldn't be happier for ye both," he said, giving her a proper hug.

"I have a favor to ask you," she said upon stepping back from him.

"Anything," Lucky said. "Name it."

Josie smiled as she asked, "Will you give me away? Outside of my friend Opal, who's back in Pullman, you're my best friend, sort of like a brother, and I would really love for you to walk me down the aisle."

Deeply touched, Lucky got a little teary-eyed as he said, "I would be honored to give ya away and I'm grateful for ya askin'."

Josie hugged him again. "Thank you."

Lucky laughed again as she shook him a little and let out a small squeal. "It does me good to see you so happy. Evan's a smart man for askin' ya. I know you'll be very happy together."

"Yes, we will. We're going to the church tomorrow to talk to the minister," she said. "We're not waiting long."

Lucky said, "And I wonder why that would be," with a wink.

Blushing deeply, Josie laughed and said, "Ok. Go to bed, Lucky."

Chuckling, he picked up his lantern. "I don't know why you're so shy about it."

She pointed at the door, but there was a big smile on her face as he left her room.

Chapter Seventeen

"If anything happens to her—"

Travis said, "Nothing's going to happen to her, Jenny. I promise you. I'd never let anything happen to her and you know it."

Jenny put a hand to her forehead and said, "I just don't understand what he wants with her."

The day beforehand, Marvin had made an odd request to have Pauline come for lunch. Travis knew that it had really been an order, however.

"He's just going to have lunch with her and I'll be right there the whole time. She's going to be with me all morning. I won't let her out of my sight," Travis said, putting his arms around his wife.

"Promise me that you won't lose sight of her," Jenny said.

Tipping her head up so he could look in her eyes, Travis said, "I promise." He kissed her and let her go.

Pauline came running down the stairs of their two bedroom house and said, "I'm ready, Pa."

Jenny gathered their little girl to her and said, "Now, you stay right with your pa and don't be bothering Mr. Earnest, ok?"

"All right, Ma. I'll be good," Pauline said.

Jenny kissed Pauline and forced herself to loosen her arms from around her daughter. "Have fun."

Travis gave her a last reassuring smile and held out his hand to Pauline. "C'mon, honey. I don't wanna be late."

"Ok. 'Bye, Ma," Pauline said, following her father.

Travis grinned as Pauline sang and chattered the whole way to the Earnest ranch. She'd never be a great singer, but her voice was sweet and her witty comments about people around town made him laugh.

"I decided I like boys now," she told him.

"You did, huh? Do I need to be worried about you gettin' married soon?" he asked.

"No, but I know who I'm gonna marry," Pauline said.

"Who's that?" Travis asked, going over the possibilities of potential suitors down the line-provided Echo still existed by the time Pauline would be old enough to marry.

"Billy."

"Billy who?" Travis asked, since there were at least two boys with that name in her age group.

"Billy Two Moons, Pa. He's a handsome boy."

Travis' amusement increased. "Oh, so you like him?"

"Yeah. He has long hair and I like it. It's pretty," Pauline said.

"So it's important to you that your husband has pretty hair?"

"Sure. I don't want his hair to be ugly and Billy's isn't ugly. Don't you think Billy has pretty hair?" Pauline asked.

Travis supposed she was right. Billy's hair color was not the typical coloring for someone of his heritage. It must come from whatever white blood he had, Travis reasoned. "Sure, it's pretty, I guess. But men don't really notice that kind of thing about other men, honey."

"Oh. That's a shame. I notice if a girl's hair is pretty or not. Why don't men do that?" Pauline wanted to know.

"I don't know. We just don't," Travis said, carefully avoiding that subject.

"I can't wait to see Barkley. Is he still fat?" Pauline asked.

Their conversation ran in much the same vein until they got to the ranch. Travis was dismayed to see Marvin sitting in a rocking chair on the front porch. In his gentleman's clothing, Marvin was a striking figure with his golden blond hair and fine features. Travis pulled his horse to a stop and swung out of the saddle.

Pauline waved at Marvin. "Hi, Mr. Earnest!"

Travis lifted her from the horse and sat her down. "You can say a quick hello, but then I gotta get to work."

"Ok," Pauline said and took off running toward the house.

Travis followed at a more sedate pace, wanting to appear nonchalant to Marvin.

Marvin watched the little girl hurry towards him, her black hair flying behind her. Sheer joy filled him at the beautiful sight she made.

"Well, Miss Pauline," he said as she gained the porch. "Look how much you've grown since I've seen you last."

Pauline had always like Marvin and she ran over and hugged him around the neck. "I have. Half an inch, Ma says. You look handsome."

"Thank you and you're more beautiful than I remember. Your pa tells me that you're quite a busy little woman," Marvin said as he picked her up and sat her on his knee.

"Mmm hmm," Pauline said. "I help Ma and I play with my friends."

Travis came up on the porch and smiled at Marvin even though he was on the alert for one wrong move from his employer.

"I'm not surprised that such a pretty girl is popular," Marvin said.

She beamed at him. "Are you flirtin' with me?"

"And just what do you know about flirting?" Marvin teased her, enjoying her laugh of response.

Hearing a dog bark, Pauline turned around to see Barkley over by the barn. "I have to go," she announced as she slid off Marvin's lap.

Marvin laughed as he watched her descend the steps and take off to go see her canine pal. "Travis, you're a lucky man. She's a delight. Thank you for bringing her to see me."

"Sure. Well, I'm gonna get started," Travis said.

"There's no hurry, Travis," Marvin said.

"Well, actually—"

Marvin cocked his head a little at Travis as he interrupted his foreman. "I said, there's no hurry. Sit down."

Travis' apprehension grew as he sat in the rocking closest to Marvin. "What do you want?"

Marvin eyed his foreman, assessing his mood. Although Travis was fairly good at hiding his thoughts, Marvin was adept at reading the nuances in expressions and body posture and he could tell that Travis was on edge.

"I've been thinking," he said.

Travis became even more alert. "What about?"

"I've decided to increase your pay by five dollars a week."

"Why?" Travis asked immediately.

Marvin couldn't say he blamed Travis for being suspicious. There were certain things that he accepted about himself, one being that he rarely did anything out of altruistic motives.

"Because even though you hate me, you've done something that brings me much pleasure."

"You're talking about Pauline." It wasn't a question.

"Yes. She's a delight and I'd like to see her more often."

Travis had had enough. "Look, you can torment me, insult me, and treat me like crap all you want, but I'm not going to have you do anything to my daughter. I'm not using her as a bargaining chip."

Marvin admired Travis' candor and his protectiveness of Pauline. That was as it should be. "I'm glad to see that you have the stones to stand up to me in order to ensure your daughter's safety. However, your fear is unwarranted. I am many things, Travis, but I would never harm a child. I adore them."

"You adore them? You're a bald-faced liar," Travis said. He was no longer mincing words. "Do I gotta remind you about Louise?"

Travis watched the pleasant mask on Marvin's face slip away to be replaced by an expression of such fury that it made the hair stand up on his arms.

"Do not speak of Louise. I am well aware of what everyone thinks about that situation, but no one knows the truth except me and one other person," Marvin said, his blue eyes blazing.

Travis pushed through his fear and said, "And just what is the truth?"

In a blindingly fast movement, Marvin slammed his hand down on the arm of his chair, making Travis jump. "Do you *really* want to know the truth? Because I don't think you'll like it very much, Travis."

Travis forehead wrinkle in confusion. "What are you talking about?"

"Ask your wife about what really happened with Louise." Marvin's face began returning to its former serene countenance.

Through gritted teeth, Travis asked, "What's Jenny got to do with this? You leave her out of all this."

Marvin regarded him calmly. "That's all I'll say about it. Now, back to our agreement. I will increase your pay five dollars a week provided you bring Pauline to see me once a week. You have until tomorrow to give me an answer. Talk it over with Jenny tonight and tell her to remember a conversation we had a long time ago. She'll know what that means and that it's perfectly safe to bring Pauline to visit."

"You're insane if you think I'm going to subject Pauline to your craziness," Travis said.

Marvin laughed and the sound chilled Travis' blood. "That's your decision to make. I'm offering you an opportunity to make enough money to have another baby."

"What the hell do you care if we have another baby?" Travis' mind spun in confusion.

"You will. I care about Pauline and I want her to have a sibling. I know what it's like to be an only child and it's a lonely existence. I don't want that for her," Marvin said.

Travis shook his head as if trying to clear his mind. "So you're paying me to have a kid?"

Marvin's face took on a look of distaste. "I would prefer to say that I'm encouraging you. Paying you sounds so tawdry, don't you think?"

"Why do you care about Pauline so much? And what's all this about Jenny?"

"Pauline is a very sweet child and being around her makes me happy. I want her to be happy, too. I think a brother or sister would make her happy and if I have to pay you more to make that happen, then so be it," Marvin said. "It's that simple."

Travis held Marvin's gaze. "Nothing with you is ever simple. You said your accountant told you to cut back. Was that all just a bunch of crap?"

With a smile, Marvin said, "That's true, I'm afraid. I'll admit that I am a complicated man. As for finances, let's just say that I'm in the process of freeing up some equity that I hadn't planned on using until now. That's enough chitchat for now. I think you mentioned having some work to do?"

It took supreme effort for Travis to squelch his anger over Marvin's abrupt dismissal. He wanted to punch the man in the head and choke him to death. Knowing he was hanging onto his composure by a gossamer thread, Travis had to get away from his employer before he did just that. He made no response to Marvin as he got up and left the porch. He called to Pauline, who was playing on the lawn and took her with him to the barn.

As he sat rocking in his chair on the porch, Marvin grinned as he thought about the events he was setting in motion. It was going to be very entertaining watching it all unfold. Yes, very entertaining indeed.

Dr. Sean Everett was startled when his wife ran into his study loudly calling his name.

"Sean! We're going to Montana!" she said, running over to throw her arms around his neck.

He laughed and embraced her, pulling her onto his lap. "Montana? Why are we going there?" he asked as he looked into her pretty brown eyes.

She kissed him and said, "Because Evan proposed to Josie! They're getting married, Sean! Isn't that wonderful?"

Grinning, Sean said, "It sure is! I'm really happy for her. When's the wedding?"

"The first Saturday in September," Opal said and bit her lip. "Please find a way to cover things so we can go. I don't want to go alone, but I will if I have to. I'm not missing her wedding, so one way or another, I'm going."

Sean knew how stubborn Opal could be about things like this and he had no doubt that she meant what she said. It was a little over a month away, so he supposed that would be enough time to get things squared away at the practice so that his patients were taken care of in his absence. Besides, he'd missed Josie, too, and he'd love to be there when she got married.

"I'll get things shifted around so we can go. I know how much this means to you and I want to go, too," Sean said. "Check the train schedule and see when we would need to leave so I can start getting things set up, ok?"

Opal hugged her husband and pressed an enthusiastic kiss to his lips. "Thank you. I'm going to go write Josie back so she knows that we're coming." She slid off his lap and said, "Don't be long coming to bed."

He laughed at her saucy wink and watched her practically skip from the room. With a sigh, Sean then turned back to his work, intent on finishing as quickly as possible.

⌒‿⌒

"Hello, Shadow," Marvin said. He sat out on the porch as lightning streaked across the sky and thunder growled in the distance.

"Marvin," his visitor said. "How are you?"

"I'm fine. What news do you have to tell me?" Marvin asked.

"Nothing of interest to you," Shadow said. "Petty things that aren't anything you could ever use."

"Has he talked to her?" Marvin asked.

"No. I listened the past several days like you wanted me to, but he hasn't. Why don't you just tell him yourself?" Shadow asked.

Marvin looked over at Shadow. "I've told you that it's more fun this way."

Shadow smiled. "I guess it is."

Lightning turned night into day, illuminating Shadow's features, his face a mirror image of Marvin's. The only two differences between the two men was that Shadow's hair was dark brown and he wore it long. If not for that fact, it would been almost impossible for anyone to tell them apart. This was only one reason Marvin's twin was called Shadow. The others were due to his preference to only be out and about at night and his ability to sneak around and remain hidden.

"Do you think it's actually going to rain?" Marvin asked.

"So now we're discussing weather?" Shadow replied.

"I suppose so since you don't have anything exciting to impart."

"No Phoebe tonight?"

"No, damn it."

"I don't understand why you love her," Shadow said. "She's sleeping with Thad, too. You should find someone of your own."

"I love her because she loves me unconditionally. She doesn't want to change me. She appreciates me for my quirks," Marvin said.

Shadow laughed. "You mean your insanity?"

"Yes," Marvin agreed and they laughed together. "Why don't *you* find someone?"

"Well, I would, but unless she's a vampire, I don't think it'll work out. I'm content as I am," Shadow said. "Did you hear the good sheriff is getting married?"

"Oh, yes, it's all over town. It's nauseating how happy about it everyone is," Marvin said.

"You're just jealous. You've always wanted to get married and have children," Shadow said.

"Yes, but, again, there are reasons why I can't. Besides, I won't ever find anyone like Phoebe," Marvin lamented.

"You could pay someone to be like her," Shadow said.

"No! It has to be real. Besides, any other woman would run the first time they got a glimpse of the real me. No, Phoebe is my true love."

"So you're willing to share her with McIntyre?"

"Yes. You wouldn't understand," Marvin said. "I don't think you have any capacity for love of any kind."

Shadow's face registered his hurt. "That's not true. I love you, don't I?"

"That's different. Do you want to fall in love with a woman?"

"Possibly. I don't know. Maybe I really don't have it in me to truly love someone that way," Shadow said. "Now you have me thinking about women. The sheriff's fiancée is a very pretty lady."

"Don't you dare. If you do, you'll bring him down on me a second time. While I'm not afraid of him, it would be a terrible inconvenience to have him in the middle of my business. Last time was more than enough," Marvin said. "So the Irishman and his Indian pal haven't found any silver?"

"No. I heard Lucky talking about it at Spike's the other night. He said it's good that he has some savings or else he'd be dead broke. The boy said much the same thing. If it weren't for selling his art, he wouldn't have any money because with the two little kids, his parents don't have extra to give him."

Marvin frowned. "I do feel badly for them. Such a horrible thing for young children to go through."

Shadow let out a loud laugh. "You really crack me up with that stuff."

"You ought to feel the same way after … everything."

"Oh, you mean basically being locked up in a cage for the first sixteen years of my life?" Shadow asked. "I got over that a long time ago,

Marvy. As soon as you let me loose that night, I made sure I'd never be put back in there again, didn't I?"

"Yes, you did," Marvin said, smiling as he thought about it. "And what a glorious night it was."

"It truly was."

"Shadow?"

"Yes?"

"Follow our Irish fellow some time and see what he's up to," Marvin said.

"That means I have to be out in the daylight," Shadow said, a thrill of nerves trickling down his spine. "You know I don't like that."

Marvin reached over and patted Shadow's powerful forearm consolingly. "I know, but it's important."

"I just told you what he's up to."

"No, that's what he *says* he's up to. I have a hunch about it, though," Marvin said.

"Do you think he found silver?" Shadow asked.

"I don't know. That's why I need you to follow him"

"But I don't think—"

"Shadow! Do you remember our agreement? I get to do the thinking and you get to do the things you enjoy," Marvin said.

Thinking about those things, Shadow said, "I remember. I'm not stupid, Marvin."

"Of course not. I wasn't implying you were. I'm merely saying that we have different talents. Mental strategy and business aren't yours," Marvin said. "Just as the more physical side of things aren't mine. I don't like them, but you do. That's why we make the perfect team."

"Opposites. Like light and dark," Shadow said with a smile. "Isn't that what Phoebe said the last time she was here?"

Marvin laughed. "I should have known you'd be skulking around somewhere."

"I saw her arrive and followed her inside. She never knew I was there. She's very pretty, I'll give you that," Shadow said.

"Yes, she is. You didn't come in my room, did you? You know I hate it when you do without me knowing you're there," Marvin said.

Inside his mind, Shadow felt his twin's cold anger. "No, Marvy. I know you don't and I won't do that. I'll do all kinds of other stuff to annoy you, but I always respect your privacy. The same way you respect mine."

The cold anger receded.

"Thank you, Shadow. Well, I suppose I'll go to bed," Marvin said.

"I'll go find a good place to hide until Irish and the Indian leave to go to the mine, if that's really where they're going," Shadow said. "I'll let you know what I find out."

"Good," Marvin said with another pat to Shadow's arm as he rose. "See you tomorrow."

"Goodnight."

Chapter Eighteen

That night after supper, Evan decided to take Josie to Spike's again. She'd been a couple of times with him and had enjoyed it.

"Oh, good! That'll be fun," she said, her eyes lighting up at the idea. "I'll take my guitar. Maybe they'd like to hear some music."

Evan smiled. "I think that's a good idea. We'll see if Billy wants to go. Lucky, too."

Josie rinsed off a plate and gave it to Evan to dry. "Great. We'll make a night of it, but we shouldn't stay out too late so you can get some sleep."

"Yes, ma'am," Evan said with a smile.

The four of them entered Spike's to find that it was a slow night. Spike greeted them as they took seats at the bar.

"Well, what can I get you? I have beer, whiskey, and more beer," Spike said.

Josie smiled at his witty statement and said, "Well, then, I guess I'll have a beer."

"A beer for the pretty lady," Spike said.

Evan said, "I think that's what we're all going to have."

Lucky and Billy nodded their assent and Spike poured their drinks.

"So what's new and exciting in Echo?" he asked.

Josie said, "My friends Opal and Sean are coming to the wedding."

Spike smiled and said, "That's good news. When are they gettin' here?"

"About a week before hand. I can't wait. I've missed them."

"Well, there's some people that look like trouble," said Jerry as he strolled through the door.

Lucky smiled and said, "Take a look in the mirror, lad. You're trouble if I've ever seen it."

Jerry laughed and sat down. "My usual, Spike."

As he poured Jerry a shot of whiskey, he said, "How's Sonya?"

"She's good, thanks. Busy with the Ladies' Auxiliary tonight, so I thought I'd stop in."

Evan pointed at Josie's guitar case. "It's a good thing you did. We're in for a treat tonight."

Jerry looked at it and asked, "You playin' for us tonight, Josie?"

She nodded. "Yes. I thought you might enjoy it. I haven't performed in front of an audience for a while though, so I might be a little rusty."

Spike said, "I doubt that. Well, what are you waiting for? Break out that guitar and let's hear it."

Josie smiled at his gruff tone. "Yes, sir."

Evan walked with her over to a good place for her to sit so the sound carried well. He held up his hands and said, "Everyone, I'd like to ask you to quiet down. My beautiful fiancée is going to play for us, and her voice is as pretty as she is."

Josie blushed at his praise as she sat down and readied her guitar. She warmed up by doing a couple of scales. Evan sat at the table closest to her, not wanting to miss a thing. The other men began crowding around. Josie waited to start until all the scuffling and noise from chairs had quieted.

She decided to start out with some familiar favorites and soon the sound of tapping toes accompanied her. Lucky sat next to Evan and Billy, and during the second song he could hear Billy humming along. He nudged Billy and motioned that he should go sing with her. Billy shook his head and stopped humming. He hadn't even been aware he was doing it.

He was soon humming along again, though, and Lucky prodded him again. Evan looked over to see what was going on.

As soon as Josie finished the song she'd been playing, Lucky said, "Josie, would ya mind if Billy sang one with you?"

Billy glared at him. "What are you doing?" he whispered.

Josie smiled. "Billy, I didn't know you sang."

His face was slightly flushed. "I don't. Not really."

Lucky said, "Now, don't be lyin'. Ya have a beautiful voice. Go on, lad."

"Please come sing with me," Josie encouraged him. "I haven't sang with anyone in a while and it'll be a real treat for me."

Feeling everyone's eyes on him, Billy reluctantly rose from his seat, giving Lucky dagger eyes the whole time. He pulled his chair over to sit with Josie. They quietly conferred until they came up with a song they both knew.

"What key is best for you?" Josie asked.

Billy shrugged. "I don't know. I've never done this before."

"You don't read music?" she asked.

"No."

"Can you do harmony?" Josie asked.

"Sure. You just play and I'll jump in," Billy said. "I just sing by ear."

"All right. Let's just see what happens. I'll sing the melody and you come in wherever you're comfortable."

He nodded. His palms were sweaty and it felt like there was a horse galloping inside his chest. He'd never sang in front of anyone but his parents and the Tafts before and it was nerve-wracking. Josie started the song intro and then began singing at the appropriate place. Billy waited to start until she came to the chorus, giving himself time to work up to it and really get the harmony in his head.

Hesitantly, he started out, not daring to look at their audience. He knew if he did, he'd fall apart and be humiliated. Instead, he focused on Josie, who smiled encouragingly at him. His confidence grew and he began getting caught up in the song and blending his voice with Josie's. Before too long, he didn't care very much about the audience.

Josie enjoyed singing with Billy immensely. Lucky had been right about Billy's voice. Its timber was very pleasing and he had a good ear for harmony. She could just imagine what he could do if he had some training. When the song ended, applause broke out.

Lucky whistled and others followed suit. "I told ye he could sing and together they sound like a couple of angels."

Billy smiled bashfully at the praise from the small crowd and also from Josie.

"I had no idea you could sing like that. You have an excellent voice and great instincts—we should sing together more often," she said.

"I don't know about that," Billy said. "I'm not all that good."

"Yes, you are. I wouldn't just say that, Billy," Josie said.

His eyes smiled as he said, "So you'd tell me if I stunk at it?"

Josie laughed and said, "Yes, but I'd be nice about it."

"Thanks," he said as he got up.

"Where are you going?" she asked. "Sing another one with me."

"I don't know," Billy hedged.

Rob Rickmers spoke up. "Yeah, go ahead, Billy. I didn't know Injuns could sing like that."

Josie watched as Billy's smile slowly faded, the happy light in his eyes replaced by anger and hurt. He got up and quickly moved towards the door. Josie rose and went after him.

"Billy, don't leave. Just ignore him," she pleaded.

Billy didn't heed her plea, however, he walked faster until he reached the door. He opened it and slammed it shut again. Josie became enraged.

Turning around, she walked straight over to Rob and said, "You cruel, ignorant, imbecile. How could you do that to him?"

"What? I told him he was good," Rob said, confusion stamped on his rough features. "Seems like his white blood came through there somewhere."

Josie's vision blurred with her fury and she delivered a hard slap to Rob's face. Never before had she struck another person, but her anger was so great that all rational thought had fled her brain.

Pandemonium instantly ensued. Rob stood up, reaching towards Josie. Evan intervened, pushing Rob back down in his chair, while another man hurried towards the sheriff. He was met in mid-stride by Lucky's fist and the man went down, unconscious before he hit the floor.

"That's enough!" Evan shouted. "Next person to throw a punch is getting locked up!"

His angry glare touched on each person who'd been in motion and who had frozen. This included Lucky. Evan held his eyes and Lucky relaxed his hold on another guy, stepping back and holding up his hands. There was something in the sheriff's eyes that told Lucky that he was not a man to be trifled with and since Evan was also his friend, he didn't want to get on his bad side.

Lucky said, "Sorry about that, Evan. I guess I got a little carried away there. Seems as though we all did. Right, lads?"

As Evan continued to aim his laser sharp gaze around the room, more men began relaxing, a few nodding their heads in agreement with Lucky. Josie hadn't backed off very far, so angry that she would have gone toe-to-toe with Rob despite the fact that he could have knocked her out in seconds. She didn't care. He'd hurt one of her friends in the worst way and she just couldn't stand by and let it slide.

Spike, wishing to restore order, said, "Well, I think we've had enough excitement for tonight. C'mon and have a round on me, boys. Except you, Rob. You get the hell out and don't come back until you can behave yourself."

Rob gave Evan a mutinous stare.

"You heard the man," Evan said, his voice a malicious growl. "Get out or I'll haul your ass in. No man hits a woman in my presence."

"She hit me first, Sheriff. It's me that ought to be pressin' charges."

That was the wrong thing to say. Loud laughter broke out; the idea of a man wanting to have a woman arrested for merely slapping him caused great amusement. Evan didn't have to warn Rob to leave again. The men laughing at him did if for the sheriff. Rob strode angrily from the bar amid the hilarity.

The bar was once again a peaceful, if lively place. Evan turned to Josie.

"Are you all right?" he asked her. He took in her stormy blue eyes and the high color in her cheeks.

"No, I'm not. I only wish I was stronger and so I could have knocked him right on his ass!" she declared. "It's no less than he deserves. Poor Billy is sensitive enough about his heritage and that, that …" she couldn't think of a strong enough swear word at the moment.

"Bastard," Evan supplied. He was trying not to smile. This was a whole other side to Josie and he was enjoying it immensely. It was exciting to see that she had that kind of fire in her.

"Yes, that bastard only made it worse," Josie said. "You know what the saddest part is?"

"Tell me," Evan said.

Her lip actually curled as her temper rose again. "I'm sure he wasn't the only one in this room who thought the same thing or something similar!" Her voice had risen and some of the men turned to her. "Didn't you?" she challenged them.

Evan felt the same way she did, but he didn't want a second confrontation to occur so he pulled her over with him to her guitar. Keeping his voice low, he said, "Honey, I'd have liked to have smacked Rob around, too, but it's best if we go for the night. Things are calmed down now, so I'm asking you to help me out here and keep it that way."

Looking into his eyes, she saw his sincerity. She gave him a curt nod and began packing up her guitar. Once it was safely stowed in its case, Josie picked it up and began walking toward the door. As she passed the bar, she paused and looked at the man nearest her. He held her fiery stare for a moment and then dropped his eyes. Impulse struck again and Josie took the shot of whiskey that sat in front him and drank it down all at once. Then she slammed the glass back down on the bar and continued on her way. She met each man's eyes as she walked onward and most of them also lowered their eyes.

Somehow, Josie was able to hold the cough in until after they were outside. She felt like someone had lit her insides on fire and she gasped for air. Evan patted her on the back as she coughed and wheezed. When she'd regained her breath, she looked at Evan and saw the amused look on his face.

Some of her temper had cooled and shock over what she'd done set in. She burst into laughter and asked, "Did I really just do that?"

Evan laughed with her and said, "You sure as heck did. It was a thing of beauty, too. I should hire you as a deputy. There's nothing like a woman's scolding to bring a man down. You smacking Rob was something to see, too."

This sent Josie on another wave of laughter as they walked to their horses. "I don't know what came over me. I was just so furious."

"You're not the only one. I know that if you hadn't done it, Lucky would have. You should have seen the look on his face. I might have had to lock him up for murder if you hadn't gotten to Rob first," Evan said. "Remind me not to get on your bad side."

She mounted as he held her guitar for her. "I've never been so angry in all my life," she said, taking it from him.

"Well, I hope you don't get angry like that again for a long time," Evan said, swinging into the saddle.

Josie burped, repeating the whiskey. "Ugh! How do you drink that stuff? It's awful."

Evan chuckled. "Once you drink about three of them, you don't notice the taste much."

"I would hope not," Josie said. "I don't think I'll be drinking any more of it."

"Well, at least I don't have to worry about you becoming a drunk," Evan said.

"Nope. I wonder how poor Billy is," she said, sobering.

Evan sighed. "Me, too. I noticed that Lucky had left. Most likely to go after him. He'll take care of him."

"I know," Josie said.

They fell silent, both thinking how much nicer the world would be without prejudice and injustice.

Chapter Nineteen

Remus and Arlene jerked upright in bed upon hearing an incredible ruckus downstairs.

"What the heck is that?" Arlene asked.

"I don't know. You stay with the kids while I go see," Remus said as he got up.

He went out in the hallway and looked down over the banister. It didn't seem like there was anyone in the parlor, so he crept downstairs as he heard another crash. It came from Billy's studio. Carefully, Remus opened the door. The sight that met his eyes froze him in place for a few moments.

Billy was destroying his paintings and easels, smashing the canvases down over the three-sided point at the top of the wooden structures. Remus rushed into the room.

"Billy! What the hell are you doing?" he demanded.

Breathing heavily, Billy stopped and glared at his father. "Why did you do this to me?"

Remus was shocked by the level of anger in Billy's eyes and the fact that it was aimed at him when he couldn't think of anything he'd done to make his son so furious.

"What are you talkin' about? I didn't do anything to you," Remus said. "Why are you doing this?" He gestured at the destruction around them. "You've been working so hard on these? Why would you destroy them?"

Billy's voice came out in a harsh rasp as he said, "Because it doesn't matter how hard I work, how talented I am at anything, I'll always be an Indian! I'll never be good enough for anyone!"

Remus asked, "What happened?"

"Only what was bound to happen sooner or later," Billy said. "Who are my parents? I mean my real parents. Where are they? Where did I come from? Why would you take me from them? Did I come from an orphanage? *WHERE DID I COME FROM?*" he screamed.

Remus stepped back a step, completely unprepared for both Billy's question and his vehement outburst. "Billy, you have to calm down, son. I'll tell you, but you have to calm down."

Billy stepped around Remus, going to his work table where he picked up a pair of scissors. To Remus' horror, he began cutting off his hair.

"Billy, stop that!" Remus said.

Billy kept cutting, however, ignoring his father. Remus grabbed Billy from behind, his big arms surrounding him.

"Get off me! Let me go!" Billy demanded, struggling against him.

They fought for the scissors. Remus was able to knock them from Billy's hand. They clattered to the floor just as Lucky came hurrying in the outside door to Billy's room. He saw the two men wrestling and began helping Remus hold Billy in check.

"Billy, stop! Please?" Remus said. "You're going to scare your ma and the kids. C'mon, son. Calm down and we'll talk about this. Please."

Remus looked at Lucky in a questioning manner. Lucky closed his eyes and shook his head in a sad gesture.

"Billy, come, lad. Listen to your pa," Lucky said. "Ya don't want to scare the little ones, do you?"

Some of the fight left Billy as he thought about the kids and his mother. He relaxed in his father's grip and said, "Fine."

Remus released him. "Now would you please tell me what this is about?"

Facing him, Billy said, "It's about who I am. Who am I really? Where are my parents? Why did you take me from them? Why would you raise me in a white town where no one would accept me? How could you do that to me?"

Remus' heart broke, not only for Billy, but for him and Arlene, too. They'd always known this day would come, but not like this. Not with Billy so full of anger about it. He couldn't find the words at the moment and stood mute in the face of Billy's questions.

Billy glared at Remus for several moments and when his father remained silent, he turned and went out the door into the night. Remus looked at Lucky and then around at all of Billy's ruined work.

"Ok, Lucky, you need to explain to me what happened tonight," Remus said.

"Aye," Lucky said and began the story.

Although it was late, Win was still awake. He sat reading in the main room of his cabin. It still wasn't quite finished, but enough that he could stay in it. He now owned a small kitchen table with three chairs, a loveseat, and coffee table, all of which were secondhand, but still in fairly good condition. Billy and Lucky had procured the furniture for him since it would have looked suspicious for him to be buying furniture since everyone knew that he didn't have a permanent place of residence.

There was also a bedroom, but Win had yet to get a bed. For now he was content to use a bedroll, but it was so hot that he mostly slept outside anyway. There were several books about animal husbandry on the coffee table as well as a couple of others on various subjects, but those weren't what Win liked to read.

Win might not be religious at all, but he was a secret romantic and his mother had gotten him on to reading romance books. His father had never known it. It was something that only he and his mother had shared. She was the one who had taught him to read and write English and she would often sit in the evenings reading romance because it gave her an escape from the stress of her real life. When he'd been about fourteen, Win had picked one up and started reading it out of curiosity. Fifty pages later, he'd been hooked and he'd been reading them ever since.

He was just getting to a good part when he heard the dogs bark. Springing up, he hid the book under one of the loveseat cushions and snatched his rifle from where it stood by the open door. By the time he stepped through the door, he had it up to his shoulder, ready to fire at a moment's notice.

A horse approached and slowed down. "It's me, Win," he heard Billy say.

Win relaxed and lowered the gun. "What are you doing here?"

Billy ascended the stairs onto the porch and said, "I'm staying here tonight."

Something sounded off about Billy and Win's gaze settled on him as the lantern light from within the cabin hit him. Win noted Billy's half-chopped hair and the wild light in his eyes.

"Well, that's an interesting haircut you have there," Win said.

Billy just smirked at him and walked past Win into the cabin. "You got anything to drink?"

Win frowned and followed Billy inside. "What's eating you?"

"Nothing," Billy said, flopping down on the loveseat. "I just needed to get away."

Anger radiated from the boy.

"Away from what?" Win said, walking into his bedroom and coming back out with a bottle of scotch.

"Everything. Everyone," Billy said.

"Mmm. Who gave you the haircut?" Win said as he looked over the jagged locks hanging down around Billy's ears.

"I did," Billy said. He took the bottle of liquor from Win and drank down a couple of healthy swigs.

"You didn't do a very good job," Win said with a deadpan expression.

Billy swallowed and stared at Win. Both men started laughing at the same time. When their mirth was exhausted, Win said, "I'll fix it as best I can while you tell me what happened. C'mon."

"You can fix it, but I don't want to talk about it," Billy said.

Win did an imitation of his father. "No talk, no fix," he said with a heavy Chinese accent.

Billy smiled and said, "Fine."

He went out to the table, taking the bottle with him. Sitting down, he took another pull from it and sighed. Win retrieved his scissors from his bedroom and started turning Billy's head this way and that. As he began cutting his hair, Billy's tale poured forth.

In the morning, Josie knocked on Lucky's door. When he answered it, he was just putting on his shirt. "Hi, Lucky. You weren't here when I came home last night. How is Billy?"

Lucky's face settled into grim lines, giving Josie her answer. "He was in a bad way. Completely destroyed all his paintings and such. Cut off a bunch of his hair before Remus could get the scissors away from him."

"Oh my God. Did you get him calmed down? Is he hurt?" she said, coming into his room and shutting the door.

"He's not hurt that I know of. He took off after screamin' and causin' a ruckus. He wants to know about his biological parents and I'm afraid that's my fault," Lucky said.

"What do you mean?" Josie asked. "How is that your fault?"

"The day after we got here, I brought it up to him. I didn't know that he didn't know, ya see. I just wondered what had happened to them. He said he'd never asked. He didn't have a reason to really," Lucky said as he finished with his shirt and tucked it into his pants. "I think I started him thinking about it and with what happened last night, well, it just all came to a boil."

"Oh, how awful. Where do you think he went?" Josie asked.

"I'm guessin' out with Win. It's the only place I can think of. I'm heading there now," Lucky said.

Josie wished she didn't have two cleaning jobs to do. She'd have gone with him. "Please let me know when you find him." They left Lucky's room.

"I will. Don't worry yerself over it. It'll all get straightened out," Lucky said. After kissing her forehead, he jogged down the stairs and strode out the door.

Josie descended at a more sedate pace, her mind on her young friend. Going into the kitchen, she encountered Phoebe and Thad kissing. She stopped dead and turned around, leaving again. In shock she left the house and decided to stop at the diner for breakfast. Walking up the street, she saw Marvin and groaned to herself.

"I should have stayed in bed today," she said under her breath.

Marvin smiled at her. "Good morning, Josie."

Despite the hot day, she shivered inside over hearing him say her name. "Hello, Marvin. I'll have the last of my payments this week."

Marvin put a hand to his chest and asked, "Why is it every time I see you that's one of the first things you say to me? Did I ask about the payment?"

"Well, no," Josie said.

"No, I didn't. I was merely being social. I see that Evan has poisoned your mind against me, however. That's fine," he said, the hurt in his eyes seemingly genuine. "Have your sheriff bring it like always so that I don't snatch you up in my evil clutches. Congratulations on your upcoming nuptials, by the way. Good day, Josie."

Josie watched him walk away, his back straight with anger. She didn't know why, but she felt a moment's sympathy for him. "Marvin! Wait!"

Perplexed, he turned around and looked at her as she caught up with him. "Yes?"

"I'm sorry," she said. "I shouldn't have been so abrupt with you.

I'm just a little upset this morning." She didn't want to get on the man's bad side.

"Oh. What's wrong?" he asked.

Josie didn't know why she did it, but she said, "Something happened last night at Spike's with Billy and I'm a little worried about him. I'm afraid it's put me a little bit of a bad mood. Forgive me?" She gave him a small smile.

Cocking an eyebrow at her, Marvin said, "On one condition. Have breakfast with me."

"What?" His request was completely unexpected, and she now regretted trying to rectify things with him.

"Have breakfast with me at the diner," he repeated.

She conjured a smile from somewhere. "That's a very nice gesture, but I have to get to work. I'm cleaning today and I'd like to get started before it gets any hotter."

"I see. Well, that's too bad," Marvin said. "Tomorrow morning then?"

Josie could see that he wasn't going to let her get out of this and she mentally kicked herself. "What about lunch today?" she asked, thinking to get the meal with him over as quickly as possible.

His eyebrows rose. "Lunch? Well, I really wasn't planning on coming back into town. I have a meeting at the bank, but then I was going home. I know. I'll have my cook make us something nice. We can eat out on the veranda. It's quite cool there under the maple trees."

Josie was trapped and she knew it. The cat had cornered the mouse and was ready to close in for the kill. Then she thought about what she'd done at the bar the previous night and decided that maybe the mouse had some fight in it. "That would be lovely. What time should I arrive?"

Marvin was very surprised by her acceptance of his invitation; he'd expected her to make some excuse as to why she couldn't come. "One o'clock. Do you remember the way or should I have Travis come get you?"

"I remember the way," she said.

His face broke out into a wide grin. "Wonderful. Well, I'm looking very forward to it. I haven't had a lunch guest in quite a while. Is there anything in particular you'd like to eat?"

She shook her head a little dazzled by his beauty. *Good God! It really is too bad he's the way he is. Who could resist him when he smiles like that?* "No. I'm sure whatever your cook makes will be fine."

"All right, then. I'll let you get underway. I don't want you to suffer heat exhaustion. Until later," Marvin said, giving her a parting smile.

"What have I done?" she mumbled to herself.

No longer hungry, Josie went to the sheriff's office to face the music known otherwise as an angry Evan.

Evan didn't yell, he didn't stomp around, or gesture wildly as Josie had expected him to. Once she finished telling him about her encounter with Marvin, he sat calmly. The only way she knew he was irritated was by his narrowed eyes.

She sat looking back at him and the longer he was silent the more uneasy she grew.

Finally he said, "Ok. Have a nice lunch."

"What?" she said. "You're letting me go?"

"Oh, were you hoping that I'd forbid you from going?" he asked.

"Yes. I mean, no. I don't know! It happened before I knew it," Josie said. She was completely flustered by his permissive attitude.

"Exactly," Evan said. "That's the way Marvin works. He's a master at it. He makes you do and say things that you never thought you would and he makes you think it was your idea. I've never seen a better manipulator, Josie. Now he has you right where he wants you."

"It'll be fine. I'll just go have lunch with him and that'll be it. I'll send you with my payment like always and then I'll be free of him," Josie said. "Travis or someone will be around."

"Are you sure you want to be? Done with him, I mean," Evan said.

"Of course, I do. How …" She gazed into his eyes and saw the fear in them. "Evan, don't read anything into this. I swear to you that I can't stand him and that I'm only doing this to get him off my back. I'll only stay as long as I have to in order to not appear rude."

Evan's anger threatened to boil over, but he couldn't be too angry with her. Marvin was incredibly slick and Josie had no real prior experience with him. "You're supposed to be there at one o'clock, right?"

"Yes," she said.

"If you don't come here to the office by two-thirty on the dot, I'm coming after you. Two-thirty. Do you understand me?"

"Yes. I'm not an idiot, Evan. I'll be here by then. I promise," Josie said, going to him and giving him a lingering kiss.

As soon as she left the office, Evan picked up his coffee mug and threw it across the room where it hit the wall and shattered into a dozen or so pieces. Then he raked his hand through his hair and pounded the desk a few times just as Thad came in the door. He watched Evan continue to vent his frustration on the desk.

There was only one thing that made Evan that furious. "What did Earnest do this time?"

Billy closed his eyes against the piercing light as he sat up on the loveseat where he'd slept. At first he had no recollection as to where he was and then remembered coming to Win's last night. He went to run a hand through his hair only to discover that he had very little left. Alarmed, he opened his eyes again and stood up too quickly.

The room tilted and his stomach rolled. Staggering to the doorway, he stumbled out onto the porch and hurried over to the railing as dry heaves hit him. When he was back in control of his body, he looked around and saw Win sitting in a chair on the other side of the porch.

"Where's my hair?" he asked.

Win smiled. "I cut it for you after your failed attempt to do it. Remember?"

The events of the night before came back to him and he groaned. "I do now. What does it look like?"

"Well, considering that I'm not a barber, it doesn't look too bad. There's a mirror in my bedroom. Go take a look."

Billy walked slowly to Win's bedroom and went over to the small mirror on the wall. Although Win had given him a haircut that most white men would have been happy with, Billy was horrified by the way he looked. His misery rose again as he looked at the close cropped style. Tears stung his eyes as he turned away from the mirror. He went back outside and sat on the porch steps, burying his face in his hands.

Lucky was just riding up. As he dismounted, Billy looked up and Lucky froze in place. "God Almighty!"

That did Billy in and he started crying in earnest. Win never moved.

Lucky looked at him. "Aren't ya goin' to do somethin'?"

"What would you have me do?" Win asked. He was not good at dealing with this sort of thing.

"It's called comforting someone," Lucky said, sitting down by Billy and putting an arm around him. "It's all right, lad. It'll grow back."

"I look ridiculous," Billy said.

Win said, "That's why God made hats."

Billy started laughing through his tears.

"See, Lucky, I know how to comfort someone. Laughing is a sure cure-all for tears," Win said.

Lucky laughed and said, "I can't believe ya actually said God made something, even if ya did mean it as a joke."

Billy brushed his tears away and said, "I'm going to find my parents. My real parents. I want to know why they gave me up."

"You need to talk to your ma and pa first," Lucky said. "Don't just take off."

"I don't understand why they took me. They should have left me with my first parents. Then I'd be where I was accepted," Billy responded.

Win said, "I'm sure they had their reasons. Hear them out first."

Billy ran a hand over his hair and started getting upset again. "Yeah. You're right. I need answers."

Lucky said, "Billy, I know what happened last night hurt, but ya can't let them get to ya like that. You know the truth of who ya are. Don't let other people decide who that is."

Nodding, Billy stood up and said, "See you later."

He mounted his horse and rode away.

Sweat ran down Josie's spine as she got closer to the Earnest ranch. It was not all heat-related, though. A couple of times, she was tempted to turn around and go back to town, but her pride wouldn't let her. She also refused to give in to her fear.

As she rode up the drive, Barkley ran out to meet her. He was such a cute dog, Josie thought as she rode up to the house. Marvin had already descended the veranda steps and he took Captain from her.

"Good afternoon, Josie. I'm glad you were still able to make it," he said, tying Captain to a hitching post under the trees. Marvin was a contradiction in almost every way. Although he might not know much about animal quality, he enjoyed them and was very considerate of them. Putting the horse in the shade showed his compassion for the animal.

"Me, too," she said, her heart hammering in her chest.

Marvin could hear the stress in her voice and smiled. "I'm surprised that your fiancé gave his blessing."

Josie opted for the truth. "Well, he wasn't pleased, but I'm a grown woman and I can make my own decisions."

"Yes, you can," he said, motioning for her to go up on the veranda.

Josie hesitated for a moment and then ascended the steps. She saw that a very nice table had been set up there. A nice arrangement of flowers in a crystal vase stood on the table that was covered in a white tablecloth. Fine china plates and silverware shined to perfection kept company with the vase of flowers.

Despite her misgivings, Josie had to admit that she was impressed with all the thought that Marvin had put into the appearance of the table.

"Please have a seat," Marvin said. He held a chair for Josie.

She let him help seat her. He put hand on her shoulder and she jumped a little. Marvin seemed to ignore this. He sat opposite her as a servant came out carrying a bottle of wine, which Marvin took from her.

"Thank you, Fiona," Marvin said, with a smile.

Fiona smiled back a little and left again.

"I chose a nice Pinot Noir. I assume you do drink wine," Marvin said, opening the bottle.

Josie nodded. "Yes, but only a little."

Marvin poured some in a glass, swirled it around, and sniffed the bouquet. It was apparently to his liking because he sat the glass down and then poured more in another glass for her. After handing it to her, he sat the bottle down and looked at her.

Josie met his eyes, trying not to flinch from his gaze.

"You really are a very beautiful woman, Josie. And I say that from a purely platonic point of view. I don't want you to think that I have designs on you. That's not why I invited you here," Marvin said.

Josie took a tiny sip of her wine and enjoyed the taste. "Why did you invite me here?"

"A very good question. You see, I know how Evan thinks. I suppose by now he's told you the terrible tale of how I stole Louise from him and the rest of it," Marvin said, reining in his temper. "I would like to tell you my side of things and let you judge for yourself whether or not I'm the evil man most people believe I am."

Looking into his wide blue eyes, Josie couldn't detect a hint of dishonesty, but she'd been warned about Marvin's ability to win people over and she kept that in the back of her mind. Still, she couldn't help but be curious. "As long as we're being truthful, yes, he did tell me about it. He said that you got Louise pregnant and that you made her have an abortion."

She saw anger flash in Marvin's eyes and then disappear. "It's true that I did sleep with Louise a few times. She was a very beautiful woman and I'm afraid that I succumbed to her charms. And very enticing she was. At the risk of shocking you, I will tell you that she wasn't a virgin. A man can tell these things."

Josie almost choked on the sip of wine she'd taken. Her face turned pink with embarrassment. "I see," she managed to say.

"She lied to Evan about that particular detail. I think she had rethought marrying him because of that lie. I tried to convince her that Evan was the forgiving sort and that she should go through with the wedding," Marvin said. "Believe it or not, I like Evan, and I was trying to look out for his welfare. Even after sleeping with Louise, I tried to rectify that by insisting she marry him."

"She'd already been unfaithful to him. Why on earth do you think she deserved him?" Josie asked, her disgust clearly stamped on her face.

"Because he loved her. I think he had an inkling, but he didn't want to believe it. So he turned a blind eye to the situation."

Fiona came back out carrying a tray of delicate cucumber sandwiches and a pitcher of water. She sat them down and left again.

Marvin continued. "You have my full permission to tell Evan about everything we discuss here today. I have nothing to hide. I was not the father of Louise's baby."

Josie's eyes widened. She couldn't believe that he was being so forthcoming about everything. "Then who was? Evan said they hadn't been intimate."

Marvin laughed. "Isn't it such a double standard about sex? I've never subscribed to the idea that a woman must be a virgin when she's married while men can fool around whenever they want to. I find it ludicrous, don't you?"

Unprepared for his question, Josie said, "I don't really believe in relations before marriage whether the person be a man or a woman."

"So it doesn't bother you that Evan has been with women before you?" Marvin asked. When she hesitated about answering, Marvin said,

"Come now, Josie. I'm being honest with you. You owe me the same courtesy."

She raised her chin a little and said, "I suppose it does bother me a little, but I don't really think about it most of the time."

"Ah, I see." Marvin said as he took a bite of a sandwich. "Mmm. I'll have to tell cook what a good job she's done with these."

The sandwiches were very delicious and Josie ate a couple of them with relish. "Yes, they're very good."

"Getting back to Louise's baby. The reason I know that I was not the father was because I can't have children. Not to be blunt, but I can be physical with a woman, but nothing will come of it," Marvin told her.

Josie decided not to pull any punches with him. Her fear of him was beginning to abate. "How can I believe you? This could all be a fabrication, something to trick me into believing you."

Although annoyed, Marvin had to admire her courage. She sat in the lion's den with the lion himself encircling her and yet she still challenged him. "Yes, I could be lying, but I'm not. I have no reason to. What advantage would that possibly give me? Evan will never believe me and I'm not telling you this so that you can convince him of my innocence. I'm merely trying to make you see that I'm not what many people try to make me out to be."

Josie poured some water in her glass and sipped at it before asking, "How do you know that you can't father children?"

"Because I have intercourse on a regular basis and I have yet to produce a child," Marvin said. "I know there are methods to control such things, but I have no need of them."

Josie was glad that she didn't have anything in her mouth because his blunt statement would surely have made her choke. "I see."

He laughed, her discomfort amusing to him. "I am sorry to offend your sense of decorum, but I am simply getting everything out in the open."

"I appreciate that. Who was the father?" Josie asked.

"Well, now there's where things get a little complicated," Marvin said. "I promised Louise that I wouldn't tell anyone who it was."

"That's a little convenient, don't you think?" Josie asked.

Marvin's admiration of Josie rose at her head-on handling of the situation. "Yes, I suppose you could look at it that way. It's just that when I make a promise to someone, I always keep it. My promise to you is that I will never harm a hair on that pretty head of yours. I'm sure that Evan is worrying about your safety right at this moment."

Unable to refute his last statement, Josie said, "So you promised Louise that you would keep the baby's father a secret. She told Evan that you forced her to get an abortion."

Marvin's mouth curved in a resigned smile. "I told her to tell him that. Better he think badly of me than of her. I was holding out hope that he might forgive her and marry her, but that didn't happen, fortunately for you."

Josie leaned forward a little. "So you set yourself up as the bad guy? Why would you do that?"

Marvin leaned back and spread his hands wide. "I suppose it's because I can't resist helping a damsel in distress. I didn't force Louise to get an abortion. She asked me for the money to get one and I gave it to her. That's what she told Evan, but it's not what really happened."

Fiona came back with their entrée of salmon steaks, asparagus, and new roasted potatoes. The food smelled delicious and Josie began eating as she thought over everything that Marvin had told her.

"Is it to your liking?" Marvin asked.

"Yes," Josie said. "It's excellent."

Marvin nodded as he sampled the salmon. "Yes. Quite good. So I'm sure you're trying to figure out whether or not I'm lying to you."

"I am," Josie confirmed.

"I expected no less. Well, that is something only you can decide. However, there is no benefit to me telling you this except to make you stop avoiding me whenever we meet," Marvin said, looking injured. "You have no idea how lonely it is. I could move elsewhere and start over, but our family has owned this ranch for generations and I have no wish to leave it. I'm working hard to restore it to its former glory."

"Evan said that your family lost quite a bit of money when the mines left," she said.

"That's true. I've invested in some ventures that seem promising and I'm hoping to recoup some of that loss," Marvin said. "Now, just to show that I am not a heartless, unfeeling man, I am writing off the rest of what you owe me for that horse."

"No, no," Josie said. "I'm paying you what I owe you. I won't go back on my agreement. I don't want to be beholden to anyone."

"While I appreciate your independence and integrity, I insist," Marvin said. "I'll write it up and you don't have to sign it until Evan approves it."

Something flickered in Marvin's eyes and her fear of him returned a little. "All right. Thank you."

His smile was pleased. "Now, let's move on to more pleasant matters, shall we?"

"Certainly," Josie said, hoping to get the rest of the lunch over with as soon as possible. She didn't want to be late getting back to Evan.

For the next half hour, Marvin told her amusing stories of his time at boarding school and college. She couldn't help but laugh as he relayed to her some of the outrageous things he and his friends had done together. Josie couldn't figure the man out. Everything he was telling her rang true and his laughter was genuine. His eyes lit up, his enjoyment evident as he recounted these stories to her.

Finally, when dessert was over, Josie made her excuses to leave, but she couldn't truthfully say that she hadn't enjoyed herself somewhat.

"Josie, it has been a delight lunching with you. I do hope you'll come back some time. You're always welcome here. Not that I really expect to see you here again. Come inside so I can give you a copy of your agreement," Marvin said.

He waved her inside the house and guided her to his office even though she remembered where it was. Going over to his desk, Marvin sat down and pulled out a drawer. Once he found the appropriate file, he took out their agreement and with great flair wrote "paid in full" on it.

He stood up and came to stand by her, holding out the paper to her. "There you are. Just as promised. You are free and clear of any obligation to me whatsoever, so there is no need to mention it to me any longer."

Josie looked up into his eyes and said, "Thank you."

"As I said, have Evan read over it and if he finds anything amiss, have him let me know," Marvin said.

His nearness filled her with a cold dread and yet there was a part of her that felt sorry for him. "Thank you. I'm sure it's in order," she said and moved towards the door.

Marvin followed her outside, walking her to Captain. Gallantly, he held the horse while she mounted. "Don't be a stranger," he said stepping back.

Josie smiled and said, "I'll think about it."

Marvin chuckled. "At least you're honest."

"Goodbye, Marvin," Josie said and turned Captain around.

Marvin watched until she was out of sight and then went back to his office. As he shut the door, he jumped upon seeing Shadow behind it.

"Why must you do that?" he complained.

Shadow smiled. "Because it's fun."

"You shouldn't be up here right now," Marvin said, sitting down at his desk.

"You like her," Shadow stated, ignoring his brother's remark.

Marvin frowned. "Don't be ridiculous."

"You can't lie to me," Shadow said. "I know you too well. Despite what you say, I know there's a part of you that is attracted to her."

An annoyed expression settled on Marvin's face and then was replaced by a grin. "I suppose you're right, but don't read anything into that. There are many women I could say I have a passing interest in, but I love Phoebe. Now, you need to go back to your lair before anyone sees you. You don't like being up during the day anyway."

Shadow shrugged one of his powerful shoulders. "I was curious to see what she was like. She's very pretty."

Marvin cocked his head. "Yes, she is. Now, enough of this. I have work to do and so do you tonight, remember?"

Shadow smiled and stepped over to the closet in the office and opened the door. Pressing on a hidden button, he waited for the secret panel to slide open, stepped through and closed it again.

Marvin chuckled and started on some paperwork.

Chapter Twenty

Evan was just stepping toward the door of the office when Josie came inside.

"Hi," she said. "I'm on time."

He felt faint with relief, embracing her and holding her close. Kissing the side of her head, he said, "I've been worried sick about you. I haven't been able to think straight."

She hugged him back. "I'm fine, Evan. I knew I would be."

Needing reassurance, he pulled back and looked into her eyes. "He didn't try to hurt you or anything?"

Smiling into his eyes, she said, "No. Nothing happened. We had lunch. He did tell me some interesting things, which he said that I should tell you because he knew you'd want to know what we discussed."

Evan couldn't deny that he was curious. "Ok. Sit down here and tell me."

Josie related their conversation to him. "Evan, unless he is the devil incarnate, a lot of what he said rang true. I couldn't sense any lies. I really don't know what to think."

Letting out a snort of derision, Evan said, "Josie, I keep trying to tell you that he is a master at this. I can't tell you how many lies he fed me that I swallowed because I had no idea he was lying. I don't believe a damn thing he told you."

"He said you would say that," Josie said.

"See? He thinks of everything," Evan said. "I don't believe for a second that he can't father a child."

"There's no way to verify that one way or another," Josie said. "Well, it doesn't matter. I won't be going back there and neither will you." She took the agreement that Marvin had given her and handed it to him. "He doesn't want any more money for Captain. He wrote off my last payment."

Evan looked it over and could find nothing amiss with it. "You hang onto this. I don't want anything coming back on you, on us, about it. Earnest doesn't do anything without some kind of twisted motive. I learned that the hard way."

Seeing how upset Evan was becoming, Josie said, "It's over and done. Let's not worry about it anymore." She ran a hand over his jaw. "I'd rather do something else right now than talk about him."

Seeing the desire in her eyes, Evan said, "I think we're thinking the same thing."

Josie leaned close to him, brushing her lips over his before whispering, "Yes, we are," against his mouth.

Evan's arms came around her as he deepened the kiss immediately. His need of her was almost more than he could contain. Everything about her felt incredible to him. Having her in his arms reassured him that she was safe, but it also lit his fiery passion for her.

Josie encircled his neck with her arms and kissed him back for all she was worth, her own desire rising swiftly. She couldn't get close enough to him and pressed against him, running her fingers through his hair. Then she remembered that someone could come through the door at any moment and pulled back from him.

"I have to go," she said. "I have some work to finish up."

Evan smiled even though he was reluctant to let her go. "And I need to go have a look around town now that I know you're ok."

She pressed another kiss to his mouth and said, "I am. See you tonight."

"Yeah. Tonight," Evan said.

Josie gave him one last kiss and then left the office before she couldn't find the strength to do so.

When Billy entered his studio he stood transfixed by the sight of the havoc he'd wreaked the night before. Nothing had been cleaned up and knowing his parents, that had been deliberate. He began sifting through the mess, seeing what could be salvaged and what was completely ruined. Making two piles, he began organizing it, angry with himself and everything else, too.

He took the ruined stuff outside to be burned later on. When he went back inside, his mother stood in the studio. She gasped upon seeing his short hair.

"Billy! What did you do?" she asked, coming over to him.

He twisted his lips in a wry smile. "I tried to give myself a haircut, but it didn't go so well. Win fixed it as good as he could."

Arlene's eyes filled with tears as she ran a hand over it. "I wish you wouldn't have done that. It looks so strange. I almost thought some stranger had just come through the door. I heard you out here and wanted to come make sure you were ok."

"Not really, Ma. I have a lot of questions and I'm mad at you and Pa," Billy said, moving away from her touch.

Arlene pursed her lips. "Well, we're not too pleased with you, either, right at the moment. Let me know when you're finished out here and then we'll talk."

He nodded and went back to work. Arlene stood watching him for a moment and then left him to it. A half hour later, he had things back in order, although he was minus a good amount of almost completed work. He'd have to work hard to make up for it and then he thought, what was the point? His artwork was never going to help him get past the stigma and prejudice he would deal with all of his life, so why bother creating it?

Done with the job, he found his mother dusting in the parlor. She saw him and looked up. "All finished?"

"Yeah."

"Let's go back out there and talk," she said.

Billy led the way and they sat on his bed.

"Now, I know you want to know about your birth parents," Arlene said. "Your father and I always planned on telling you, but you never asked, so we just let it go. We weren't trying to hide anything from you."

"Ok."

Taking a deep breath, Arlene said, "Remus was in the military, as you know. He and his unit were in South Dakota rounding up Indians. He didn't like it, Billy, not one little bit, but he had his orders. I want you to know that he never harmed any of them and if it had been up to him, he would have just left them be."

Billy nodded his understanding.

"One night a bunch of the men had gotten drunk and went after a small Indian camp. Your pa tried to talk them out of it, but they wouldn't listen to him. He fought with a couple of them and they knocked him out. By the time he'd come to, it was too late; the damage had been done." Arlene pressed her hands together to keep them from shaking. "He went to the camp to see what had happened and he was sick over all of the people who were dead. He started looking through the camp to see if there was anyone he could help, but they were either dead or dying."

Tears started in Billy's eyes as mental images of what it must have been like came to him.

Arlene cleared her throat and went on. "There was one woman who was very badly injured but still alive. She saw your father and started yelling at him in English, telling him to go away, that the army had already done enough damage. After talking to her for several minutes, he convinced her that he wasn't one of the men responsible for the slaughter. She pulled her buffalo hide away from her and there you were in her arms.

"She knew she was going to die and begged Remus to take you and care for you. He tried to explain that he had to go back to his regiment, but she insisted that he take you, pleading with him to save her son from death. She said she could die in peace knowing that you were safe. Remus asked her your name and she said, 'Two Moons' because you were born on the second month of the year.

"So we used that as your last name and named you William after my father. She was married to a brave who was a mix of Lakota and Nez Perce. She was three-quarters Cheyenne and a quarter white. Your father died trying to defend their village from the army."

"How did we come here? What did Pa do with me," Billy asked. Tears ran down his face at the thought that his parents had perished.

"This is something you can never repeat to anyone, Billy. At least not for a long time," Arlene warned. "He deserted. Right then and there, he took you and ran away back to me. He told me what happened and said that he couldn't take you back to his unit because someone would have killed you and they most likely would have, too. We packed up and moved to Canada for a short time."

"We fed you cow's milk, goat's milk, or sometimes we were able to find a new mother who was willing to feed you. It was a relief once you were older and could eat regular food," Arlene said.

"Pa deserted so you could raise me?" Billy asked. "Why didn't he just find some Indians to give me to?"

Arlene said, "It would have been hard to locate them and you needed fed right away. It was too risky for him to be running around searching for Indians when he was wanted by the military. We did what we had to in order to save you. You've been the biggest joy to us, Billy. I've never been able to have children and after two miscarriages, well, we just knew that it wasn't meant to be. But we had you."

Feeling ashamed, Billy lowered his head as tears fell from his eyes.

His parents had loved him enough to run away from the army and live in another country just to keep him safe. "How did we wind up here?"

"Well, Remus heard there was work to be had here from a friend of his. We thought it would be a good place to live because all of the Indians had been moved away from here and we wouldn't have to worry about the military finding us since they wouldn't have any reason to come here. By then, no one knew who your father was anyway. You were three when we came here," Arlene said.

Billy raised his head and looked her in the eyes. "I'm grateful to you and Pa for doing what you did, but Ma, I don't fit in anywhere. No one around here will ever see me as anything but an Indian and it'll be the same no matter where I go. I can't go to a reservation because I don't belong with Indians, either. Don't you see? I'm stuck between both worlds and there's no place for me in either one."

"Your pa told me about what happened at Spike's last night and I'm so sorry about it. I know it must be hard for you, and it breaks my heart, but I'm not sorry about keeping you, Billy. So you can be angry at us all you want, but my feelings won't change. You have to decide if you're going to back down from the people who act like Rob did or if you're going to stand your ground and not let them get to you when they say things like that," she said.

"But how am I supposed to not react? How do I just let it go?" Billy asked. "I was so embarrassed and it really showed me that no one outside of my family and a few friends will ever accept me because of what I am."

Arlene smoothed a hand over his hair again and said, "I wish I could help you with that more, Billy, but I'm afraid that's something you have to figure out on your own. All I can tell you is how proud we are of you. You're a smart, talented, kind, handsome young man who's always been so funny and good-natured and I'd hate to see all of that change. It would kill me to see you become bitter and angry all the time. You should be proud of yourself and not let anyone decide your self-worth, but you."

She embraced him and kissed him before going back in the house again, leaving him to think over all she'd told him.

Chapter Twenty-One

Finally the day came for Evan and Josie to go pick up Opal and Sean. Win went with them, however, he had his own things he planned to do, so he'd informed them that they were on their own once they reached Corbin and that they could do whatever they wanted to do. There would be no judgement from him.

Evan and Josie had laughed at his cavalier attitude, but said they had no plans to do anything inappropriate to which Win had responded, "That's too bad. No piece of paper should keep you from enjoying yourself, but that's up to you."

They hadn't been in Corbin very long until Win had taken off. He told them he'd meet them at the hotel for breakfast the next morning and to not worry about him.

"He's a very strange man," Josie said as they headed for the train station to meet her friends.

Evan shrugged. "Maybe. He's had a lot to put up with over the years and he just decided to do things his way and the hell with anyone who didn't like it. He doesn't believe in God or any other god, either."

Josie looked at him. "He's an atheist?"

"Yep. He needs evidence before he'll believe something and since there's been no evidence in his life of that sort of thing, he doesn't believe in it," Evan said.

"That's terrible," Josie said. "I feel badly for him."

Evan smiled as he pulled the wagon to a stop at the station. "Don't. He's happy as he is, so that's all that matters. He and Lucky argue about it constantly. It's pretty funny to hear them."

Josie didn't answer because she spotted Opal and climbed down from the wagon without waiting for Evan to help her. She flew towards the depot.

"Opal!" she called out. "Opal! Over here!" She waved frantically at her.

Opal's eyes lit up as she caught sight of Josie. With a little cry of delight, she left Sean to run to Josie. The two women embraced, tears of joy running down their faces as they talked over each other and laughed.

Sean and Evan introduced themselves to one another as the women talked. Then Josie introduced Evan to Opal.

"My goodness, you certainly found yourself a rugged, handsome man, Josie," she said, her brown eyes twinkling.

Evan grinned. "I like a woman who flatters me. Feel free to keep going."

Opal giggled. "And he has a sense of humor, too. Always an important quality in a man."

Josie said, "Yes, he's quite a good catch. I'm a lucky woman."

Evan returned her look and the love between the two of them was very evident to Opal and Sean. They were both very happy for Josie.

The men loaded their suitcases into the wagon. By now, Evan had taught Josie how to drive not only a buggy, but the wagon as well since there were going to be times when she would need to take it somewhere. She and Opal sat up on the wagon seat while the men sat in the back.

As they pulled out onto the street, Opal said, "Look at you, driving a wagon and all. You've become a real frontier woman."

"I don't know about that, but I'm certainly very self-sufficient now thanks to Evan and Lucky. And Thad and Billy. Well, there's really a lot of people who have been helpful in educating me about the best way to do things in Echo," Josie said.

"I can't wait to meet all these handsome men—and Edna, too."

Josie smiled. "You'll love her. She's so feisty and funny."

"So you've said." Opal looked surreptitiously at the men. Since they seemed engrossed in their own conversation, she leaned closer to Josie and in a low voice asked, "Will we meet this Marvin? I want to see how evil he is for myself."

A chill ran through Josie at the mention of the man. "I'm sure we'll run into him at some point, although I would prefer not to."

"Is he really that bad?"

Josie nodded. "Yes. You stay away from him," she said, giving Opal a serious look.

Opal was fascinated. "All right, but if I'm with you, it'll be fine. I can't help but be curious."

"Once you meet him, you won't be curious anymore," Josie said. "He's no one to fool with. I've learned how to handle him, but I wouldn't want you to fall for his pleasant act."

"I won't," Opal said.

The subject was dropped before Evan overheard what they were saying. Josie avoided talking about Marvin because the mere mention of the man angered Evan. She'd run into him quite often ever since she'd lunched with him and he always extended an invitation to her to come back, but she neatly rebuffed him every time. He always chuckled and went on his way.

Josie turned her thoughts away from Marvin and concentrated on her friends and fiancé. They all checked in at their hotel and took their luggage to their rooms. That done, they went to eat at a nice restaurant Evan knew and had a wonderful time. Evan liked the other couple very much and it seemed as if they felt the same about him.

Evan then took them to a saloon that ran a cleaner operation than many and they danced and had some drinks. It was late by the time they got back to the hotel. Opal and Sean bid Evan and Josie goodnight and went to their room.

Leaving Josie for the night was difficult for Evan and he almost gave in to his craving for her, thinking that their wedding was only a week away, so what would it matter if they made love now? Her kisses and embrace were intoxicating, much more so than the liquor they'd drank, and he always felt like he was drowning in a pool of passion. He found the strength to pull away from her and go to his own room. Sleep was a long time coming as he lay burning for her.

The morning of their wedding day, Evan whistled to himself as he got dressed in his tuxedo at home. Since it wasn't far to the church, he'd opted to get ready at home—it was just easier than carting his suit there. Besides, he wanted a little time alone to quiet his nerves.

Edna had been picked up by Tansy and Sonya and the three women had rode away in Tansy's carriage, laughing and teasing each other. Evan had smiled as he'd watched them ride away. He was glad to see his aunt get out of the house for a while and he decided to talk to Josie about helping him talk her into doing it more often. Josie had a way of convincing his aunt to do things.

Looking in the mirror, Evan made sure his tie was straight and smoothed his lapels as he hummed and sang. He didn't care that he sounded horrible, he enjoyed it anyway. Evan was an excellent lawman, he could cook, clean, and crochet like nobody's business, but when it came to anything musical, he had no talent. He was always awed by Josie's singing and guitar playing and he hoped that their children would inherit her musical abilities.

They'd joked that maybe they'd have guitar playing deputies. He laughed thinking about it as he went out to the parlor. His eyes swept over the parlor, making sure that everything was in order. Lucky had volunteered to stay with Edna while Evan and Josie went on their honeymoon in Helena for two weeks. Thad was once again filling in for him as lawman, with Lucky also willing to play deputy if need be. He'd said that since him and Thad were Irishmen, they had to stick together.

Seeing that everything was as it should be, Evan moved towards the front door, his excitement over the wedding mounting. His thoughts were so centered on his bride-to-be that he never heard someone come up behind him. All he knew was that one moment, he'd been about to walk out the door and the next he was hit on the back of his head. Even though he went down, he kept consciousness somehow.

However, his assailant wasted no time in making sure he didn't get up again. They pinned him down with a knee to his back and shoved a chloroform-soaked rag into his face. Evan tried not to breathe, but eventually his lungs needed oxygen and he had to inhale. Swiftly, he descended into blackness.

Josie stood in the church office being fussed over by Opal, Tansy, and Sonya.

Sonya had done her hair and was putting the finishing touches on it. "You look beautiful, honey," she told Josie.

Edna said, "I agree with Sonya. Evan won't know what hit him."

Peering into a mirror, Josie said, "Thank you. I'm so nervous. What if I can't be a good wife? I don't want to trip or make a mistake saying my vows. I can't do this! Why did I think I could?"

Opal took Josie by the shoulders. "Deep breaths. Don't hyperventilate on us. I felt the same on my wedding day, remember? Look how that turned out. I couldn't be any happier. It'll be the same with you and Evan. You've found your perfect mate and everything is going to be fine."

Josie nodded. "Ok. You're right. I mean, being a wife isn't too much different than being engaged, except that we're not living together. We've been together so much that we might as well have been."

Tansy chuckled. "That's true. You two already act like a married couple, except for, well, you know what I mean."

"Sex," Edna said bluntly. "Why do people have such trouble with that word? It's not hard to say and there's nothing wrong with saying it."

Sonya giggled and said, "Well, in polite society, it's not really acceptable."

"Well, we're not in polite society so there's nothing wrong with saying it," Edna retorted. "Besides, I never had any time for polite society."

Josie laughed. "We can tell."

Edna just grinned.

———

Thad looked at his watch again and looked out the church doors to see if Evan was coming down the street. Pastor Sam Watson came to stand by Thad.

"No sign of him yet, huh?" he asked.

Thad turned towards him, finding himself face-to-chest with the man. "Hey, Sam, can you back up a little?"

"Oh, sorry," Sam said, moving away slightly.

Sam was around six-foot-seven and built like a brick wall. When he wasn't being a preacher, Sam made extra money for his wife and family by doing some logging and other heavy labor. His brown eyes looked down the street, but he didn't see Evan, either. However, he did see Billy coming their way.

Sam smiled and said, "Here comes, Billy. His hair is starting to grow back."

"Yeah. He's really happy about it. That'll teach him to cut it again. I'll be glad when it's long again. He looks weird without it," Thad said.

Billy's expression was grim as he mounted the church steps. "He's not at home and the buggy is gone, too. I went in the house and everything. Nothing looked wrong. Neat as a pin like always."

Thad said, "Something's wrong. Evan's never late. You can set your clock by him. Where the hell would he have gone? Some kind of trouble must have come up that he needed to handle, but I can't figure what it would be."

Billy took off his suit jacket and gave it to Thad. "I'll go get my horse and start looking for him."

"Ok. We'll stay here in case he shows up," Thad said.

Billy nodded and replied, "Right. If he does, don't wait on me. Go ahead and start. Josie's already nervous enough without having to wait longer than necessary."

Sam said, "Ok."

Billy jogged out of sight to the back of the church where the horses were tied. Thad looked at his watch again and sighed. His gut was telling him that something drastic was keeping Evan from his wedding and his instincts were rarely wrong.

"Where is he?" Josie said as she paced back and forth in the church office.

Evan was half an hour late, which wasn't like him at all. The whole time she'd known him, Evan had never been late anywhere. He was as punctual as he was neat.

Edna was very concerned, too, but she tried to keep Josie as calm as possible. "I'm sure he'll be here. Whatever it is must be very important. You know how much he loves you and he'd never let anything keep him from your wedding. He'll be here."

Josie nodded as Tansy and Opal exchanged glances. Someone knocked on the door and Sonya opened it. Lucky stood on the other side with a grim expression on his face.

He looked over at Josie with sadness in his eyes. "I'm sorry, but he's still not here, lass."

Beginning to panic, she said, "How could he do this to me? If he wasn't ready or he didn't want to marry me, why wouldn't he tell me?"

Lucky entered the room and said, "Evan would never stand ya up. Your weddin' is all he's talked about. Somethin' musta happened."

Josie was hurt and humiliated. "He's almost forty-five minutes late. He's not coming. Now I have to go out there and tell all those people that there won't be a wedding today."

Lucky said, "Let's wait a little longer."

Tears brimmed in her eyes. "No. He's not coming and we all know it. Billy said the buggy is gone and that everything looks fine. He's taken off somewhere."

Edna said, "He might not be coming, but I don't believe he ran off, sweetheart. We can't think like that."

"I'm trying not to," Josie said, sitting down by Edna.

Edna took her hand and said, "Let's do what Lucky said and give him a little longer."

Josie nodded, but kept her eyes downcast. The others in the room exchanged glances, but they weren't much more hopeful than her.

Evan came to gradually, rising up through fuzzy layers to full consciousness. His head ached so badly that it hurt to open his eyes. Finally he managed it and discovered that it was dark and that he laid on the ground out in what he thought were the woods. He couldn't move and discovered that it was because he was bound and gagged.

He took in huge breaths of night air through his nose, trying to clear his mind. He needed to figure out where he was and the exact nature of his situation. Although his head still throbbed, he could put coherent thought together. Fortunately, his hands were tied in front of him instead of behind his back. It would make it easier to untie his legs.

Rolling up onto his elbow, he felt the sharp stab of a knife against his left palm and made a noise of pain and surprise. Looking down, he discovered that whoever had tied him up, had left a knife for him so he could get loose. He didn't question it right then, instead taking advantage of the knife.

From a young age, he'd been schooled in how to get out of all sorts of restraints: ropes, handcuffs, shackles, and chains. He made quick work of the rope around his wrists and then untied the gag from his mouth. Once his feet were free, he tried to stand up, but staggered and fell down onto his knees. Waiting for several minutes, Evan grabbed a tree next to him and hauled himself upwards, leaning against it for support while he gained his bearings.

The whole time he kept a good grip on the knife, ready to use it if need be. It was second nature to him to brush himself off and as he did so, he discovered a piece of paper safety pinned to his suit jacket. Ripping it off, Evan tried to read it, but it was too dark for him to make out what it said. Then he realized that his hand was wet from where he'd touched his suit. Smelling it, he realized that he was soaked with whiskey.

"What the hell?" he asked no one.

He took another couple minutes to catch his breath and let some more of the pain in his head recede. Starting out, he was determined to get out of the woods so he could figure out where he was and get back to town. As his brain became even more alert, he stopped walking, remembering that the reason he was wearing a tuxedo was because it had been his wedding day.

"Oh, no," he mumbled. "She's gonna think I stood her up."

His eagerness to get to his fiancée fueled him, giving him the strength to move faster through the forest. Dread filled him as he thought about how hurt and angry Josie was bound to be. How was he going to explain this? He didn't know, but he would do anything to make her see that he would never have left her at the altar.

Upon coming out of the woods, Evan was surprised to see that he was in back of the Burgundy House, the saloon on the other side of Echo. He now heard music and laughter as he came closer to it. This was not helping him to figure out what had happened. That someone had kidnapped him he knew, but to what end?

As he walked through the lot out back, men and saloon girls walked past him. A couple of them recognized him and even spoke to him. Evan never answered them, intent on getting back home. Looking over at the line of horses and buggies by the hitching post, Evan noticed his own buggy with Smitty hitched to it.

Things were getting more and more bizarre. Why was his horse and buggy at the Burgundy House? He knew he hadn't come there today. The last thing he remembered was getting ready to leave for the church and then everything had gone dark. Making his way over to Smitty, he patted his horse, who nickered at him.

Evan untied the reins and backed him out from between the other horses. Then he stopped and took the piece of paper out of his pocket. There was now enough light for him to read it.

> *Evan, I'm so sorry to do this to you, but I didn't know any other way. You were right about me and Marvin. I didn't know how to tell you. I hope one day you'll be able to forgive me.*

Evan read the note five times, but each time it said the same thing— betrayal. He stuffed it back in his pocket along with the knife. Fully alert now, Evan got in the buggy and put Smitty into a canter, so he could get to the boarding house as soon as possible and confront Josie.

At the same time, Thad, Lucky, and Jerry descended on the Earnest ranch. Marvin was sitting in the parlor when the front door smashed open and the three men entered the house. Although greatly startled, Marvin stayed put in his chair. Recovering, he offered them a smile as they came into the parlor.

"Hello, gentlemen. How are you this evening? I thought you'd be at the reception or passed out drunk somewhere," he said, laying aside the book he'd been reading.

Thad pulled out his gun and pointed it at Marvin. "Where is he? Tell me now or I'm going to put a bullet in your crotch."

Marvin frowned. "Must you be so uncouth? Couldn't you just shoot me in the leg?"

Thad blinked once. "No. It'll hurt worse in the crotch and then you won't be able to reproduce."

Marvin sighed as though bored. "Very well, but before you do, would you care to enlighten me as to who you're looking for?"

"You know damn well who," Thad said, coming closer.

Marvin cocked his head a little and said, "No, I don't. If I did, I wouldn't ask who it is. That would be a waste of time. Now, who is it?"

"Evan," Lucky piped up. "He's missin' and we know ya have him."

"I do love your accent," Marvin said, with a smile. "Are you all playing some joke on me? Shouldn't he be with his wife on their wedding night? Why would he be here?"

Jerry said, "He didn't show up for the wedding and no one can find him. You did something to him. Now where is he?"

"Mr. Belker, I don't have Evan. I mean, do you really see me overpowering him? I'm strong, but I don't have his fighting capabilities. Besides, I've been here all day. How could I kidnap Evan from here?"

"Jerry, guard him. Lucky, you and I are going to search this place from top to bottom," Thad said. "Let's go."

Unperturbed, Marvin simply re-crossed his legs and said, "Jerry, why don't you have a seat while we wait?"

"Sure," Jerry said, sitting down on the sofa. "I can shoot you just as well sitting down as standing up."

"Of course you can," Marvin stated in a reasonable tone of voice.

Thad watched the way Marvin acted. The man wasn't jumpy or nervous in any way despite the fact that they were going to search his house. He couldn't figure out if it was Marvin's unique ability to lie and present a pleasant demeanor when he wanted or if it meant that he was actually innocent.

"Let's go, Lucky," he said and the two men began their search.

Marvin looked at Jerry and asked, "Would you like some brandy? There's some over on the table over there. It's some special stock that I recently bought."

Jerry said, "You make me sick. You pay your hands such low wages even though they deserve a lot more. Then you buy all this expensive crap. You oughta be ashamed of yourself."

Marvin gave him a smile and said, "Well, first off, since it *is* my money, I guess I can spend it any way I choose. Secondly, I just gave Travis a very nice raise not long ago, or hadn't he told anyone?"

Jerry's eyebrows climbed high on his head over that. "You gave him a raise? Why? What's in it for you?"

An annoyed look crossed Marvin's face. "You know, contrary to popular belief, I do appreciate Travis and he does a good job around here. I merely wanted to show my appreciation. I think it's strange that he hasn't mentioned it, though. Why would he hide it?"

Jerry had to admit that it was strange. Most guys would have bragged about getting a raise, but Travis hadn't said a word about it. "I don't know. Travis can be private sometimes."

"Oh, well, I didn't realize I was divulging private information. I'll apologize to him on Monday. I hope you don't think it rude of me to go back to my reading while we wait? I'm at a very good part and I'm anxious to see what happens."

Jerry said, "Suit yourself."

Marvin smiled and began reading again.

Chapter Twenty-Two

Thad and Lucky's search of Marvin's house turned up nothing. They searched each and every room thoroughly, along with the huge basement and the attic. There was no sign of Evan anywhere. They entered Marvin's parlor almost forty-five minutes later.

"Ok, he's not here. You could still be holding him somewhere else," Thad said.

"To what end?" Marvin said. "Why would I do that knowing full-well that I'd be the first person you'd blame for his disappearance? That would be idiotic of me, wouldn't it?"

"Who knows with you, Earnest? Why do you do anything? You're twisted in the head and you like to screw with people just because you can," Thad said. "You could have paid someone to do your dirty work."

"Yes, I certainly could, but I didn't. I have no issue with Evan. I don't bother him and he doesn't bother me."

Lucky stepped forward. "Maybe ya want Josie for yerself and figure that with Evan out of the way, ya can win her over."

Marvin actually laughed over his remark. "I can assure you that I have no romantic interest in Josie. She's not my type at all. I like someone a little more ... experienced, I guess you'd say and it's easy to see that Josie is very innocent in that respect."

Thad could hear the ring of truth in Marvin's voice, but said, "That didn't stop you from messin' with Louise."

Marvin stood up and came right over to Thad, disregarding the fact that the older man was aiming a revolver at him. "I am so tired of people bringing that up to me. You know how much I adored my father. On his life, I swear that I did nothing that Louise didn't want me to do and that I was not the one who instigated it. I also swear that her virginity was already gone by the time she got around to me. I was not the one to take it."

Staring back into Marvin's eyes, Thad saw the conviction there and thought that maybe he was telling the truth. It was hard to say with Marvin, who told lies so easily and convincingly. However, he did know that Marvin still worshipped his father and that for him to swear on his old man was the one sure way to know that he was telling the truth.

"So swear to me on your father's life that you have no idea where Evan is and that you didn't do anything to him," Thad said, narrowing his eyes.

Stepping even closer to his unwitting competitor for Phoebe's affections, Marvin said, "I do not know where Evan is, I did not hire someone to do anything to him, and I have no wish to harm him, nor do I have any designs on Josie. I swear it on Father's life."

Thad stared back at him for several minutes and then put his gun back into his holster. "Let's go, men." He turned and walked out the front door again.

Jerry and Lucky looked at each other and then at Marvin. He smiled at them and said, "Have a pleasant evening, gentlemen. I hope you find the good sheriff and that he's all right."

Lucky scowled at him and followed Thad and Jerry out the door. Marvin shut it, but didn't lock it. He never bothered locking his doors. Sighing, he went into his office and opened the closet door. Stepping into it, he found a different hidden button than the one used to open the secret panel. It was rigged to a bell system that alerted Shadow to various things. Marvin pressed it only once; their signal that he wanted to see his brother.

Marvin sat on the edge of his desk to wait. Soon, the hidden panel slid open and Shadow stepped through it.

"What have you done now, Shadow?"

Josie sat in her room with Opal, misery weighing her down as though a steamboat anchor hung around her neck. Her head and eyes hurt from all the crying she'd done. Someone knocked loudly on the door, making the women jump.

"I'll get it," Opal said.

She opened the door and gasped as she recognized Evan. He was bedraggled, dirty, and smelled like booze.

"Evan! What on earth?" Opal asked, stepping back slightly.

"That's why I'd like to know," he said.

Josie stood up upon hearing who it was. She saw him and her heart sped up. "Where have you been? How could you just leave me there like that?"

Evan moved past Opal. "How could you do this to me? How could you lead me on like this?"

Josie's eyes widened at his accusatory tone. "What are you talking about?"

Evan took out the note and thrust it at her. "This is what I'm talking about."

Josie took it and read it, her mouth dropping open. She looked into Evan's green eyes that blazed with anger. "I didn't write this and I would never ... I could never ..."

"Never marry a lowly sheriff when you could have him and he could give you money and keep you in style? So you could have a better life, move up a station or two?" Evan growled.

"Of course not! You stood me up at the church!"

"Only because you had someone kidnap me and leave me in the

woods so that I missed the wedding. It was nice of them to leave me a knife so I could get loose. Was that your idea?" Evan asked in a cruel voice.

Josie paled in the face of his rage and then hers began burning bright. She yelled, "I didn't do anything to you and I'm not sleeping with Marvin! I haven't ever been out to his place except for that one day. I love you or I did! I am not a cheater!"

"Liar!" Evan shouted back. "I don't know how you managed it, but I'll find out and then I'll slap cuffs on you and haul your sweet ass to jail as an accomplice to kidnapping and assault! Mark my words, I'll get to the bottom of it if it takes me years to do it!"

By this time, a crowd had gathered outside the room. Arthur stepped inside it and took Evan by the shoulders. "Evan, you need to leave. I know both of you are upset. Everyone needs to cool off right now and we don't need our other guests upset by all of this."

Evan turned to Arthur and shrugged him off. "I'll go. I have nothing more to say. Just remember what I said." He gave Josie a glare and then pushed his way past Arthur and Sean, who'd also come to make Evan leave. He'd almost made it to the door when he felt something hit him in the back of the head. Turning he looked down at the floor and saw Josie's engagement ring lying there.

Finding her eyes through the people between them, he raised his foot and brought it down hard on the piece of jewelry. Removing it, he saw that diamond hadn't broken, but the ring was bent out of shape. Turning again, he stomped from the room and ran down the steps. He slammed the front door shut behind him.

Edna was shocked when Evan came in the door in such poor shape.

"Good Lord, Evan! Where have you been? What happened to you?" she asked, rising stiffly from her chair.

Staying right inside the door, Evan began stripping. "I'll tell you as soon as I get cleaned up. Will you make some coffee? I'll be back

3

shortly." He walked quickly to his bedroom, snagged his robe, and took off his underwear before wrapping the robe around him. He took all of his clothes and dumped them out on the back porch before going down the path to the creek to bathe.

When he returned to the house, he put on underwear and his robe before going out to the kitchen. He poured both him and Edna a cup of coffee, put a splash of whiskey in both of them and carried them into the parlor. After handing one to his aunt, he wearily sat in his chair. His head still throbbed and he was exhausted.

Edna stayed quiet, letting him drink some coffee before telling her what had happened. It was apparent that he didn't need medical attention, so some of her fear had abated.

He cleared his throat and told her what had occurred. When he was done, he said, "I can't believe she did this to me. I can't believe he did this again. Why does he hate me so much?"

Edna said, "Evan, you're not thinking clearly right now. Josie would never do that to you."

He gave her a mirthless smile. "She would if Marvin got his hooks into her. Look at what he did with Louise."

"That was Louise. Josie is not the kind of woman to do something like this," Edna said. "I think you need to get some sleep and look at this with fresh eyes in the morning."

Just then the door opened and Thad, Lucky, and Jerry entered the house.

"Evan!" Thad said. "Are you ok? Where the hell have you been?"

Evan rubbed a hand over his face and motioned for them to sit down. Once more he recounted his story.

"None of this makes any sense," Lucky said. "We were just out at Earnest's place and searched it for ya. We didn't find anything, of course, since you're here, but we didn't see nothin' amiss, either."

Thad said, "Evan, I saw your clothes outside and they reek of alcohol. Are you sure you just didn't get cold feet and go on a bender somewhere no one would suspect you'd go?"

Evan's eyes glittered with rage. "I've never chickened out of anything, Thad, and you know it! Why would I chicken out on marrying the woman I love?"

Thad countered with, "Why would the woman who loves you cheat on you with someone as slimy as Earnest?"

Lucky said, "Evan, you're wrong about Josie. I was with her today and there's no faking the kind of anguish she's been in. I'm very offended that you'd think somethin' like that about her."

Evan's temper rose when he saw that Lucky was also getting angry. "Maybe it was you?"

"Me?" Lucky asked. "What are ya talkin' about?"

"You've been sniffing around her ever since you got here with her. Playing the hero and befriending everyone," Evan said. He knew on some level that he was being irrational, but he couldn't seem to stop himself.

Lucky laughed and said, "Lad, if I'd have wanted Josie for my own, I'd have had her by now. No, Josie loves *you* and all I feel for her is friendship. I'm gonna go before this gets any worse. Goodnight, everyone. Get some rest, Evan. Things'll look better in the morning."

Once Lucky was gone, Jerry said, "Evan, Earnest swore to us on his father's life that he had nothing to do with what happened to you and I gotta say that I believe him. You know how he is about his father."

Thad nodded. "He lies and schemes about all kinds of stuff, but when he swears on his father's life about something, you know he's telling the truth. He swore that he has no interest in Josie and I believe him."

"Who else would do this to me?" Evan said. "Who else would wanna keep me from getting married? What's in it for them?"

"I don't know," Jerry said. "None of it makes any sense. You're right; if not Earnest, then who?"

Thad said, "Well, we're not gonna find any answers tonight. Like me and Reb always taught you, Evan, sometimes you have to regroup and get your mind right again so you can look at something with fresh eyes. Meet me at the office in the morning and we'll get workin' on it, ok?"

Getting up, he patted Evan's shoulder and gave Edna a kiss. Jerry did the same and followed Thad from the house. Soon after, Edna and Evan went to bed, but Evan never went to sleep, instead turning things around and around in his mind but getting no closer to an answer.

He cried silent tears as he thought about how he should be laying with Josie in his arms right then instead of alone and miserable in his bed. It was supposed to have been the happiest day in his life, but instead it was the most miserable since he'd lost his family. He cursed whoever had done this to him and vowed to find the culprit.

Chapter Twenty-Three

E van wasn't the only one who'd had a sleepless night. Josie had lain all through the night, her eyes wide open, staring sightlessly at the window. It didn't really register with her when daylight came. She had no more tears to cry, but she ached inside and her heart still shed tears.

Someone knocked on her door, but she didn't respond or move. They knocked again and then opened the door. Opal appeared in her line of vision, but she didn't greet her friend.

"Josie? Are you hungry? Would you like some coffee or tea?" Opal asked.

Josie blinked and whispered, "No." Her throat hurt from all the sobbing she'd done the day and night before.

"How about some water?" Opal said. She was worried sick about Josie and hadn't slept well herself.

"No. Please just leave me be," Josie said. "I need to be alone."

Opal said, "Josie, I know you're hurting very badly, but you have to at least drink something."

Knowing that Opal wasn't going to go away until she got what she wanted, Josie snapped, "Fine! Just coffee."

Opal said, "Ok. I'll be back."

Suddenly rage overtook Josie with surprising force. "No, on second thought, I'll be down soon." She rose from bed and said, "I just need to freshen up and then I'll join you."

Opal was shocked by the abrupt change in her. "Are you sure?"

"Yes. I have something I need to go do," she said. "Shoo, Opal."

Opal gave her a doubtful look, but left the room.

Evan thought that he was seeing things when Josie walked in the door of the sheriff's office. She walked over to his desk, her eyes burning with rage. She slapped the piece of paper that had been pinned to his tuxedo jacket down on the desk and snatched up a pencil that was lying on his desk. Right underneath the last words of the note, she wrote the exact same thing.

"Since we wrote so many letters to each other, I'm surprised that you didn't realize the handwriting on this note and mine are nothing alike," Josie said. "Sometimes when people say they're innocent, they're telling the truth, just like I am. You should look in the mirror if you want to see a guilty person."

Then she turned on her heel and stomped from the office, leaving Evan and Thad sitting there in stunned silence.

"Why do you want to go all the way up here?" Billy asked. "If you wanna see the sheep, we should have gone the other way."

Josie huffed and puffed as she followed Billy. "I'm not going to see the sheep. I want to see the mine."

"Why?" Billy asked.

"I've never seen it since I always go the other way to see the sheep, and I want to see it before I leave," Josie said.

Billy turned around. "You're leaving?"

"Yes. There's nothing for me here now. I mean, I know that I have friends, but I couldn't stand seeing Evan all the time," Josie said.

"Can't you guys work it out? Evan wasn't in his right mind yesterday. He was drugged and kidnapped, after all," Billy said. "I'm not saying that some of the stuff he said was right, but I don't think that he really meant them."

"Oh, he meant them, Billy," she said. "No. I'll be going back to Pullman. I'll miss everyone, but I'll write to you."

Billy had come to think of Josie as sort of a big sister. "It won't be the same. Who's gonna teach me guitar now? I don't want you to go." She'd been showing him how to play the instrument and he'd been making good headway on it.

"I wish I didn't have to, but it's clear to me that as long as I stay here, Evan will always be worried that I'll develop feelings for Marvin," she said. "I can't live like that." She put a hand on his arm. "You're doing so well with your guitar playing that you'll be fine if you just keep practicing. I'm sure there's someone in Dickensville who can teach you."

He just shrugged and began moving again.

They reached the summit and stood looking down over the valley where the sheep were located. They saw Win and waved to him. He waved back at them.

"When we're done here, we'll go down so I can tell him goodbye and see the sheep one last time," Josie said. "So this is the mine, huh?"

She looked at the entrance and saw that the support beams were in poor condition. They looked about to give way any moment. Although curious about the inside of the mine, she knew better than to go inside it. "It's not very exciting, is it?" she remarked.

Billy smiled at her as the wind ruffled his growing hair. "No. I told you it wasn't."

Josie said, "Well, at least now I can say I've seen one."

She took out the engagement ring that Evan had given her and looked at its bent form. The diamond still glittered, but to Josie it had lost its shine and was no longer beautiful. She no longer wanted it, and since Evan didn't want it back, she was going to put it where no one would ever find it.

Billy saw what she was about to going to do and said, "Aw, Josie, don't do that."

Josie didn't respond. She drew her arm back and threw the ring as hard as she could into the mine. It made no sound and Jose surmised that it had gone too far into the mineshaft for them to hear it make contact with anything. It drove home to her that all of her dreams of a life with Evan were also gone.

"I wish you wouldn't have done that," Billy said to her.

"I wish I wouldn't have had to. He didn't want it and neither do I," Josie said.

"You could have sold it," he said.

"No. I would always know where the money came from. It's better this way. Let's go see the sheep."

With a shake of his head, Billy started for the other side of the mine. As he looked down at the scene below, he thought how idyllic it looked with the lush green grass and white, fluffy sheep. Win's cabin only added to the picture and he thought this would be a good vantage point from which to paint a picture.

He saw the sheep beginning to get restless and the dogs started running to and fro. Then the sheep bolted, their loud bleats reaching their ears.

"What's wrong with them?" Josie asked.

Billy scanned the area and saw nothing that would alarm the sheep. He waved to Win and made a questioning gesture to him. Win made the same gesture back to him right before the earth beneath them heaved, throwing them down onto the ground. It did it again and stopped. Billy and Josie lay there afraid to move.

"Was that just an earthquake?" she asked, breathlessly.

"Uh huh."

Just as they got to their knees, it happened again, only this time it was much stronger and they were hurled towards the edge of the mountain.

Win hung onto a tree he was standing by, his powerful muscles keeping him upright even as the ground bucked and shuddered. He tried to keep a watch for Billy and Josie, knowing that they were in grave danger. As he looked up to where they had been, a hole opened up in the side of the mountain facing him and he was almost certain he saw them slide into it.

Slowly the world settled down again. Win waited a few minutes to make sure it wasn't going to start up again as soon as he let go of the tree. Then he ran to his cabin, grabbed two ropes, a lantern, matches, and a shovel. Armed with his supplies, he raced across the pastureland and began to scale the mountain.

Fortunately, most of Echo was spared great damage from the earthquake. Most of it centered on the eastern end of town. There were people hurt, however, and Evan and others tried to do their best to help them. Once again, Evan cursed the fact that the town had no doctor. He was just finishing up bandaging the leg of a little boy as best he could when Win ran up to him.

"Evan, you need to come with me and we need to take a bunch of men with us," he said.

Evan looked into Win's wide, dark eyes and saw terror in their depths. Nothing ever rattled Win, so something had to be dreadfully wrong for Win to act like this. "What is it?"

"It's Billy and Josie. I don't know why, but they were up at the mine. I think they were just getting ready to come down to my place when the quake hit. The mine caved in on my side and they were thrown down in it. I went up with ropes and stuff, but I couldn't find them. I need help."

Evan blanched and felt dizzy with fear for the woman he loved and his friend. Getting a grip on himself, he went back into sheriff mode and said, "All right. Go find Jerry and tell him we're gonna need that horse of his and as much rope as he has. I'll get some rope and grappling hooks that I know Sam has in his barn. Hell, I'll get Sam, too. He's about as good as a draft horse and we sure can use the extra manpower. I'll meet you and whoever else is free to go help up there."

Win set out without wasting time on a response. Evan explained to Tansy, who had been helping with injuries, what had happened and where he was going. She wished him luck and said she'd pray for all of them.

Fortunately for Billy and Josie, they had landed on a shelf that jutted out into the ruined shaft. It wasn't very wide, but it was enough for them to lay on. Billy hadn't lost consciousness, but he wished that he had. He was certain that one of his legs was broken judging by the fact that it hurt so badly that he would have rather just cut it off than deal with the pain.

Feeling around him, his hands encountered Josie. "Josie? Are you ok?"

She didn't answer him and he shook her again, praying that she wasn't dead. Then he remembered that he had matches in his pocket. He always kept them on him because they came in handy to him on a lot of occasions, but he'd never had to use them for this reason. He also always carried his knife.

Lighting a match, he tried to take stock of where they were. The small flame revealed the ledge on which they lay and that Josie didn't look too bad. She had some cuts and bruises, but other than that, it looked like she was all right. Of course, he was no doctor and she could have internal injuries.

When the ground had opened up, they'd grabbed onto each other before falling. It had been his instinct to protect her and it seemed that it had been hers to protect him. As he tried to twist to turn more fully to her, he felt a pain in his back that took his breath away. Flopping back on his back, he concentrated on catching it again.

No daylight reached him and Billy had the sinking sensation that they lying in what would become their tomb. Josie began stirring beside him and he put his arm around her so she didn't roll off the ledge.

"Josie, don't move much," he warned her.

"Billy? Where are we?" she asked, feeling fuzzy.

"Inside the mine somewhere. We're on a ledge of some sort, but it's not very big. I can't see any light so I don't know how far down we are," Billy said. "Are you hurt anywhere?"

Josie moved various body parts, but aside from being sore and her head hurting, she felt fine. "No, I'm ok. You?"

"Not so good. I think my leg is broken and my back is messed up," he said.

"Oh, no. Am I closer to the drop off or are you?"

"You are. I'm right up against the wall."

Josie rolled over towards Billy and propped up on an elbow. "Is there something I can do to help you?"

Billy said, "Not without something to splint my leg with and I don't know if it would do any good right at the moment anyway."

Josie sighed and laid down again. "I guess there's nothing to do but wait and pray that someone finds us."

"Win knew we were there. I'm sure he'll go get help," Billy said. "I just don't know if we're close enough to the top to be helped. This could become unstable any second."

"Ok, quit being the voice of doom," she said.

Billy said, "Just being practical."

Sighing, Josie said, "Let's try to be positive for the moment."

"Ok," Billy said, but didn't sound convincing.

Both of them fell silent knowing that there was nothing else they could do to improve their situation at the moment.

Chapter Twenty-Four

Digging through the rocks and boulders was a delicate task. One wrong move could cause a shift in the mountainside again and any hope of rescuing Josie and Billy would be dashed. Several horses, including Alonso, Jerry's Clydesdale were harnessed and rigged to pulley systems that could be used to remove the larger boulders so they just didn't roll down the incline and cause an avalanche.

Everyone prayed that there were no aftershocks, but the likelihood of that happening was slim. Lucky and many others kept praying that the Earth would remain calm. Finally around early afternoon, they succeeded in breaking through into the mine shaft. Evan lit a lantern and held it out into the open space before poking his head and shoulders through the three foot diameter hole.

He couldn't see much of anything since the lantern didn't do much to dispel the darkness in the huge cavern.

"Hello?" he shouted. "Josie! Billy! Can you hear me?"

From far below, he thought he heard a shout. He waited and faintly, he heard "We're here!"

"Ok! Stay put! We'll get you out!" he screamed so they could hear him.

Down below, Josie said, "Billy! They found us. We're gonna be ok."

Billy smiled as his teeth chattered. He'd gone into shock by this point. "Good."

Josie stopped smiling at his quiet reply. "Billy? Are you all right?" She felt him trembling next to her.

"C-cold," he said.

Josie shifted closer to him and, still being mindful of his leg, she laid partially on top of him to lend him her body heat.

Billy managed to laugh a little and say, "I had no idea you felt that way about me."

She laughed and said, "Shut up and save your energy."

"Listen, if I don't make it promise me a couple of things."

"Don't you dare talk like that, Billy. We're both making it out of here."

"Josie, we don't know how long it's going to take them to get down to us. You'll be all right, but I'm not doing so good, so please just humor me here."

"Ok."

Billy drew in a breath. "Please tell my parents that I love them so much and how grateful I am to them for saving me and for loving me. Tell them that I know how much they sacrificed for me and that I couldn't have any better parents."

Tears stung her eyes. "Ok. I'll tell them, but you're going to be fine."

"There's something else you have to promise me."

"What?"

Billy took another deep breath and said, "After you get out of here, you'll fix things with Evan."

"Oh, Billy, I can't promise you that," she said.

"Yes, you can. This is proof that life is something delicate and that you should be thankful for it. You both deserve to be happy. You're both just stupid and stubborn, that's all. You haven't stopped loving each other, right? You still love him, don't you?"

There was no sense denying it. As much as Evan had hurt her, her heart still belonged to him. "Yes, I still love him, but—"

"No 'but' about it. Where there's love, there's hope. I think Ma told me that one time. It's true. As long as you love each other, you can work things out. Promise me you'll at least try. I love both of you and I want you to be happy. Please promise me you'll try," Billy insisted, starting to feel faint.

Facing the reality of their situation, Josie began to cry, but said, "I promise, Billy. I promise I'll try."

He smiled. "Ok. Thanks."

Josie felt him relax under her. "Billy? Billy?" She shook him a little but he didn't respond. She could feel that he was still breathing.

Looking upwards she screamed, "Hurry! Billy's hurt!"

Hearing her, Evan shouted back his understanding. "We got to get them out quick. Josie said that Billy's hurt."

Win thought of both of his friends and said, "I'm just as strong as you, but I weigh less because I don't have as much bone density weight since I'm shorter. Rig me up and lower me down. I'll bring them back up."

Evan said, "No, I'll go. I'm the sheriff and I should be the one to go in case something happens."

Win said, "That's exactly why you shouldn't go. We need a sheriff around here more than we do a vet and let's face it, no other sheriff will come work here for what we pay you."

Evan chuckled at his wisecrack.

"He's right, Evan. Let him do it," Lucky said. "Win, I promise we won't drop ya."

Win said, "That's comforting."

"Aye, and with me here, you'll surely have good fortune in getting them up out of there," Lucky said.

"That's some ego you got there," Win said, with a smile. "Ok, let's get a move-on."

Slowly, Win was lowered towards his two stranded friends. Hanging out in midair the way he was, Win felt a strange sense of freedom. Where most people would have been scared of plummeting to their death, he found the experience exciting. His only fear was that something would happen before he could get Josie and Billy to safety. Loss of people he loved was the only fear Win had in life.

"Josie, I'm on my way down. Talk to me so I can get a fix on where you are," he shouted.

"Ok. We're over here. I can't see you," she responded.

"I can't see you either. I have a lantern, but I don't want to light it in case I drop it. I'm afraid it might hit you guys. How bad is Billy?"

Josie said, "I think one of his legs is broken and something's wrong with his back. I'm all right. I have some cuts and things like that, but nothing's broken. Billy's unconscious."

Win pursed his lips. "Shock, mostly likely. How long has he been out?"

"Since shortly after Evan first called down to us."

"Ok, so about a half hour. Can you rouse him at all?" Win asked.

"No. I've tried. He's breathing."

"Is it shallow?"

Josie listened to Billy's breathing. "Not too bad. I'm lying on top of him to keep him warm. It's cold down here."

"Good girl. That's what he needs," Win said.

He could tell that he was getting closer to them. He could feel the temperature drop the further he was lowered.

Josie took the book of matches from Billy's hand and lit one so Win could pin point where they were. "Can you see that?"

"Yeah. Good," Win said and saw that he wasn't too far away. He only hoped that things remained stable.

Billy sat in the middle of a field, but he had no idea how he'd gotten there. The last thing he'd known, he was deep inside the mountain, lying on a

rocky ledge with Josie. Now he was in the middle of a picturesque scene complete with a forest and a beautiful range of mountains in the background. The sunshine was warm on his shoulders and the breeze carried the scent of various flowers and plants.

He wasn't sure what he should do since he didn't know where he was, so he simply sat and enjoyed his surroundings.

"Two Moons," a woman's voice said from behind him.

Turning, he saw an Indian woman who he instinctively knew was his mother. She smiled at him and came to sit in front of him. Billy didn't say anything at first, just looked her over. Two long braids hung down her front, secured by red and blue beaded thongs. Her buckskin dress was adorned by red and blue quills and long fringes hung from the sleeves and along the bottom of the dress.

Her moccasins were also decorated and feather earrings dangled from her ears. She wore one eagle feather in her hair. Looking into her dark eyes, Billy saw that he strongly resembled her.

"Mother?"

She smiled and he thought her beautiful. "Yes, my son. You have grown into a fine young man. It is what I always wished for you."

"That's why you gave me to Pa, isn't it?" he asked.

"Yes. I wanted you to live and carry on our traditions."

Billy shook his head. "I know nothing of Indian traditions. I've been raised by white people and there are no Indians around anymore. They're all on reservations."

This made his mother sad.

"What's your name?" he asked.

"Sweet Water. There are ways for you to learn about our culture and your ancestors," she said, "but you have to have the desire to."

He let out a small laugh. "Which culture would that be? I'm a mix of three types of Indian."

"I see what you mean. Perhaps my father's people, the Cheyenne, are a good place to start. Your yellow-haired friend knows about them."

"What good will that do me? I don't fit in anywhere, Mother. I'm *doomed to live a life always on the edge no matter where I go. Don't you see? The white people don't think I'm good enough and your people probably think the same thing because I've been raised by white people,"* Billy said.

Her expression turned fierce. "You make your own destiny, Two Moons. Your father was a brave man who never backed down from a challenge, and you are your father's son. It is in you to do the same thing if only you dig deep and find the courage to do so. The opinion of others doesn't matter because the truth is in your heart, not in theirs."

"You sound like Ma and Lucky," Billy said, smiling.

"They are wise. You must listen to them. You are soft-hearted like me and easily wounded. You must try to be more like White Sun and not give in to your hurt and anger. You must not give up or you will live your life in the misery you describe. Your life is what you make of it and no one can do that for you," Sweet Water said.

Billy nodded. "Can you tell me what the future holds for me? Will I be happy?"

She gave him a kind smile. "I cannot tell you that. It is something you must decide for yourself. What I can tell you is that you have been given many gifts and talents, even ones that you haven't discovered yet. You must make your own happiness."

"I understand. So I'm not going to die?" Billy asked.

"I hope not. I want you to have the chance to grow old and have many grandchildren," she said. "But for now, you can sit here with me while I tell you some stories of our people."

"I'd like that," Billy said, with a smile.

Sweet Water took his hand and said, "For thousands of years our ancestors roamed freely over these lands ..."

Win made a large loop in the end of the second rope he'd brought down with him and had Josie lift her arms so he could put it around her. "Ok, now I want you to hold onto me and they're going to lift us up."

"What about Billy?" she asked.

"I can't take both of you. I'll come back down for him. Let's get you up first," Win said.

The ropes to which they were attached began to tremble and Win knew that an aftershock was beginning. "Shit! Josie, help me get a hold on Billy. I don't know how stable this ledge is, but I'm not taking the chance of it breaking away with him on it."

Between them, they got Billy upright and wrapped their arms around him. Tightening his left arm even more around Billy, Win found the third rope, a smaller one that was to be used as a signal rope and began tugging on it for all he was worth. No sooner had he done that than the aftershock grew in intensity and rocks and debris began falling down on them.

Up top, people were thrown around by the large shift in the earth. Evan laid down where he was, waiting for it to end. He prayed fervently that the three people inside the mine were all right. Hearing someone speaking in a language he'd never heard, he turned to see Lucky holding up his arms to the sky in a beseeching manner, speaking what Evan figured was Cheyenne. Whatever god Lucky was praying to, the sheriff hoped the god listened to Lucky.

Lucky prayed loudly, his voice filled with respect and his eyes welling with tears as he thought about the fact that the people trapped in the mountain, whom he'd come to love, might die. He pleaded with the Great Spirit to quiet the earth and give them the time they needed to bring them to safety.

Other people watched him, but had no idea what he was saying. All they knew was that he was praying. Sam also began praying aloud in English and those that could hear him lifted their voices with him.

As the tremors began to subside, Evan signaled to the others that they needed to start pulling again immediately. Sam was a tremendous help in this, his mighty muscles and two hundred and twenty-five pounds acting as an anchor. Suddenly Jerry was at his side, holding up another rope with a loop tied in it.

"Put this around you. I'm gonna use Alonso to help pull," he said. "I don't want to risk any slippage by trying to tie the two together."

"Good idea. This will be quicker anyway. I hope there aren't any more tremors," Sam said and slipped it over him to settle around his waist.

Jerry nodded and headed back down to the bottom of the mountain. He gave Alonso a hard slap on his rump. "Pull! Pull!"

Alonso tossed his head and began stepping forward, his powerful legs and haunches beginning to make headway right away.

Sam felt the rope tighten around him and he started to be pulled backwards. He used his legs to help Alonso along. "Hey up there!" he shouted to the group assembled up top. "Stop pulling! Let me and the horse do that part. Just keep the ropes from snagging!"

"Ok!" Evan hollered back.

Lucky ended his prayer with words of thanks for the Great Spirit's help in calming Mother Earth again, then turned to help with the ropes.

Meanwhile, Win and Josie clung to Billy as they watched the shelf that had been supporting them crumble and slide down into the abyss below. Other parts of the rock walls followed it and Josie thanked God that Win had had the sense for them to gather Billy in their arms. Otherwise, their young friend would have been forever lost.

As it was, their survival was tenuous at the moment and completely dependent on whether or not there were more strong aftershocks or not. They were lucky that the upheaval hadn't caused any huge boulders to fall on them. If that had happened, they would all have perished for certain.

Then they were being hauled upwards. The going was slow but steady and as they grew closer to the light coming through the opening in the mountainside, hope grew within them that they would survive the ordeal.

The Earth began to shake where Billy and his mother sat. They looked around and then at each other. Billy saw that Sweet Water was not scared. In fact, there was a serene smile on her beautiful face.

"It is time for you to return, Two Moons. Remember all that I have told you. You may see me again," she said. "Know that you take my love and the love of your father with you always."

Billy's eyes filled with tears. "I wish I had known you."

She put a hand on his cheek. "You know me now, my handsome son. Go and do great things for our people. I love you."

"I love you, too," Billy said.

She smiled again and then all went dark as the world shuddered harder.

Billy awoke with a start to realize two things; he was in great pain and there were strong arms wrapped around him.

Groaning, he asked faintly, "Who is that and where am I?"

Win said, "Welcome back. Me and Josie have you. Don't start struggling around. We're all being pulled out of here. We're still in the mine, but dangling hundreds of feet up in the air."

"Oh," Billy said calmly. "Ok. My leg is broken and I did something to my back."

"Ok, kid," Win said. "Hang on. We'll be there soon."

Evan shouted down, "I can see you. It won't be long now."

Looking up, Josie could see his head silhouetted against the sky, but she couldn't make out his features. She remembered her promise to Billy, but she didn't know if she could follow through on it.

It seemed like an eternity to Evan until they were close enough for him and Lucky to get their hands on the trio.

"Take Billy first," Josie insisted. "He's badly hurt."

"Ok," Evan said.

Once Win and Josie were sure that Billy was secure in their grasps, they let go of him, watching as he was handed off to several other men. From there, Billy was carefully borne down the mountain to the sheep pasture. Sean had finished up with the worst injury cases in Echo and upon hearing the news about the people inside the mine, he'd had another man show him its location. Not only did he want to help provide medical attention if necessary, but as Josie's friend, he wanted to know what was happening. As Billy was slowly laid on the grass, he began assessing the young man.

Next, Win gave Josie to the sheriff and the Irishman. Hurriedly releasing the rope from around Josie, Evan hauled her into his arms and kissed her long and hard. Josie responded, wrapping her arms around his neck, not caring if others saw or not.

Pulling back from her, Evan ran his hands over her, searching for injuries. "Are you ok? Are you hurt? Does anything hurt?"

Josie said, "No. Nothing serious."

Evan looked her over. Her face was dirty and sweaty, her hair matted with dirt and debris. She had a scrape on her forehead and one on her cheek, but in Evan's eyes, she was still the most beautiful woman on Earth.

"I'm so sorry, honey. So sorry. I was a complete idiot and I love you so much. I can't believe how awful I acted with you and I want the chance to make it up to you. I'm just sorry it took something like this to make me see what a jackass I was about it all," Evan said. "Please say you'll forgive me."

Tears began streaming down his face and Josie saw the deep regret in his eyes. She also saw love in the luminous green depths and her heart couldn't stay hardened against him. Her promise to Billy once again rose in her mind, but she was still a little hesitant. "Can we talk about this when we're not sitting on the side of a mountain?"

Evan laughed. "Yeah. That's a good idea." He hugged her again and then began helping her down to the meadow below. The fact that she wanted to discuss it gave him hope that maybe they could work through their differences.

Josie wasn't the only one who was kissed upon reaching safety. Lucky pulled Win into his embrace and kissed the side of his head. "Praise be to God you're all right, lad!"

Incredibly happy to be alive and unhurt, Win hugged him back, not minding one little bit that another man had just kissed him when other people were about. "It's good to see you, too, Yelling Bear."

Lucky laughed at his use of his Cheyenne name and said, "All right. Let's get off this mountain before Mother Earth gets cranky again."

It didn't take long for everyone to descend to the foot of the mountain and move a respectful distance away. There was a crowd around Billy as Sean worked on him.

Remus and Arlene stood close by as the doctor splinted his leg. When he stepped back, Sean told them, "I'm glad the break isn't a complicated one. I don't think there's anything permanently wrong with his back, either. He's not having any numbness anywhere and he can move all of his limbs. I think he'll make a full recovery."

Arlene sank down on her knees and took Billy's face in her hands. "I was so afraid that we'd lost you." Pressing kisses to his forehead, she cried over him. "I love you so much, Billy."

With a lot of effort, Billy reached up to embrace her and held her tightly. "I love you, too, Ma. I'm so sorry for being so angry with you. I had no right to be."

Arlene sobbed in his arms. "It's ok, honey. I understand. It's going to be ok now. You'll see."

"I know. I saw her, Ma. I saw my birth mother," Billy said.

Remus kneeled close to him and asked, "What do you mean?"

Billy said, "I must have died or something because I think I went to heaven and I saw her."

Remus said, "That's impossible."

"No, it's not, Pa. You've never told me her name, right?"

His father shook his head. "No, son."

"She told me her name was Sweet Water and that my father's name was White Sun. Is that right?"

Remus became very pale and swayed slightly. "Yes, but how ...?"

Lucky broke into their conversation. "Glory be, he's had his first vision."

Billy found Lucky and gave him a steady look. "Is that what it was?"

"'Twas."

"I guess I'm more Indian that we thought I was," Billy said with a weak laugh.

Sean said, "I'm sorry for interrupting, but I'd like to get Billy moved inside. Win said that we should use his cabin until Billy can be moved home."

Once this was accomplished, Sean gave him a little more laudanum and left the bottle with Win, who insisted that he could take care of Billy overnight.

Arlene said, "Win, I appreciate that, but I hope you won't mind me asserting my right as his mother to do it."

Win graciously said, "Of course not. I'm sorry I don't have a proper bed for either of you, but I wasn't anticipating guests."

Jerry stepped into the cabin and said, "I can help with that. They're single beds and straw mattresses, but they'll be better than sleeping on the floor."

Win nodded, not too proud to accept them, especially since they would benefit someone else. "Ok. Much obliged."

Jerry eyed him and said, "So a sheep herd, huh? Whose idea was that?"

"The big Irish guy's. This is all his land," Win answered.

Arlene asked, "So this is really what Billy has been helping Lucky with?"

Again Win nodded. "I'll let Lucky tell you all about it. Jerry, I'll go with you and help bring those beds back."

"Don't worry about it. Ross is already doing that. You should rest. I'm sure you're tired after playing hero," Jerry said.

Win dismissed Jerry's comment with a hand gesture and said, "There were a lot of heroes here today."

With a smile and a nod, Jerry exited the cabin.

Chapter Twenty-Five

Evan was bone-weary that evening after making sure that everything around Echo was being dealt with satisfactorily. He'd also delivered Josie safely to the boarding house so she could clean up and rest. Opal hadn't left her side, insisting that she help Josie, so Evan knew she was in good hands. Still, he couldn't rest.

He desperately needed to talk to Josie, but he didn't want to disturb her. Josie had been teaching him to embroider and he picked up the practice project she'd given him. Working on it didn't interest him, however, and he put it back down. He thought about getting just a little drunk to see if it would help relax him, but then dismissed that idea in case someone needed help with something.

Edna watched Evan roam back and forth through the house and then outside. He'd be back soon and start the process all over again. She knew what was bothering her nephew and admired him for being considerate of Josie, but he was driving her batty with his pacing.

The next time he came back in the house, she said, "Evan, if you can't sit still, go down to Spike's or something. You're making me nervous with this caged animal routine you've been performing."

He flopped down on the sofa and huffed out a loud sigh. "Sorry. I just don't think I can sleep without talking to her. I'm afraid if it's left too long, it'll be too late to convince her to forgive me and that I'll never doubt her again."

"Evan, Josie's a smart woman and a kind one, too. She'll listen to you. Despite what happened, I know she still loves you. The kind of love you two have doesn't just die overnight," Edna said. "Look at you and Louise. Even though she betrayed you, you still loved her for a long while after she left."

Evan found that although the thought of that time still rankled a little, it didn't bother him like it had before. It seemed as though he was finally letting go of it. "You're right. I did. I've put it behind me, though." Leaning forward he propped his elbows on his knees and put his head in his hands. "This is killing me."

"You have to calm down, sonny boy. You're not doing yourself any good," Edna said.

"Maybe I will go to Spike's. Maybe that'll keep me occupied for a little bit," Evan said.

Just as he reached the door, someone knocked on it, making him jump a little. Opening it, he discovered that Josie stood on the porch. He was flooded with happiness upon seeing her.

"Hi," he said, with a big smile. "I thought you'd be resting."

"I couldn't," Josie said. "I couldn't wait to talk to you."

Edna called out, "Get in here and see me first!"

Evan rolled his eyes and laughed, motioning Josie past him.

"There's my girl." Edna stood up, holding her arms open to Josie.

Josie embraced her, tears stinging her eyes. "I'm so glad to be able to see you again."

"I'm so glad to see you again," Edna said as tears trickled from her eyes. "I was scared to death for you and Billy. I love you."

"I love you, too."

Edna patted her on her back and said, "Ok. Go on and talk to your man."

Josie smiled at Edna as she sat back down and then turned to Evan, who led her outside.

"Let's go to the barn," he said.

Josie nodded and they walked in silence until they reached it.

"Evan, thank you for all you did today to help save us," she said.

Tucking a tendril of her hair behind her ear, Evan said, "I'd do anything for you and I was terrified that I was going to lose you forever."

"I need you to think about something and give what I'm going to ask you careful thought," Josie said, even as her body reacted to his touch.

Evan's expression became solemn and he nodded.

"If there hadn't been an earthquake and I wouldn't have been trapped inside the mine, with the real possibility of me dying, would you still want to reconcile with me? Please think about it seriously," Josie said.

Evan gave her query the consideration it deserved, looking deep inside himself for the answer. As he did, he felt a wave of emotion wash over him as he thought about how he'd almost lost her that day. Not bothering to fight against the tears these thoughts began, he said, "I was so angry and hurt, even though I had no reason to be. I let the past cloud my judgement of the situation and I am so ashamed that I lost control like that. I don't think I would have if I didn't love you so much. What I feel for you is a million times stronger than anything I ever felt for Louise.

"I can tell you without a shadow of a doubt that once I had calmed down, I would have come asking for your forgiveness and I would have done anything to gain it. I still would. I am sorry, though, that it took …" He broke off for a few moments. "…almost losing you to make me do it quicker. But when I thought about you down there in the dark and maybe hurt or dead, I vowed that if we got you out of there safely, I'd start begging for you to forgive me right away, even if it meant risking that you'd tell me to go to hell. If you take me back, I'll spend every day for the rest of my life making sure you never regret it."

Josie watched the man she still loved cry unabashedly as he spoke and she had a difficult time holding in her own emotions. She nodded her understanding. "All right. Before I can make a decision about that, I need to know something else that you haven't told me. What happened to your family? I think it's time you told me."

Evan knew she was right. Heaving a sigh, he said, "When I was eleven, I'd gone hunting with a couple of my buddies. At the time, we lived outside of Billings. Both my pa and Uncle Reb were deputies there. It was after dark when I got home. When I got closer to the house, I could hear my mother screaming and I ran inside. Three guys were holding her and my sisters hostage. Pa was passed out on the floor. I thought he was dead at first, but he moved a little and I didn't see any blood on him."

Evan had to pause there because he was being overcome with emotion. He paced a little and continued once he gained control again. "I still had my shotgun and I was able to get a shot off before one of the guys shot me. I'd only winged the other guy. I remember falling to the floor. My mother screamed my name and tried to get to me before one of the bastards stomped on her back and shot her—the last thing I ever heard from her was that scream."

Josie's mouth opened in horror, but no sound came out. Her shock was too great.

"Next, they killed my sisters, laughing the whole time. There was nothing I could do to help them. I was hurt too bad and I'd lost my gun. Then they slapped Pa awake and made him look at them, yelling at him about how they'd told him they'd get revenge on him. I'll never forget the way he cried at seeing Ma and my sisters dead. Then he looked at me, smiled and told me how much he loved me and how proud he was of me. He told me to look away, but I wouldn't. He yelled at me to look away, so I did, and I heard the gun go off."

Josie flinched as if she had been present and heard it. She couldn't begin to imagine what it had been like for Evan. She kept silent, afraid to interrupt his recounting of the dreadful night, knowing that he needed to get it out.

Evan closed his eyes. "When I looked again, I saw the life leave his eyes, Josie. I watched the man I admired and loved most lose his life and I lost my father at that same moment. I watched my mother and sisters die, cut down as though their lives meant nothing, and to the men who killed them, they didn't."

"I prayed that the men would kill me, too, so I could go be with the rest of my family. They didn't, though. The one guy asked their leader if he should shoot me again, but the guy just smiled at me and said, 'Nah. Leave him. He's gonna die all on his own. Don't worry about it.' They just walked out of our house like nothing significant had happened there. Like they hadn't just murdered four people and like I wasn't going to die.

"I laid there all night, sure that at any moment I was going to die. I wanted to. I was in so much pain, physical and emotional. I just wanted it all to end. Aunt Edna was the one that found us. She came by in the morning because Ma and she were supposed to do some canning together and when Ma hadn't shown up at her house, she got worried. So did Uncle Reb. Pa hadn't gotten to work, so he came looking for him. He arrived shortly after Aunt Edna did.

"I was barely conscious, but I remember how they both cried while Aunt Edna held me. Uncle Reb screamed that he was gonna kill whoever had done it and that's when I began to pray to live so that I could help him do it. God answered both of my prayers. The one where I lived and the one where I got to help put them away.

"Actually, I got to watch them hang. I was sixteen and I watched with a smile on my face as they swung from the end of that rope. It's the only time I've ever been glad to watch someone die. Before they hung, I went to see them in jail, and I told them who I was and how much I was gonna enjoy seeing their sorry asses drop through that gallows door underneath them. And I did. God help me, I did.

"Knowing that I'd helped catch the men responsible, made me feel a little less guilty about living when the rest of my family had died."

Evan stopped talking and sat down on hay bale, his shoulders shaking as the old grief that he held inside was released in harsh sobs. Josie knelt in front of him, taking him in her arms, offering him the comfort he needed. They clung to each other, him crying for his lost family and her crying for the hurt little boy still locked inside him.

When both of their tears subsided, they pulled apart and brushed away the tears from each other's faces.

Evan said, "Even if you can't forgive me, I'm glad I told you. You deserved to know."

"I have one last question. What convinced you that I was innocent?" Josie asked.

Before answering, Evan made her get off her knees and sit on the hay bale with him. "It was the way you stormed into the office this morning. I've had a lot of experience in telling whether someone is guilty or not and what you did proved that you hadn't had anything to do with what happened to me."

"Because the handwriting on the note was different than mine?"

"No. Anyone could have written the note. You could have told them what to say. So that didn't prove it to me," Evan said.

She shook her head a little. "What did then?"

"The look in your eyes and the way you held yourself. How angry you were. Your anger was genuine, not some act you were just putting on. I know the difference between when people are lying and when they aren't. If I hadn't been hit over the head and drugged yesterday, I probably would have been in a better frame of mind to believe you," Evan said. "I'm sorry about that, all of it."

Josie said, "Phoebe said that she heard that people saw you at the Burgundy House and that you were drunk. That's what made me so mad this morning. I thought you'd lost your nerve and that you'd gone drinking to forget how cowardly you were."

"So that's what that crack about me being the guilty person meant. I had no idea what you were talking about. Someone went to great lengths to make it look that way. I woke up in the woods behind the saloon, soaked in alcohol, with that note stuck to me. I found Smitty and the buggy tied there and it was close enough to the door to make sure people would see me there. Yeah, they did a good job of framing me, all right," he said.

Josie took his hand and said, "So you really did still want to marry me?"

"Josie, I've thought of nothing else but marrying you ever since the night we first said we loved each other. It was that night when I decided to propose to you and I would never walk out on our wedding and miss out on marrying the most beautiful, kind, smart, fun woman I know. I still want to marry you, that is if you'll still have me," Evan said.

Josie knew that Evan was an honorable man and she'd known the answer to her question before she'd even asked it. She'd just needed reassurance. "I'd like to apologize to you, too. If I'd been thinking more clearly yesterday, I'd have known that you wouldn't have done that to me. I was hurt and humiliated and when you accused me of cheating on you, well, I think I lost my ability to reason things out. Are you sure you still want to marry me?"

"Yes," he said emphatically. "I still want to marry you. Do you still want to marry me?"

With a beautiful smile, she said, "Yes, I want to marry you."

He ran a hand over her left hand and felt the bareness of her ring finger. "Oh, crap! Your ring! I smashed it. I'm so sorry. I'll get it fixed."

"You can't," she said.

"Why? Is it that bad? I'll have the diamond reset," Evan said. He felt terrible over having destroyed the ring.

"You can't. I threw it in the mine," she said and waited for his reaction with bated breath.

"You ... threw it ... in the mine?" he asked.

She rushed to make him understand. "I didn't want it because it had become ugly to me and I still wouldn't even if you hadn't ruined it. Do you see what I mean? It would always remind me of all of the horrible things that had happened yesterday and I don't want any reminders like that."

He did see her point of view. "I understand. It's ok. I'll get you a new one."

"No. I don't want one. The only ring I want you to put on this finger is my wedding band," she said.

Evan gave her a doubtful look. "Are you sure?"

"Positive. All I need is that one gold band. A symbol of a new beginning in more ways than one," Josie assured him.

He looked into her eyes for several moments and then nodded. "All right. If that's what you want, it's fine with me. Now, since we're both in agreement about still tying the knot, I'm not waiting any longer than need be. Day after tomorrow we're doing it. Can you be ready that soon?"

She bit her bottom lip. "I don't know. I don't want to wear the same dress, either. Is that silly of me?"

Evan thought about it. "I don't have a tux, either. The one I had was ruined. So I guess if I have to get a new suit, you should have a new dress. I don't want any bad luck, so I don't think we should have anything from yesterday. I don't want to wait, though."

Josie thought a moment and then said, "Evan, I don't care what we wear. I have a nice dress that you haven't seen. Do you have a suit I haven't seen?"

"Yeah, I do."

"Then we're getting married the day after tomorrow, like you said. We have our clothes, our rings, and most importantly, each other," she said forcefully.

Evan felt excitement build inside. "Are you really sure? I don't want you to have any regrets."

She kissed him and then said, "I won't, will you?"

"No," he said and kissed her.

Against his lips, she said, "Then we're getting married the day after tomorrow. Oh wait. What about Billy? I'd like him to be there."

Evan slumped a little and then brightened. "I have an idea."

"You do?"

When he told her, she said, "You're a genius. I'm marrying a genius sheriff."

He laughed and said, "How about kissing your genius sheriff some more?"

Josie gladly complied with his request and it was only with a supreme effort on both their parts that they didn't make love right there in his barn.

"The next time I see you, we'll be getting married," he said as they rode around to the stable in back of the Hanovers'.

She giggled. "I'm so excited."

"Me, too," he said. "You go on in. I'll take care of Captain for you."

"Ok," she said. "Thank you."

After giving her a final kiss for the night, Evan sent her inside.

Marvin listened attentively as Shadow related more of the events that had occurred around Echo that day, including that it was now common knowledge about Lucky's sheep herd.

"I'm glad that Josie and company were brought to safety," Marvin said. "It would have been a shame for them to have perished."

Shadow looked at his brother and said, "I think you actually mean that."

"I do. Unlike you, I do have a little bit of a heart. I like Josie very much. She has spirit and despite the fact that she fears me, she also stands up to me. I admire her courage. However, I did like the havoc you created for the sheriff—too bad this earthquake came along and ruined it," Marvin said.

Shadow's laugh was filled with glee. "Maybe it was a sign that we'll be able to do something bigger and worse in the future."

"Don't tell me you're getting religious on me."

"Not exactly. I don't know if I exactly believe in God, but I do believe there is something greater than us at work," Shadow said, looking up at the stars.

"Hmm," Marvin said noncommittally. "A sheep herd. I admire how cleverly they hid it from everyone. Well, except you, that is. Why did you wait so long to tell me?"

Raising an eyebrow at Marvin, Shadow said, "You're not the only one who's good at mental strategy, Marvy."

"All right. Perhaps I was hasty in saying that, Shadow. Go ahead and tell me your idea," Marvin said. He watched the vicious smile he loved spread across his twin's face and waited with great anticipation for Shadow to begin.

Chapter Twenty-Six

"Ow! Easy! Ow!" Billy yelled.

"Quit being such a big baby," Lucky said.

"I have a broken leg, you know," Billy said.

Lucky laughed. "Too bad it's not your mouth that's broke."

Win chuckled.

He and Lucky carried Billy in the wheelchair that Tansy and her husband Reggie had brought out to the farm for him. They reached the area where the wedding guests were seated and put him down gently.

"How's your back feeling?" Win asked.

"Not bad. That needle stuff you did worked pretty good," Billy said.

Win smiled. "It's called acupuncture, and my people have been using it for centuries."

Billy leaned back in the wheelchair and said, "Well, it worked. I'm glad that my back wasn't broken or anything."

"Torn muscles can sometimes feel as bad as a break, so you have to give yourself a little time to get feeling better. If you overdo it, you'll have a setback," Win warned him.

"Yes, Dr. Wu," Billy said, giving him a salute.

Lucky looked over at Win's cabin when he heard feminine laughter.

"Sounds like the ladies are havin' a good time."

"Good," Win said. "Are you going to be all right, Billy? Do you want some more laudanum?"

"No. I'm fine. Lucky's willow bark tea seemed to help. God, that stuff tastes awful," Billy remarked.

Lucky smiled. "Aye, but it works."

Win said, "C'mon, Lucky, we better make sure everything else is ready so that when the girls are, the ceremony can get started."

Inside the cabin the mood was exuberant, the women having fun as they all got ready. Upon hearing that Josie wanted a different dress, Tansy had showed her a white, off-the-shoulder dress that a customer had ordered a while back, but hadn't wanted at the last minute. It had never been out of the box and Josie had fallen in love with it when Tansy had showed it to her. It was completely different than her other dress and that suited Josie just fine.

Edna and Tansy had worked quickly to make the necessary alterations to it and it now fit Josie to perfection. She looked in the full-length mirror Sonya had carefully wrapped and had Jerry bring out so that they could use it. Instead of being nervous like she'd been two days ago, she was excited and eager to wed her sheriff.

It didn't matter to her that she still had a partially healed scrape on both her forehead and cheek. Opal had done her magic with her makeup paints and lip rouge and the scrapes were barely noticeable now. She had some bruises on her legs and back, but those were hidden by her dress.

Over and over she had thanked the Lord for coming away from such a dangerous event so unscathed. She felt badly that Billy had been injured, but she knew it could have been worse for him. And she knew that if that tremor had happened before Win had arrived, she would not be standing in his cabin looking at her reflection, about to marry Evan. She was grateful for the second chance at happiness and had no intention of squandering it.

Edna watched Josie and was thankful for the safety of the woman who had fallen in love with her nephew. Josie would be a wonderful wife to Evan and she couldn't wait until she heard the pitter-patter of little feet around their house. She knew how much Evan loved Josie as well, and to have lost her would have crushed him. It would have broken her own heart as well; Josie had become like a daughter to her the same way Evan had become her son. She looked forward to seeing their love continue to grow for however many more years she was allowed to stay on Earth.

Opal finished fussing with the lacey hem on the bottom of Josie's dress and said, "You're perfect. Evan will drool when he sees you."

Josie beamed. "Good, because I'm sure I'll drool when I see him. At least I won't be the only one drooling."

Tansy and Sonya laughed with the other three women.

Thad finished straightening Evan's gray tie that matched his suit. "I'm glad this still fits you."

"Did you think I'd gained weight or something?" Evan asked.

"You might have, what with sitting at that desk sleeping so much," Thad said, which made Jerry and Win laugh.

The men stood behind Jerry's big wagon where Josie wouldn't be able to see Evan. He and several of the men had slept out at Win's cabin on high alert. They were determined that nothing happen to prevent the nuptials from happening this time. It had been funny shuffling everyone around so that Evan and Josie never saw each other. Evan had gone off into the woods with Lucky until Jerry had come to fetch them to get ready. They'd dressed hurriedly before any wedding guests had shown up. It had been a hilarious affair and the men had laughed as much as the women did now.

"How do I look?" Evan asked, holding out his arms and offering himself up for inspection.

The other men gave him the once-over and approved of his appearance.

Jerry said, "I still think you should hold a shepherd's hook while you say 'I do.'"

"The only thing I'd do with one is whack some sense into your head with it," Evan said with a grin.

Win said, "I'd doubt that would do any good. I think Jerry's a lost cause."

"You do, huh? Well, whose idea was it for Evan to advertise for a mail-order-bride?" Jerry challenged him.

Win just frowned and remained silent.

"Uh huh. That's what I thought," Jerry said smugly.

Evan laughed. "Yeah, Jerry, you're right. If it wasn't for you, I wouldn't be standing here about to marry the woman of my dreams. I give you full credit for that."

"Thank you. At least someone knows how to show some appreciation."

"You're a smart man and a good problem solver, Jerry," Evan continued.

Jerry just grinned at his praise.

Smiling back, Evan clapped him on the shoulder and said, "Which is why I think you oughta be mayor."

Jerry's grin disappeared and his eyes bugged out. "You're kiddin', right?"

"Nope. I mean it. If this idea of yours catches on, you'll be responsible for saving Echo," Evan said.

Win laughed at Jerry's stunned expression while Thad said, "He's right, Jerry. It's a good idea."

"But I'm colored," Jerry said.

"Very astute of you," Thad said. "You really *are* smart."

"There's no way they're gonna vote for a colored man and you know it," Jerry said. "I'll be made a laughing stock."

"What makes you think you aren't now?" Win teased him.

"Be serious, now," Jerry said.

Evan took Jerry by the shoulders and said, "Jerry, you said that the fella who sold you Alonso was a successful mayor, right?"

"Yeah."

"Well, maybe God made him tell you about mail-order-brides because the Good Lord knew you were smart enough to listen to him about it and come up with the idea for us to do the same," Evan said. "You know, sort of passing things along from one mayor to another?"

"But I'm not a mayor and I wasn't at the time," Jerry said.

"Ok, from one mayor to a potential mayor then," Evan insisted.

Jerry laughed. "You're really reaching here, Evan."

"I'd vote for you," Win said. "Besides, there's lots of black mayors all over the south, so why not here? I know we're to the north somewhat, but still..."

Jerry knew that, but he'd never given any consideration to taking an office of any kind.

Thad said, "Look, Jerry, you're an educated man, you run a successful business that's vital to our town, you've got a good heart, and you know right from wrong. What more could anyone want in a mayor, colored or otherwise?"

Evan said, "At least think about it. Besides, it's not like anyone else is going to do it."

"Gee, Evan, you really know how to make a guy feel special," Jerry said, his dark eyes smiling.

"Just think about it," Evan said.

Sam appeared from around the back of the wagon. "Gentlemen, let's get into position."

"I think you're still thinking you're back in the military, Sam," Thad said. "Sounds more like we're getting ready to go into battle instead of going to a wedding."

Sam smiled wryly and said, "Sometimes weddings feel more like battles."

The group of men laughed as they followed him to where a temporary altar had been set up opposite Win's cabin. From that position, Josie would walk down the porch steps and continue straight to Evan. Baskets of flowers created a bright, pretty aisle for Josie to walk down. The whole town had been invited through word of mouth and it looked like most of it had turned out to watch their sheriff get married.

Billy sat at the front of the one side the aisle. Evan went over and crouched down next to him.

"You doing ok, buddy?"

Billy smiled. "Yeah. I'm fine. You nervous?"

"Nope. Not one little bit."

"Good. You shouldn't be. You and Josie were meant to be together," Billy said with a smile.

"I know," Evan agreed. "I can't tell you how glad I am that you're both here. I'd have hated—"

"No, Evan. Don't even say it. This is your wedding day. Only good thoughts, ok?" Billy said.

"You're right. You know, it's gonna be you in a couple of years or so," Evan said.

Billy laughed. "Maybe. I have a lot to do first. It'll happen when it's the right time. No sense in rushing anything."

"Boy, I'm surrounded by smart people today," Evan said.

"What?"

The sheriff chuckled at Billy's confused frown. He saw Lucky waving from the cabin porch. "I'll tell you later on. Right now, I have to go get hitched."

He joined his best man and his groomsmen, taking his spot closest to Sam. Pauline Desmond walked proudly down the aisle, spreading flower petals on the grassy aisle. She was followed by Opal, who looked very pretty in her light blue maid-of-honor dress. She blew a kiss to her husband who grinned and caught it, unashamed to do so in front of other people. The guests chuckled at her playful behavior.

Tansy preceded Sonya down the aisle and the women took their places by Opal.

Josie came out on the porch and took Lucky's arm.

"Ready, lass?" he asked her.

"Are you sure I look all right?" she asked.

"Josie, I can assure ya that ya couldn't look any lovelier than ya already do," he answered.

Josie nodded. "Thank you. Then yes, I'm ready."

Lucky safely guided Josie down the steps and waited for Jenny Desmond to begin playing her harpsicord. She was talented and the pretty music floated on the light September breeze.

Love and desire washed over Evan, constricting his breathing for a moment as he watched his bride walk to him. His gaze never wavered from hers as Lucky escorted her along. He thought she was perfection itself in her flowing, white dress that left her pretty shoulders bared to his sight. Her hair that had been styled in a loose, attractive mass of curls caught the sunlight, turning it into a golden halo. She smiled a little shyly at him and he sent her a wide, love-filled grin in return.

Thad saw and stepped lightly on Jerry's foot, nodding in Evan's direction. Jerry grinned at Evan's love-struck expression and thought back to the day when he'd married Sonya as he looked over at his wife. He winked at her, telling her how pretty she looked. Her smile flashed in response and Jerry knew exactly how Evan felt about Josie.

As they reached the altar, Sam asked, "Who gives this woman to this man?"

Lucky stood very erect as he said, "I do, and I'm certain Josie's father would have, too. She picked a fine man to marry."

He shook Evan's hand and kissed Josie on the cheek before giving her over to Evan. He went to stand beside Billy then.

Josie looked into Evan's eyes that seemed an even more vivid shade of green than usual and it came to her that it was his love for her that made them brighter. She hoped that he could see the same thing in her eyes. His suit emphasized his broad shoulders and strong chest. His black hair was a little windblown, but that was the way she liked it best.

Instead of being inside of a church with organ music and fancy decorations, they stood under a canopy of white clouds and blue sky, surrounded by their friends, family, and a herd of fluffy white sheep.

Their vows were exchanged amid wavering sheep bleats and birdsong.

When Sam pronounced them husband and wife, Evan took Josie's face in his hands and took his time in kissing the woman who'd just become his wife. As Evan's lips met hers, Josie felt happy tears spill from her eyes as she closed them. Placing her hands against his chest, she made no effort to pull away from him as he proceeded to kiss her more firmly. It would have been just fine with her for their embrace to continue forever.

However, Sam pointedly cleared his throat and Evan withdrew from her. In his eyes, though, Josie saw the promise of things that would occur at a later time and felt pleasant drop in her stomach at the thought.

As she and her new husband turned to face the congregation, Sam said loudly, "I now present to you, Sheriff and Mrs. Sheriff Evan Taft!"

While the wedding guests cheered and clapped, Evan and Josie turned around to look at Sam, questioning his unusual introduction of them. He just winked and grinned broadly at them as he joined the others in clapping. Breaking into laughter, they turned back around and walked down the aisle together to the playing of the harpsicord.

Dan Griffith, a younger man in the town, was fairly handy with a camera. He had Josie and Evan stand for pictures first and then the rest of the wedding party. From there, the happy couple was taken over towards some tables that had been set up under a stand of trees. They were fashioned from wooden sawhorses and planks, but they were covered in pretty cloths.

Rough benches had been put together the day before for the guests to sit upon. Sam's wife, Bea, had been asked to make the wedding cake and she'd done a spectacular job. The white, three-tiered creation was beautiful. The ladies of the town had cooked delicious food and Spike supplied the alcohol for the occasion for those who wanted some.

Sam blessed the meal and Thad stood up to give his speech. He hadn't bothered to write down anything, instead speaking from the heart.

"I've known Evan since before he was born and I'm grateful I got to watch him grow up and become the fine man he is today. Evan's the kind of man who puts others ahead of himself, works hard to protect our town, and helps anyone who asks him to. He's tough as nails, smart, and likes to chase bad guys in his underwear—all good things to have in a sheriff."

Evan groaned and put his hands over his face while everyone else laughed with Thad.

"I couldn't love him any more if he was my own son and I know that his father and all of his loved ones in Heaven are looking down on him with love and pride. It was Jerry's idea for Evan to get a mail-order-bride, and I think the Man Upstairs put him up to it in a way. Not only that, He picked Josie for Evan and I think He picked right. I'm just glad Evan was smart enough to ask her to marry him."

"Josie, you're a beautiful, intelligent, feisty girl who doesn't mind smacking people in the kisser when they insult her friends, and I'd say someone like that is the perfect match for a sheriff."

Now Josie hid her face.

"We're all very happy you came to Echo, and even though you brought that loud Irish guy with you, we still love you," Thad said with a grin at Lucky. "Everyone, join me in a toast to the happy couple and in wishing them a lifetime of happiness!"

Glasses were clinked and drained amid well-wishes. Once the meal was eaten, Arthur went over and spoke in Billy's ear. The younger man nodded at him. Next, Arthur collected Jenny and the trio gathered by Billy's chair.

"May I have your attention, please?" His bass voice carried to the others and they stopped what they were doing to look at him. "We have a surprise for our newlyweds, so please come over here. This is now our dance floor." He made a broad gesture with his hands. He turned and looked at Billy, who took over.

"I wanted to do something really special for you both and I got the idea shortly after you got engaged," he said. "Thad, would you bring that here?" Thad brought Josie's guitar to Billy, who arranged it on his lap. "I won't play this nearly as well as you do, Josie, but I hope you'll like it. This is why I had you teach me how to play, but I don't have nowhere near your talent with it. The three of us worked on the arrangement. Thad gave me permission to use your guitar, by the way."

Evan and Josie exchanged curious looks and then turned back as the trio began their song. It was the love song Josie had first sang in her hotel room the day her luggage and guitar had arrived. She'd taught it to Billy, never dreaming that this is why he'd kept insisting that she work so hard with him on it.

An amazed smile broke out on her face as Billy and Arthur began singing together, lifting their baritone and bass voices in harmony. Evan took her hand and began to dance. As they moved together, Josie began singing the song to Evan, never looking away from him as she did. He was entranced by the beauty of her face and of her voice and he rejoiced to be her husband.

If Billy's playing wasn't perfect, no one seemed to notice, so caught up were they in the romantic sight of seeing Josie sing to her sheriff. When the song ended, Evan soundly kissed Josie, drawing applause. Billy didn't know any other songs and since he was starting to tire, he said his goodbyes to Josie and Evan so that Win and Lucky could take him back inside to lay down.

Josie hugged him and said, "Thank you so much. I can't believe you did that. It was the sweetest thing and you played so well. You can be proud of yourself."

He blushed and said, "Thanks. I'm glad I didn't mess up too bad."

Evan said, "I never heard you mess up. Thanks, buddy. We'll never forget it."

"Go get some rest now," Josie said, kissing his cheek.

As Lucky and Win lifted the wheelchair, Billy waved at her and Evan.

Arthur continued to sing while Jenny played as the rest of the guests danced for a while.

As the festivities wound down, Josie and Evan said farewell to their guests. Then they mounted and rode away on their horses that had been decorated with ribbons and flowers. As they trotted away, Evan looked over at Josie and they smiled at each other. By unspoken agreement, they kicked their mounts into a gallop at the same time, racing across the ground as they hurried to town.

They were already packed and ready to go so that when they arrived, they could get underway immediately. They put Captain and Smitty in the barn at home and ran to their wagon, which Remus and Jerry had gotten ready for them that morning. Evan made Josie stay in the wagon while he hitched up Remus and Billy's horses to it. This had also been prearranged so that they had a pair of fresh horses for their trip.

Then he climbed up onto the seat with her and asked, "Ready, Mrs. Taft?"

"Ready, Sheriff Taft," she responded.

Evan picked up the reins, whistled to the team and got them underway.

By the time they reached Dickensville, the shadows were growing long. Evan had pushed the team as hard as he'd dared, intent on arriving there before dark. He was glad that they'd made it. They checked into their hotel and followed the bellboy up to their room.

Once they were alone, Evan said, "Do you have any idea how incredibly beautiful you are?"

She blushed and said, "I know you keep telling me that, so I guess it must be true."

"It is," he said, taking off his suit jacket. "I'm going to tell you that every day for the rest of our lives, too."

Josie watched him unbutton his shirt, hunger nudging her nerves out of the way as he shrugged out of it. His powerful chest looked as good as it always felt under her hands. She raised her eyes to his and her breath caught at the heated look in them. They walked towards each other, needing to be close.

Evan quickly snaked his arms around her waist and lowered his lips to hers, tasting their sweetness. He deftly began undoing the stays at the back of her dress as he plundered her mouth. Now that they were free to express the physical side of their love, Evan wanted to take his time and make Josie feel like the cherished woman she was.

Her skin smelled heavenly as Evan's lips left hers to nibble his way along her cheek until he reached her earlobe, which he gently bit. He smiled when she gasped and shivered against him, enjoying her reaction. Her hands moved over his chest and he growled approvingly as she did, letting her know he liked it.

Josie was fascinated with his body and how smooth his skin felt under her hands. Her dress became loose and Evan slowly began sliding it down. She became nervous, worried about pleasing him, and pulled back a little. He lovingly smiled down into her eyes, silently reassuring her that she was desirable. Her mouthed curved upwards in response before he took it again in a burning kiss that made her heartbeat run wild.

By the time they were both undressed, Josie was no longer shy. Evan's ardor for her made her feel confident and wanted. As they lay down next to each other, his hands skimmed over her, rousing her need for him to a fever pitch that was almost more than Josie could stand.

Throughout the night their passion for each other was expressed—each whisper, touch, and kiss filled with love as their commitment to one another was firmly sealed. By morning they were finally exhausted, succumbing to slumber as they held one another.

Epilogue

Two months after they arrived home from their honeymoon, Josie and Evan had settled into a nice routine. Josie had caught on to Evan and Edna's nightly visiting sessions on the stairs and now joined in. The three of them laughed and carried on, sometimes for twenty minutes or more, before saying a final goodnight. Josie lost her shyness about sexual matters, especially because every night Edna told them to go make her a baby to play with. Josie usually responded to her by telling her to not mind the noise, which made Evan blush.

Edna still made Lucky, Billy, and Win come in the house without a shirt on until it became too cold to do so. Billy's leg had healed well and rarely bothered him. He was the only one who still remained shirtless when he could since the cold never fazed him.

Instead of being ashamed of his heritage, Billy now embraced it. He asked Lucky to teach him what he knew about Cheyenne culture and he became an avid student. It seemed as though Billy had had such knowledge locked inside him somewhere and Lucky's teachings were the key to releasing them.

Since Lucky had lived with his wife among the Cheyenne for three years, he was well versed in their way of life, customs, and beliefs. He

283

enjoyed teaching Billy and he surprised everyone with his extensive knowledge. He was skilled with a knife, bow, and a spear. He knew quite a bit of Indian medicine, how to build a fire from sticks, and many other things. He made several bow-and-arrow sets and showed several different people how to shoot them.

There were two things that Billy just couldn't get past—blood and butchering animals. He didn't mind hunting them or cooking meat once it was removed from the animal and washed, but he couldn't field dress the animal or butcher it.

Billy had decided it was time for him to become independent and not rely on his parents to support him any longer. The sheep ranch started to turn a small profit and he used his share to put a down payment on one of the larger empty buildings on Main Street. It needed a lot of repairs, which was why the bank was willing to sell it for a low price. They were happy to get rid of it. Billy's father and friends helped him improve the building. They enlarged the windows on the second floor to let in more light since he planned on using it as his studio.

Downstairs was the actual shop and there was enough space for him to make a tiny apartment with a bedroom, parlor, kitchen, and washroom. His artwork began to sell in Echo, but he still took some of it to Dickensville. He no longer pined for Shelby, instead viewing his past relationship with her as a learning experience. Now content with his life, he felt confident that the future held good things for him.

Lucky saved money in any way he could since his savings had finally run out. He built a tipi on the other side of the valley from Win's place so he had no rent to pay, and he ate a lot from the land. Doing so made him somehow feel close to the woman to whom he still felt married and their child.

He was determined that they would all be together someday, and making as much money as he could became Lucky's mission. With that money, he hoped to be able to create his dream of bringing his family back together somehow. His agile mind was always at work, coming up with new ways to turn a profit with the sheep farm. His determination and strong conviction was admired by his friends.

Travis never did ask Jenny about the things Marvin had said he should. In his opinion, it was better to let sleeping dogs lie and leave the past in the past. In order to keep his raise, he took Pauline with him once a week, but watched over her protectively. With the extra money he earned, he kept investing in the sheep farm. By mutual consent, his involvement in the business was kept secret, thereby allowing him the security of regular employment so he could take care of his family.

As always, Thad was in and out of town chasing all manner of criminals. When he came back to Echo, Phoebe was always happy to see him, but never gave it away that she also saw Marvin on a regular basis. She knew it was wrong, but she craved the balance of good and evil and had no intentions of giving up either man.

Since Marvin loved Phoebe so much, he was willing to put up with this behavior. In fact, he greatly enjoyed knowing that he was pulling one over on Thad. He was also content to go along with Shadow's ideas and bide his time concerning the plans they were making; it turned out that his twin was better at mental strategy than he'd thought.

Shadow began to envy Marvin's somewhat twisted relationship with Phoebe and wondered if he could ever find someone who would accept him as he was. It was certainly something to think about.

Evan kept his vow to keep searching for the culprit who had almost succeeded in keeping him and Josie apart for good. The sheriff would bring the culprit to justice no matter how long it took.

Since witnessing Evan's success in finding a bride, Win decided to begin his own search. One day after writing down the bare bones of what he wanted, he took it to Edna since she'd done such a good job with Evan's advertisement. Edna thought that the requirements he'd outlined were highly unusual.

"Am I reading this right?" she asked him.

Win smiled as he sat shirtless in their parlor. "Yes, you are. Can you do something with it?"

Edna chuckled. "Just you wait and see."

Win put his shirt and coat on, thanked her by kissing her cheek, and went happily along his way.

Josie had adopted Evan's habit of sitting out on the back porch at night no matter how cold it was outside. Evan had installed a swing and they often sat huddled together with a blanket over them. Their combined body heat as they snuggled kept them warm.

On a moonlit night, they sat that way, talking quietly.

Josie looked up at the stars and said, "I am so happy."

Evan kissed her cheek and said, "Me, too. I'm glad you like being married to a sheriff."

She let out a wicked little laugh and said, "I'll show you just how much I like being married to a sheriff. I'll let you arrest me again."

Evan laughed at her playful remark. "I think I created a monster with that."

"I think so, too. But you have to admit that it's fun," she said, running a hand over his chest and under his robe.

A low growl escaped Evan.

Josie said, "I have to show my appreciation for my hero. You helped save me from certain death."

Evan frowned. He hated thinking about the day of the earthquake and how he'd almost lost her. "I didn't do all that much. Win was the real hero that day."

"Everyone worked together, so you're all heroes," Josie said.

Looking deep into her lovely blue eyes, Evan said, "You're my hero."

She gave him a perplexed look. "How do you figure that?"

Holding her tighter, Evan said, "You rescued me from the past. You pulled me out of all that misery and showed me that I had to let go of it. You also rescued me from being so suspicious all the time and made me realize that I will never have a reason to doubt your commitment to me. All of that is behind me now. Behind *us* now."

"That's right. We have so much to look forward to. You saved me from a life of loneliness and boredom. I might have married eventually, but I know that I would never have found anyone like you. I'm so glad I answered your ad."

"Me, too," Evan said emphatically. "I love you so much and I'll always try to show you how much every day. I don't want you to ever feel like I take you for granted."

She ran a hand over his cheek. "You always make me feel appreciated and loved. I never question that. And you know that I feel the same way about you."

He nodded. "I do."

Josie laid her head on his chest, listening to the strong heartbeat under her ear and Evan held his wife closer. They no longer felt the need to speak, each of them content to simply listen to the sounds of the night birds in the trees. They had rescued each other, but could they help rescue their beloved Echo? Time would tell the tale.

The End

Thank you for reading and supporting my book and I hope you enjoyed it.

Please will you do me a favor and review "Montana Rescue" so I'll know whether you liked it or not, it would be very much appreciated, thank you.

Linda's Other Books

Westward Winds (Montana Mail Order brides Book 1)

Westward Dance(Montana Mail Order brides Book 2)

Westward Bound (Montana Mail Order brides Book 3)

Westward Destiny (Montana Mail Order brides Book 4)

Westward Fortune (Montana Mail Order brides Book 5)

Westward Justice (Montana Mail Order brides Book 6)

Westward Dreams (Montana Mail Order brides Book 7)

Westward Holiday (Montana Mail Order brides Book 8)

Westward Sunrise (Montana Mail Order brides Book 9)

Westward Moon (Montana Mail Order brides Book 10)

Westward Christmas (Montana Mail Order brides Book 11)

Westward Visions (Montana Mail Order brides Book 12)

Westward Secrets (Montana Mail Order brides Book 13)

Westward Changes (Montana Mail Order brides Book 14)

Westward Heartbeat (Montana Mail Order brides Book 15)

Westward Joy (Montana Mail Order brides Book 16)

Westward Courage(Montana Mail Order brides Book 17)

Westward Spirit (Montana Mail Order brides Book 18)

Westward Fate (Montana Mail Order brides Book 19)

Westward Hope (Montana Mail Order brides Book 20)

Connect With Linda

Visit my website at **www.lindabridey.com** to view my other books and to sign up to my mailing list so that you are notified about my new releases.

About Linda Bridey

LINDA BRIDEY lives in New Mexico with her three dogs; a German shepherd, chocolate Labrador retriever, and a black Pug. She became fascinated with Montana and decided to combine that fascination with her fictional romance writing. Linda chose to write about mail-order-brides because of the bravery of these women who left everything and everyone to take a trek into the unknown. The Westward series books are her first publications.

Made in the USA
Monee, IL
22 August 2020